GET THE
SCAMMER

L E Kennedy

Disclaimer:

The characters and events in this book
are fictitious. Any similarity to real
persons, living or dead, is coincidental
and not intended by the author.

ISBN: 978-1-959446-11-8

DEDICATION

This novel could not have been written without the help, encouragement, patience, support, sacrifice, and love that my wife, Mary Ellen, has given so unconditionally. I know it was not easy for her as it took me over three years to complete this novel. I'm eternally grateful to you, Mary Ellen, and I love you eternity times infinity!

To all my family and friends who have been patiently waiting for the book's debut, your enthusiasm has kept me going. You made me vow to finish what I started. Thank you all so very much.

Table of Contents

ACKNOWLEDGMENTS

Special thanks to Mary Ellen Kennedy, Candace Giovannucci, and James Adams for their technical help. They taught this old dog new tricks and guided me safely over the minefields of modern-day technology.

Thanks to Kathy Wall, Mary Ellen Kennedy, Victoria Adams, and Marilyn Petersen for their suggestions and advice that ultimately improved my manuscript.

Special thanks to my editor, Melanie Saxton. Melanie, you took the story house I built and expertly wired it, using all the correct language tools that moved my words smoothly along and lit up my story. Then, you furnished the interior of my story house with some of your own words, making it exciting, warm, inviting, and shall I say, perfect. Thank you again, Melanie, I was very lucky to find you.

Special thanks to Holly Chervnsik of SuburbanBuzz.com. She read my manuscript and then let her creative juices flow to design the perfect cover for my book. Then she went inside the cover to format the edited version to my exact specifications. Thank you, Holly, I was very lucky to find you too.

PROLOGUE

October. The storm rumbled in the midnight sky above Seattle. Lightning turned the dark landscape into a ghostly scene, like a black-and-white negative. Rain strafed the city through the night like fifty caliber rounds.

In the morning, as the storm continued its war on Seattle, ex-Navy Seal Brody Alexander sat alone at a window in a coffee shop. He looked through the streams of silvery bullets outside and surveilled the building across the street. His attention was focused on a third-floor unit where the robo caller lived. The miscreant made the mistake of scamming money from Brody's next-door neighbor, his elderly friend, Mary.

What started as a simple investigation for Brody and his team morphed into an international crime scene. He is out for justice and retribution. How much pain he'll have to inflict to achieve that outcome will totally depend on...

THE SCAMMERS.

Chapter 1

BRODY ALEXANDER

Brody Alexander was born and raised in San Diego by loving parents as an only child. He grew up fast, hard, handsome, and huge—six foot three and over 200 pounds by the time he was 14.

As a freshman at Santana High School in Santee, an east county suburb, he proved his prowess on the football field as an All-Star tight-end. He earned All-State honors in that position all four years and planned to play college football. Maybe he'd make it to the NFL.

That all changed a month before graduation. His parents were driving home from a tour of a potential college match for him, when they were killed by a drunk driver. Brody was devastated and filled with grief and hatred for the drunk. The bastard also died in the crash. If he hadn't, Brody would've tried to kill him. At 18, there was only revenge in his heart.

For too many years after his parents died, he'd

kept the drunk driver alive through hate. He finally decided to kill him off, metaphorically, in order to move on. He did that by imagining his parents in Heaven and the drunk in hell. It worked.

Alone after graduation, Brody joined the Navy. He figured it would keep him too busy to grieve. He was right. They turned him into a highly trained military asset and extreme patriot. One quote he cherished above all others was made by Nathan Hale. Just before the British hung him in 1776, Hale said, "I regret that I have but one life to give for my country."

Brody was that guy. If mortally wounded on the battlefield, he wouldn't lay down and die. He'd continue to fight till the lights went out. Quit wasn't in his vocabulary. He was like the snake that still bites after its head had been severed. He made the Navy his career with no regrets.

Brody, now forty-eight years old, still had thick sandy brown hair, big blue eyes, and a youthful body. It made him appear ten years younger. He'd grown to six foot four, two hundred thirty pounds, and his frame was solidly muscled with no obvious damage...until he was shirtless. A variety of scars and remnants of compound fractures were souvenirs from thirty years of service to his country. What doesn't kill you makes you stronger. He was mended and good to go.

Women looked at him and swooned, disarmed by his dimpled smile. Men beheld him with a tinge of fear. His stare alone was intimidating.

He retired at the rank of Navy Seal Command Master Chief Petty Officer and was living the single life in a two-bedroom bungalow in the North Park area of San Diego. Being deployed all over the globe and away from home didn't help build lasting relationships. None progressed further than friends with benefits. Women learned that Brody's first commitment was to his Navy career. Some tried to change him, and those who stayed the longest were the most stubborn about giving up.

After a few months of retirement, the bachelor tried some online dating. He preferred that method of contacting and socializing with the opposite sex. It was convenient, easy, and without pressure, and allowed him to learn about a woman anonymously through her profile. Friends told him to be careful. Catfishing trolls lurked on sites to take financial advantage of gullible men. Brody weeded those out by using resources not available to the regular citizenry.

He had some good dates and some bad. It was better than trying to hook up in a bar or nightclub. That was never his style. He wasn't interested in one-night stands. Although his door was always open for female companionship that was meaningful and beneficial to both parties, it was on hold for now.

***

Brody liked how the salty mist from the nearby Pacific washed over his face as he ran through Balboa Park. It kept him cool. He ran early every morning since retiring. One thing the Seals taught him was to always stay in shape. He did so religiously and thrived on the endorphins produced by working out. He was free now to do whatever he wanted. He loved that his days were filled with want-tos instead of have-tos. But today something was different.

This morning, he couldn't shake the feeling that this new-found freedom was going to reverse direction and take him back to the rigors of his old Seal life—sacrifice and constant danger. He ran through the park's five-mile trail, wondering what would make him do that. Go back. Only two things came to mind. World War III, or someone close to him in desperate need of his military skills. Neither was on his radar. *That's not it.*

The cool, overcast morning was about to become blazing hot. He checked the forecast before leaving his bungalow. A September Santa Ana wind would blow in hot from the desert at any minute. He hated the Santa Anas, but that would only change his attitude—not his life. *That's not it either.*

Balboa Park was directly across from the San Diego Naval Medical Center. A place he became very familiar with through many painful stays as a patient. Sailors and Marines called it the Balboa Body Repair Shop. He could see the facility through the trees as he ran. Lurking, watching him. Like the Grim Reaper. *Am I having a premonition of my death?*

Brody loved the serenity of the trail as it wound through the dense trees and bypassed the world-class zoo, various exhibits, and museums. Even though it got to be a daily routine, he never tired of the view. But today, it seemed like it was looking back at him.

Had he become too predictable? After all, he was still on a few foreign adversaries' hit lists, as were many other military personnel. He knew they would never stop looking for him. That's why the lightweight backpack strapped to his back held his 9mm Glock with two extra clips. *Are they finally closing in on me?*

Now he was tense, anxious, and full of foreboding. That voice coming from his mind had a warning tone. That same voice helped him stay alive through war and life, so he wasn't going to ignore it. He heard it as...*caution, a change is coming. Your cushy civilian life is about to morph into a hybrid version of your old one, and you need to be ready. But why?*

As he ran, he looked around with suspicion instead of fun, and didn't like that at all. He strained his eyes to find some reason, some proof for his paranoia. He always ran at a fast pace. Other runners couldn't keep up, so as usual, he was alone on the trail. *Stay sharp. Stay alert.*

There. A shadowy shape moved into the trees to his right for concealment and stopped, just on the outer edge of his peripheral vision. He didn't dare move his head in that direction. He wasn't going to give up his tactical advantage of spotting the hiding place. He exaggerated the pumping of his right arm to distract the watcher from him reaching back with his left hand to unzip the backpack and reach for his Glock. He could shoot equally well with his left or right hand, as all Seals were trained to do.

He was ready. The trail ahead curved sharply to the right. That would close the gap between him and the hidden. Suddenly, the figure bolted out from behind a 10-foot-high pine and ran up the slope to his right and away from him. *False alarm. Just a California mule deer.*

He completed the right-hand curve and headed down a quarter mile straightaway with the adrenaline spike easing up a bit. The trail would curve again to the right at the end of the straightaway and empty into the parking lot where his F-150 Raptor was parked.

About fifty yards down the trail on his left, he saw a smallish woman sitting on a bench. She wore a wide-brimmed hat and a white sundress down to her ankles. Her head bent forward, chin tight to her chest, as if in prayer, asleep, unconscious, or? Definitely not a normal sitting position. *Is she hurt? Has she been mugged? She doesn't look like a threat. But then traps never do.*

He looked ahead in a 180-degree arc to see if anyone was making a getaway from her. With each footfall, he got closer and more concerned. She hadn't moved a single muscle since he spotted her. He couldn't even tell if she was breathing. He kicked into a full run, then braked hard to a stop when he got to her.

"Ma'am! Ma'am!" He shouted.

Hearing his yell, the lady lifted her head up to look at him. Her face came out from under the large hat and gave him a jolt. He knew her. It was his 75-year-old neighbor, Mrs. Mary Charbenau. And she was sobbing.

"Mary, what's wrong?"

She stood and faced him, wringing her hands. "Oh, Brody, I'm ruined," she cried out.

Mary's confession caused her to hyperventilate, go limp, and collapse into his chest. Standing there on the trail, he quietly held her in his arms. He never knew what to do in these situations. He could lead hundreds of men into life-and-death battles without fear. But when a female of any age was crying, he was the deer in headlights, frozen in fear. These were the only times in his life when he felt completely helpless.

While in his catatonic state, Brody thought back to the first time he'd met Mary. He was moving into his bungalow next door to hers, carrying loads from the back of his Ford Raptor, when she walked up with a plate of Madeleine cookies and introduced herself. The tiny gray-haired woman had a bright and cheery smile.

Mary was widowed, and her husband Zeke had gone to heaven 10 years earlier. A retired nurse, she had worked her whole 42-year career at Mercy Hospital and helped thousands of patients get better. That was her greatest reward. He couldn't have wished for a better neighbor.

Finally, after what seemed like eons, Mary's breathing settled, and her shaking subsided. She took a deep breath, looked back up at him, and began to tell her story. Thankfully, this freed him from his paralysis.

"Brody, I found out yesterday that someone took all the money out of my bank account. Last night I was so upset I couldn't sleep. Early this morning, I saw you leave in your truck. I was too nervous to drive, so I walked down to the park. I know you come here to run, and I've been waiting, hoping to see you."

Brody had definitely compromised his security. He'd become lax, complacent. Even Mary knew his jogging routine at the park. *How could I overlook the fact that this is the perfect place for an ambush? Huge wake-up call, Brody.*

"My Zeke was the one man in my life who always knew what to do. I know you're smart, just like he was, and I hope you can give me some advice. Plus, you're a good neighbor."

"Sure, I'll definitely help if I can. What happened?"

"I'm afraid it's a long story."

"That's okay. Let me drive you to my place. I'll make some coffee, and you can take your time telling me all about it."

***

Mary sat at Brody's kitchen table. As she continued to regain her composure, he fixed two cups of coffee and looked at her with pain in his heart. She wasn't the spry Frenchwoman he'd grown accustomed to. Today, she seemed frail and defeated, as if the ordeal had aged her. After taking off her hat, her white hair, normally styled perfectly, was a mess. Her root beer brown eyes, normally bright, were dull and sad. Only her full white teeth and olive skin survived whatever happened to her. He hoped her usually beautiful and welcoming smile would also return soon.

"Tell me everything."

"Well, it started simple enough. Just a voicemail. A man said he was from the Social Security Administration and my monthly check was on hold pending verification of my identity. When I heard that, I almost had a heart attack. I need that check, Brody. It's what I live on. He repeated a phone number several times and said to call as soon as possible. I was so worried. I called the number right away."

Scare tactics. Not a good sign.

"Did the man answer?"

"Yes, and I could tell it was the same man by his voice. I told him who I was, and I asked him why my check was on hold."

"Okay, try to remember everything he said. Take your time and be as specific as you can."

"I'll try. The man said, 'Mrs. Charbenau, I have your file right here. Thank you for calling back so soon. Some people don't and then call in a panic when their checks stop coming. Let me explain what happened. We received a directive from

Washington that affects everyone on social security. There have been instances of mail fraud where social security checks were sent to different addresses other than the payees. Then those checks were fraudulently cashed. So, now we have to verify everyone's personal information before we send out more checks. It's for your protection, Mrs. Charbenau. Don't worry. This'll only take a minute, and we can check you off our list.' I was so relieved, Brody."

The bastard set her up. He knew she'd tell him whatever he wanted to know to keep her check coming.

Brody's hands balled into fists.

Mary sipped some coffee and continued.

"I gave him the information he wanted. Social security number, driver's license, address, phone number, etc. He told me it all matched my account and that he released the hold. I was so happy. I thanked him and said God bless you. He said, 'You're welcome, Mrs. Charbenau, and God bless you too.' I really like it when I hear people say God bless you. It makes me feel that they're honest. Finally, he said, 'Before I let you go, I have one more question.'

Here it comes.

'Would you like to do direct deposit and bypass the problems with the mail? Your social security money will go right into your account. Then you won't have to worry about this happening again. You can do it right now; it only takes a couple of minutes.'

"I told him yes, let's do it. It was so easy, Brody. He did it all for me. He just needed my bank account number, ID, and password."

The hammer.

"After I gave him the information, he said, 'All right, Mrs. Charbenau, you're all set. You'll see your monthly benefit go directly into your account on the very next cycle date. If you have any questions or concerns, just call me at this number.' We said our goodbyes and hung up. That was two days ago."

"You said yesterday you found out your money was missing. How?"

"I went to my bank to get $40 for my church bazaar. When I got the receipt, I saw that my balance was just $110. I told the teller there must be a mistake and please double check my balance. She did, and I started to shake. I almost fainted. The teller could see I was upset and asked if I wanted to talk to the manager. I said yes. She walked me over to his office and introduced me. I sat down, and she closed the door."

"You're doing great, Mary. I'm impressed."

"Thank you, Brody. You've calmed me down and made it easier for me to remember. The manager asked me what the problem was. I told him I had $25,850 in my account and that I didn't take any of the money out except the $40 that morning. He brought up my account and turned the screen towards me so we could both look. There was only a balance of $110. He showed me that the day before, at 4:09 p.m., there was an online transfer of

$25,700 to an off-shore bank account number. I told him I didn't do that. He asked me if I gave someone access to my account. I told him no."

"I think you did, Mary. You gave that social security guy all your account information. This is more than a glitch in the bank's system," Brody said.

"Yes, I remembered that as soon as I told him no, and my heart started racing, and I got butterflies in my stomach. I told the manager that I did talk to a Social Security agent about my account so he could set up direct deposits for me. The manager didn't see any activity on my account for that, just the online transfer, which passed all the bank's protocols. He said, 'I'm sorry, Mrs. Charbenau, it looks like you're a victim of a scam. Let me transfer your $110 dollars into a new account and cancel the old one. There's nothing else I can do except call the fraud department and have you talk to one of our agents.' I talked to the agent and opened a claim. I don't know what to do now."

This is it. This is what my sixth sense was trying to tell me earlier. How did it know? Was it fate? This could just be a coincidence...if I believed in coincidences.

Mary didn't know what to do, but Brody did. Put his civilian life on hold. Strike up a military mission. Find the asshole who scammed Mary, and get her money back.

What he said next would commit him to that end, and there'd be no turning back. However, she was one of the two things that would make him go back

to being a Navy Seal—she was a friend in need.
   He dove in.

Chapter 2
THE COMMITMENT

"Mary, I see this the same way your bank manager does. I believe you've been scammed by a professional. Filing a claim probably feels a little underwhelming, but there's nothing else you can do. However, there may be something I can do. Do you still have that phone number he gave you?"

"Yes, it's in my call log. I tried to call it several times, but it's disconnected."

"That's all right. Let me have your phone for a couple of days. I have some friends who might be able to trace the call. We'll start there and see what we can do."

"I didn't mean for you to get involved with my problem, Brody. I just hoped you could tell me what you think I should do if anything."

"Believe me, Mary, I want to help, and I know my friends will too. In the meantime, is there someone who can help monitor your calls, texts, emails, and regular mail for potential scams? There are so many these days it's hard to keep up and easy to fall for

GET THE SCAMMER

one. Especially a trusting person like yourself."

"I do have a niece in Las Vegas, Jane Peltier. We used to write letters, but now we text. We also talk on the phone the first day of each month. That was her idea to stay connected more often, and it's worked out very well. She always tells me to give her a call if I need anything. I know she'll help me."

"Sounds good. If something comes up that you're not sure about, and for some reason Jane can't help, just let me know. I'll check it out for you. For now, the best thing to do is not to give anyone your personal information until you get a second opinion, agreed?"

"Agreed."

Brody walked Mary next door. When they got to her porch, she asked, "Would you like to come in? I have some cake. I feel like I owe you something, taking up your whole day."

"That's quite all right. I'll have the cake some other time. I'm gonna call my friends and get to work on tracking down that call. I'll keep you updated. And Mary, I don't want you to worry about money. I have plenty saved up, and I can loan you whatever you need with no interest. I say loan because I know you won't accept it any other way."

"I don't know what to say. You've made me feel so much better, and you've given me hope. Thank you!"

"I'll try to do more than that, I promise. Talk to you later."

Brody hustled home. He knew he had to find the

scammer, and fast. And he knew he'd need backup. Fortunately, he knew two of the best people in the world who could help him find the low life that changed Mary's life—his surrogate brothers.

Back when Brody's parents were killed by the drunk driver, he had no blood relatives left in the world. But through the Navy, he found what he considered to be two blood brothers. He excelled throughout his Boot Camp training and was selected to try out for the Seals. On the bus to the training facility, he met Shawn O'Conner and Nick Barbo.

The three bonded instantly and became best buddies. They helped each other through the trials and tribulations of becoming Seals, and all three received Trident Insignias after completing the course with the highest honors. From then on, Brody referred to them as his brothers from other mothers. They served together as an exclusive Special Forces team their entire careers.

Shawn and Nick retired around the same time Brody did. He knew they were both in town without any current commitments and would call them individually to ask for their help. Then each would decide without pressure from the other. This mission would take them back to a life they had left and away from their new routines. That was a lot to ask, and Brody knew it.

If anyone could trace the scam call, Shawn could. Brody called him first, knowing many considered him the best communication specialist the Navy ever had. Brody tapped the combination on his phone, envisioning the fair-skinned, red-headed, American-Irishman who sometimes answered calls with a fake but funny brogue.

"What's happening, mate?"

"Hey, how'd you like to knock off the rust and join me on a mission?"

"Lad! You're talkin' in riddles. Keeps me mind sharp. How's about a tad more info." Shawn hiccuped.

"You must be drinking your favorite Connemara single malt Irish whiskey…"

"Sláinte!" Shawn confirmed.

Brody laid the whole story out as quickly as he could.

"So, as you can see, time is critical if we're going to find this guy before he moves on or gets another gig. I'll be doing the leg work and need your expertise to get me there. It's a big ask, so I'll understand if you don't want to take it on. No worries if you don't, my friend."

"I'm in, Brode. You know I hate scams. Let's get the bastard. Give me the number, and I'll get on it straight away. When I track him down, you got someone in mind to do the breakdown on him?"

"You know I do. I'll let you know if he comes on board. I'll text you Mary's number, the scam number, and the time the call was made. Thanks again, buddy."

"No problem. I'm ready to rock."

After Brody texted Shawn the info, he called his other brother from an Italian mother, Nick.

"Hey, Brody, it's not poker night, is it?"

"Hi, Sofia. No, it's not poker night. Are you covering your Hubby's phone while he's eating some of your fantastic homemade lasagna? I know he likes it while it's hot."

"No, dinner's still in the oven. Five-cheese this time. He's actually on the throne. I think he goes in there just to hide from me. And... what do you know? The king has returned. Nice to hear your voice, Brody. Come on by. I'd love to cook you up a feast."

"Thanks, Sofia. You know I can't get enough of your cooking."

"Here's your bud. Bye, Brody."

"Hi, Brody. Is it poker night?" came Nick's baritone voice.

"That's funny, your better half asked me the same thing. No, it's not poker night. I wish it was. I have a huge favor to ask, and it's kinda your fault. If you weren't the world's number one expert at gathering and interpreting intelligence on people and places, retired or not, I wouldn't be asking. I'm not trying to kiss your ass...I'm calling because you're the best."

"Dude. You must be in some serious crap to shower all that sugar on me. What's going on?"

Brody told Nick the whole story, but left out the part about Shawn volunteering.

"That's a terrible story, Brody. I told you about Sofia's sister being conned out of $50,000 by a guy she met on one of those dating sites. She thought they were going to get married. Once she gave him the money, she never heard from him again."

"Yeah, I do remember that. How's she doing?"

"Never really recovered, even though we caught the bastard and got most of her money back. It's just that, well, she lost faith in men and hasn't dated since. All because of that lowlife. So, count me in, Brody. Helping your neighbor is the least I can do. When do we start?"

"Whoa. Don't you think you should talk this over with Sofia first?"

"I will, of course, but she'll be on board. She hated what that guy did to her sister. Besides, she's always supportive when someone's in need."

"Well then, I can tell you the mission is already in motion. I called Sha—"

"What? You called Shawn first? After all the number one stuff you just laid on me?"

"Hold on! We both know Shawn has to trace the call before you can do your magic."

"I know, I know. Just teasing, buddy. You got the best man to do that job."

"Yeah, I gave him the phone number, and he's working it. Also, I want you to know that I called each of you separately on purpose. I didn't want either of you to feel pressured. It's gonna take a good deal of time and effort."

"I get that, and I appreciate the sentiment, but I think you know nothing would stop the two of us from joining you in this fight."

"Thanks. Feels good to be back in the fray with

you guys. I'm feeling pretty confident about our chances now that you're in. I'll be setting up a meeting at my house. I'll let you know when after I talk with Shawn."

"Sounds good. Talk to you later, bro."

Brody went to his makeshift office in a corner of his master bedroom and got his desk ready to lay out a battle plan. As he moved things around, he felt angry, once again, that no one in the government was doing anything to stop scams. Every agency knew it was a huge problem. Everyone was losing money because of it—banks, businesses, and the general public. Yet nothing was ever done. It made him wonder if the politicians were profiting from the fraud too. Scum, if they were.

It looked like he and his friends would have to do what the government wouldn't. Brody called the guys back and set a meet at his house for early the next morning.

***

Nick and Shawn arrived at 7 a.m., right on time. Brody had veggie omelets and hash browns in hotpots on the stove. The green tea, coffee, and doughnuts were to snack on later.

"Help yourselves, guys."

Brody took a full plate of food to the table and sat down.

"Mighty nice of you, Brody. Next up, salad for lunch and salmon for dinner, am I right?" Shawn asked seriously. He knew Brody was a bit of a health nut.

Nick raised his hand.

"I second that. Sophia and I have been slacking off in the health food department."

"You got it brothers. I always say a healthy body, mind, and spirit prepares one for a fight. Good way to kick off this mission. I'm real thankful you guys are taking this on with me. I know you'll keep me in line like you've always done. We all know I can be a bit impatient."

Shawn and Nick both confirmed their commitment to the cause and agreed to keep Brody in check. After morning chow, they cleaned up and got started.

The day was spent brainstorming and arranging tasks. They came up with a simple plan. Shawn would find out where the target was, Nick would find out who he was, and Brody would confront the asshole. Shawn, the lead, already made contact with two active-duty guys who could get him access to military satellite networks. They'd cut through the red tape and get him whatever he needed as fast as possible. This was a very good start.

If Shawn was successful, then Nick would take over and compile Intel on the target, and figure out how to get Mary's money back. At that point, it would be Brody's part of the mission to make contact with the scammer.

They were confident they'd find him. After all, that was exactly what they had been trained to do. The three of them were responsible for eliminating several of the world's most wanted terrorists.

Monsters that planned out and executed heinous acts of violence, including blowing up school buses, hijacking civilian passenger aircraft and flying them into high-rise buildings, and many other crimes against humanity.

They were finalizing their contingency plans over the remnants of salmon steaks and steamed broccoli when the doorbell rang.

"Excuse me, guys," Brody said as he went to open the door.

Mary stood there smiling and holding a freshly baked pie.

"Hi, Brody. I just felt like I had to do something for you since you offered to help me. I baked one of my specialties, and it's still hot from the oven."

"Mary, you shouldn't have. Thank you, it smells great. Please come in. I want you to meet my two best friends. You've probably seen them come and go, but now it's time for formal introductions. They've agreed to help me get your money back."

"Oh my, you're making me feel so important. I'd love to meet them and thank them personally."

Brody took the pie and led her to the kitchen. After the intros, they all enjoyed coffee and slices of Mary's homemade peach pie delight. When they finished, she stood and teared up as she spoke.

"I just can't thank you wonderful men enough for what you're trying to do for me. I don't know how I'm going to repay you. But, I want you to know, if it doesn't work out, well, please don't worry. The fact that you're trying has lifted my spirits and made me feel so much better."

Brody, Nick, and Shawn stood and gave her a group hug. They told her not to worry, that they would do everything they could to make things right.

Brody walked her to the door. "Mary, the guys and I agree that your wonderful pie will suffice as the retainer for our services, and if we get your money back, we'll need a blueberry pie for final payment. Deal?"

Mary started to say something, and Brody held up his hand to stop her.

"Please, we want to do this for you, and we're actually doing it for ourselves, too, okay?"

"Okay."

"I told you I'd keep you in the loop, and here's your first update. We've been discussing how to approach this situation since early this morning, and we've formulated a preliminary plan. We'll refine it once we have all the information we need. Everything we already talked about will be set in motion first thing tomorrow, and Mary, we're pretty confident about our chances to succeed."

"Thank you so much. I can't believe this. It's all happening so fast. Please tell Nick and Shawn I said thanks again and that it was so nice to meet them. I'll be praying for you boys every day."

Brody went back to the kitchen and relayed Mary's message. It was getting late, and Nick and Shawn had things to do at home. They decided to break up the tribunal, and the guys left.

Brody went out to the backyard and laid out in a lounge chair on the open patio. With his hands behind his head, he pondered the barely visible stars through the huge eucalyptus tree in the middle of the yard. The wind blew through the leaves, a fluttering sound that was soothing, putting him almost to sleep. The fresh air and quiet always revitalized his mind, body, and spirit. It helped him think about things objectively.

It was true what he told Mary. He was fairly certain they'd find the scammer. When they did, he was going to have to control his anger and apply just enough pressure, both mentally and physically, to get the job done. He hated that he had to make another transgressor pay for choosing to exploit people because of greed.

If the scammer and the rest of the humans on the planet would use their energy and skills to work together, the achievements and rewards would be as plentiful as the stars. But in order to accomplish that, the battle between good and evil has to be won. Evil is selfish, controlling, narcissistic, and egomaniacal. Someday the battle will be fought on a full scale. For now, I'll fight the small skirmishes.

He rose to go inside.

Goodbye, stars. See you soon, scammer.

Chapter 3
PAST ENEMIES

Inside, Brody poured himself a glass of Merlot, got comfortable in his living room recliner, and began to reminisce. He recalled the most significant mission he, Shawn, and Nick had done together. It was a highly classified, top-secret mission to eliminate the sadistic leader of a terrorist group and his minions.

The CIA had confirmed through their Israeli sources who the leader was and his location. The Israelis learned the group was planning to place car bombs in the parking structure at the Mall of America in Minneapolis. At the same time, they'd plant bombs in various locations inside, including the food courts, to kill as many Americans as possible. They planned to do it on a Sunday, the busiest day of the week.

If the terrorists succeeded in carrying out the attack, it would cause panic and fear not only in Minneapolis but all over the nation. Besides the death toll and destruction, people would be afraid to shop anywhere, and the U.S. economy would suffer greatly. That was the idea for attacking the Mall—kill as many civilians as possible, and kill the U.S. economy at the same time. "Death to America" was their mantra.

At the time, the Israelis didn't know when it was going to happen, just where. The DHS beefed up security, but that wouldn't stop a determined terrorist. The only way to prevent the attack was to take them out first.

The leader of the terrorist group was one Aahil Aydin. He was making his deadly Mall plans in the back room of a brothel located in a small town surrounded by mountains outside of Damascus. The brothel's customers were serviced by young Russian girls who had been kidnapped and trafficked out of southern Russia through Turkey. It is a sin against Islam to have a brothel with Muslim girls, but not if the girls were Russian or any other nationality they deemed to be infidels. The Muslim men and women could enslave or do whatever they wanted to those girls with Allah's blessing.

Brody, Nick, and Shawn trained with the Israeli Mossad for the mission and were ready to go in just two day's time. It was a joint operation, and the plan was to hit the brothel with a coordinated attack. The Israelis were going to come through the front of the brothel during the early morning hours when it was closed. The girls and their guards inside should all be asleep during that time. Brody's team would hit the rear where the terrorists were planning the deaths of innocent American men, women, and children. The Israelis were going to rescue as many of the girls as they could and deliver them back to the Russians.

The gesture might secure some quid pro quo if they ever needed a favor from the Russians, diplomatic or otherwise. This rescue operation was a brilliant means to keep their friends close and their enemies even closer.

Brody and the guys planned to break into the back and immediately kill all the terrorists there. Laptops, hard drives, cell phones, and any paper documents would be confiscated, and then they'd race back to the drop zone.

On the day of the mission, Brody, Nick, and Shawn dropped from the bay of a B-2 stealth bomber. Using radar-absorbing flying suits, they glided down to 2200 feet above the landing area and deployed their chutes undetected. They landed at the base of a mountain, just one mile east of the brothel at 2 a.m. They had to be in and out before sunrise.

They secured the extraction zone and radioed the exact GPS coordinates to Army Captain Dan Knapp, who became a lifelong friend to them after the mission. He'd be piloting the Blackhawk chopper that would pick them up. The timing had to be exact. If the mission got stalled for any reason, the noise of the chopper coming in through a narrow pass in the mountains would alert the terrorists and risk the extraction. If they were successful, Knapp would pick them up and fly them out to a friendly base in

Turkey.

From the secured zone, they double-timed it through the one-mile stretch of desert and arrived at the back of the brothel at 2:25 a.m. They saw a single sleeping terrorist sitting by the back door. His head tilted back against the wall, exposing his neck. Brody walked right up to him and with a single swing of his KA-BAR knife, sliced through the carotid artery. The rapist and murderer of children died instantly and was probably looking around in Allah land for his 70 virgins. Instead, Brody believed he would be tormented by fire and anguish in a nightmare that would never end.

At 2:40 a.m., a trash truck with six hidden Mossad commandos and two disguised in city work clothes hanging off the back, pulled up to the curb in front of the brothel. Brody let the Israeli leader know his team was in position in the alley waiting outside the back door. On the street, two filthy Israelis in stinking trash company uniforms stepped off the putrid truck and headed to a couple of trash cans on the sidewalk. Two terrorist guards with AK-47s sat at each side of the brothel's front door, smoking cigars that choked the fresh night air. They laughed at the two garbage men.

In sync, the two Israelis (now completely ignored by the guards) reached out a hand to grab a can, then pivoted. They pulled out silenced Glock 19s from their pockets and double-tapped each guard in the head, followed by a single tap to the heart just to be sure. Liquefied chunks of brain slowly dripped down on signs taped to the brothel windows behind them, advertising in Arabic the sexual fantasies that could be had inside for a few Syrian liras.

Seconds later, Brody got the go signal from the Israeli captain, and both teams hit their entrances.

The eight-man Mossad team entered through the main entrance in the middle of the building. It opened into a large room with a reception desk directly across from the door and chairs and couches on both sides of the room. Four men slept on cots, two on each end of the room. All were shot dead before they could make the slightest move.

An opening to a hallway draped by beads was in the middle of the room next to the desk. They quickly went through and into the hallway. The team leader could see a closed door at the very end of the long hallway about 60 feet away. The Israelis knew that on the other side of that door, the Americans were doing their part of the mission.

Six rooms faced each other on each side of the hallway, doors closed. The team would have 12 rooms to clear. The first eight rooms just past the beaded entry was where their informer told them the girls were being kept, forced to do unspeakable things while being videoed. Their captors got money from walk-in customers and then sold the explicit videos on the black market for additional cash.

The team knew the last four rooms at the end of the hallway were where the scums in charge lived. There'd be no mercy for them. The commandos would clear those rooms first because the ones inside would be armed.

They rushed down the hallway to bring justice to the enslaved, tortured, and abused girls, positioning themselves in twos outside each door. With a synchronized hand signal, the four two-man teams kicked in each door and sprayed silenced nine-millimeter rounds into every monster inside.

In one of the rooms, a man and woman who were having sex jumped naked from their bed and reached for two Ruger Mark IV pistols on the table next to them. Only the man managed to get a hand on one of the guns before he and the madam were fatally riddled with bullets and sent into the afterlife to face the fires of hell.

In the other rooms, the pimps and kidnappers were still sleeping when the Israeli UZIs took their lives. The Israelis made sure no one was left alive before they went back to the first eight rooms to retrieve 16 young girls, two to a room. The rooms were bare except for beds. The commandos did their best to calm the frightened and naked teens, grabbing bed sheets to cover them as best they could. Then they rushed them outside and into the back of the garbage truck and sped off.

Meanwhile, Brody, Nick and Shawn, donning night goggles, charged into the back room. Brody covered the middle, Nick covered the left flank, and Shawn the right. There was no hesitation as they put bullets into sleeping terrorists lying on floor mattresses spread around the room. Two were light sleepers and woke just in time to shut their eyes permanently with three-round bursts in their heads.

The plan wasn't to take Aahil Aydin or anyone else alive. They knew from experience they couldn't extract any more information from the terrorists. Most interrogation techniques were banned by liberal U.S. politicians. Besides, the terrorists were more than happy to spread disinformation as another tool to succeed with their demented plans.

They secured the room and checked each body for a pulse. Not finding any, they went over to a large table in the center of the room with two computers and three laptops. They removed the computer hard drives and stuffed the laptops in their backpacks. In a file cabinet under the table, they found Google satellite photos of the Mall of America and paper files. They grabbed it all, including all cell phones and surveillance camera recordings. Then they went back to the body of Aydin, took his picture, cut off his hands for fingerprints and DNA, put them in a dry ice bag, and left.

Knapp was waiting for them at the extraction site. They hopped in and Dan quickly took off without incident. The mission was a phenomenal success. The Russians got their girls back with indebtedness to Israel. The plan to attack the Mall was thwarted by Brody and team with acquired assets from the brothel. Three embedded cells near the Mall planned to carry out the attack. FBI teams took out each cell without a single FBI fatality or injury. However, several terrorists decided to be martyrs, and the FBI gladly accommodated them.

As Brody replayed this memory, he also knew that the terrorist battle would never end as long as some believed their God sanctioned the killing of anyone who didn't believe the way they did. In addition, there would always be those tyrannical Marxist dictators terrorizing the world to gain control at the cost of millions of lives. What absolute horror the world would have been spared if only a single bullet had pierced the head of Hitler before he rose to power.

Aahil Aydin wasn't a Hitler, and Brody's team made sure he'd never become one. Brody was proud of his guys. With the success of that mission, they proved to be one of the world's most elite teams for finding and eliminating terrorists who were hell-bent on death and destruction. They used the same method of operation over and over again—learning everything about their target, finding out where he was hiding, and quietly taking him out. They were so good at it they had the freedom to develop their own detailed plans, including logistics, strategies, tactics, and backup contingencies.

They'd use those same skills to find Mary's scammer.

Chapter 4

THE SEARCH

It was like old times for the three of them. Each was energized and glad to be back in the saddle. They couldn't wait to correct another wrong in the world. Over the years, Nick and Shawn had retained contacts that they could rely on for help, no questions asked. They were primed and ready to get started on this new mission.

Shawn, with his expertise in communication, would take the lead and trace the cellular signals left by Mary's scammer. Those signals would lead back to the exact location they were transmitted from. Then Nick would go to work with his intelligence gathering experience, techniques, and connections. He would learn everything about that location he could. The hunt was on!

It only took Shawn around ten hours the next day to work his magic. He isolated and captured the signal that came from the phone used to leave a voicemail for Mary. Then he converted the signal into its digital identification code, much like an internet IP address. That way, he was able to track the signal back to any source of transmission, even if it came from a burner phone. That's the secret that militaries, intelligence services, and law enforcement agencies around the world don't want criminals or terrorists to know. Their burner phones are not completely safe.

Using his security clearances, Shawn uploaded the code into a highly classified GPS satellite. Then he coaxed the satellite database and servers through intricate electronic calisthenics to get to the signal's starting point. The task wasn't easy. In fact, it was one of the most formidable challenges Shawn ever faced. He needed to cut through multiple layers of digital cover—firewalls, smoke screens, red herrings, and other roadblocks—before he was able to expose the path the signal took. The signal originated from a highly encrypted computer and bounced off numerous cell towers and satellites. It pinballed back and forth around several geographic locations, both inside and outside the U.S.

Whoever set up the system tried very hard to avoid detection and would have if not for Shawn's skill and resources. He knew the scammer deleted the number he used to call Mary as soon as he got her money. Cell providers have trillions of numbers in their systems. When scammers drop a number, they just pick a new one and start over. Nevertheless, Shawn recaptured the deleted number's signal and its path and nailed the spot where the transmission started. He double-checked himself, and when he was 100% certain he was right, he shouted out, "GOTCHA you schmuck...your RF waves and electromagnetic field made a one-of-a-kind electronic signature—yours!"

He immediately did a double cross latitude and longitude on the location and zeroed in on an area of about 760 square feet. He still had the magic, and man it felt good. He emailed the information over to Nick, and then called him.

When Nick picked up, Shawn couldn't wait to start bragging. "Hey, brah! You get my email?"

"Yeah, I'm looking at it right now. Is this what I think it is?"

"But of course, mate. I located where the bastard made the call. Seattle, Washington, USA, at the precise coords I sent you."

"Brody and I always joke that you could locate someone by forensically analyzing their farts."

"Ha! Yeah, I did some heavy lifting on this one. The signal was cloaked behind some serious cover. This ain't just one guy working out of his garage. He had a lot of technical support to keep from being found. We'll have to be on top of our game when we go after him and whoever he's working with."

"Now that we know where the call was made, all I have to do is find out who made it."

"Piece of cake, right?"

"For me? You know it, buddy. Thanks for the heads up on the serious cover. I'll go at this like it's the toughest safe I've ever had to crack. Good work,

Shawn. You gonna update Brody?"

"Yeah, as soon as I hang up. I'm feeling good about our chances now that you've got the ball. You are one tenacious pit bull when you have something to bite on. Glad to throw you the bone."

"Thanks. Tell Brody I've already got my teeth into it. See ya."

When Shawn hung up, Nick thought to himself, *I knew Shawn would get a hit. He never failed to locate someone, as long as they use some kind of electronic device or transaction. Phones, credit cards, radio, GPS, computers, emails, and social media were his bread and butter. It was simply a matter of time. Good thing the location is in Seattle and not somewhere in Russia or North Korea.*

Nick was excited and energized. Using Shawn's precise coordinates, he'd find out everything there was to know about that specific location in Seattle and anyone associated with it. They were hot on their target's tail, and now it was his job to corner him. At his supercomputer, Nick's fingers danced over the keyboard through a choreographed sequence of moves that only his mind knew how to compose. With a final click, he was connected to a military GPS satellite with a top-secret classification. Instantly, a split screen appeared and showed a geographical map with 360-degree views of the location.

He saw 3D digital images of the area out to a 10-mile radius marked by a red pin on his screen. Optional features were listed vertically in a margin on the left and in the search box at the top. All information on the area had been recorded 29 days earlier. Typically, the satellite would reimage and update everything in that zone automatically every 30 days.

So it wouldn't be reimaging this area for another day. However, every time the satellite was in range, Nick could override its programing and get real-time images with stills and video. He was also authorized to use the satellite's advanced thermal imaging and infrared cameras with the latest penetrating technology. That technology could detect a variety of heat signatures, whether outside or inside a building, even below the surface to a depth of two hundred feet. If a heart was pumping blood anywhere in the satellite's range, he'd see it.

He slowly scanned every corner of the map and examined the details of every building, street name, address, geographical elevations, and businesses. Finally, he clicked on the targeted red pin. The map spun around, zoomed in, and gave him a street view facing a five-story building. The satellite isolated the 760-square-foot area on the third floor of the building and highlighted it with a pulsing green light.

The building's address was 88 First Avenue, Seattle, Washington. The marquee above the main entrance said, LUXURY CONDOS BY THE PETERSEN COMPANY. In the upper right corner of the highlighted area, the number 348 flashed in white, indicating a 760-square-foot condo unit on that floor.

This was it. The unit where the scammer placed the call to Mary. There was no doubt about it. Who lived there? He was about to find out.

Nick pulled up the condo association's Conditions, Covenants and Restrictions—CC&Rs. As he read through, he made an interesting discovery. Unit 348 was owned by a private charity, the Lentini Foundation. The CC&Rs only allowed a private charity to rent or sub-lease a unit to an employee, agent, or board member of their foundation. An individual owner couldn't rent or lease out their unit. The rules were very strict. Proof of occupancy was required by every unit on an annual basis.

The association's records for unit 348 showed that it was leased to and solely occupied by an employee of the Lentini Charity Foundation. That employee's name was Juan Martin.

Now Nick knew the identity of their target, bogus as it no doubt was, and his exact location. He wanted to call Brody and Shawn and tell them right then, but he knew it would be premature. No, he wouldn't call until he could answer most of the questions he knew would be coming from Brody.

Brody's deep thinking generated questions nobody else thought of. He always insisted each of them carry a notepad and write down things that needed to be acted on in a timely manner. He was relentless in following up and getting updates. He could be a real pain in the ass with it, but he and Shawn let it slide. This was one of the qualities that made Brody a great leader, and it ultimately made them much better at their jobs.

Nick had a lot of work to do to get prepared for Brody. He wanted to completely answer all his questions without having to do more research. If he did, it would be the first time. He took the street view on his screen and rotated it 360 degrees so he could see the whole street.

Foremost, it was a commercially active street lined with businesses, with a few residential high-rises sprinkled in. The street itself had two-way traffic with parking lanes on both sides. There were traffic lights every couple of blocks. Obviously designed to slow traffic and give businesses a chance to advertise their goods and services in their storefront windows.

As Nick rotated his view 180 degrees from the scammer's building, he hit the jackpot. Another five-story building was directly across from the target's building, and it was a hotel, an ideal base of operations for Brody. Nick entered the addresses for both buildings into his one-of-a-kind architectural database. It held the designs and specifications for every building in the world, including the White House, Kremlin, and every other country's capital. It didn't take him long to find the perfect unit in the hotel from which Brody could observe the target's unit.

Nick checked that off as one of the main items on his list. He continued through the next 180 degrees and ended back at the starting point without seeing any red flags or concerns. That done, he clicked off the GPS and database and went to work to learn everything about the scammer and the building he lived in.

On a yellow legal pad, Nick listed the systems associated with the unit and the building he would hack—the building's management company, state and city property tax records, utility providers, construction plans, general contractor (including all subcontractors), city inspectors, and security systems on the building and individual units.

Nick loved this stuff. He couldn't wait to investigate all the different parts and assign a value to each one, like chess pieces. Then he'd arrange them on one of his special mission boards. When he completed it, he and the guys could maneuver the pieces around the board and formulate an opening, middle, and end game. He knew he was under the gun. They needed to get to the target before he moved on to another location. Nevertheless, he'd take the time to be thorough. Missing a small detail could cost the lives of his friends or innocent civilians.

Nick hacked into the HOA's system first and got property tax records for unit 348. The condo unit was purchased with cash by the Lentini Foundation. It listed a Seattle address. The charity paid for all the utilities, HOA fees, and taxes for unit 348, and they leased a black Ford Expedition for Juan. His name was added to the registration and insurance as the primary driver. This was a huge gift to the mission. Shawn would hack into the dealership's GPS system and track wherever Juan went. Perfect!

All those expenses were a big investment for just one guy. So Juan must be running a bigger operation for the charity than scamming individuals out of his unit. A charity is the perfect front that a variety of illegal activities can hide behind, and at the same time, launder the illicit monies. The mission was going to be more complicated than simply going after one scammer.

Nick wondered, *besides a scamming operation, what other crimes for profit was the Lentini charity involved in?*

Chapter 5

LAS VEGAS

Out on a rural desert road 40 miles north of the Las Vegas strip, Dean Setlock, 67, and Maggie Setlock, 66, were driving through a heavy downpour on their way home from their favorite Thursday night restaurant. Both retired, they loved being able to go out and enjoy dinner during the week when most people were on their way home from work.

The wipers weren't keeping up with the amount of rain, and Dean was having trouble seeing through the sheets of water cascading down the windshield.

"Dean Earl, slow down and put your night driving glasses on, right now!"

Maggie used to call him honey when they dated back in high school and for the first 25 years of marriage. Then one day it just stopped, like all the honey had been eaten up, and there was nothing left. Just Dean Earl.

"Okay, okay. You're right. I forgot to put them on."

Dean took the glasses out of the little compartment in the headliner and slipped them on. When he looked in the rearview mirror to see how cool he looked, he saw red and blue flashing lights coming up fast from behind.

"Oh, man."

"What?" Maggie asked.

"Doggone it all, looks like a cop's gonna pull me over."

"What for?"

"I don't know. I was doing the speed limit, and there sure as hell aren't any traffic lights or stop signs way out here."

Dean slowed down and pulled off to the shoulder. The flashing lights rolled right up behind him and stopped just a few feet from his rear bumper. Dean looked in his side mirror and saw an officer in rain gear get out of what looked like a big Suburban or Expedition. He was walking towards him on the driver's side as Dean pulled his license out of his wallet.

"Mags, get the registration and insurance papers out of the glove box. I want to get this over fast so we can get home."

Dean hit the button to lower his window when the officer reached them. He had to scrunch down in his seat to look up to find the face of the biggest police officer he'd ever seen.

"What's the problem, officer?" Dean asked.

"Safety stop, sir. One of our famous washes filled up with rain water and jumped the road up ahead.

Must be a foot of water. Could cause you to hydroplane and lose control."

"Oh. Yeah, I know the wash you're talking about. It's a couple of miles further down the road from where we turn off for home. So we'll be fine."

"That's great news, sir. I'll still have to see your driver's license and yours, too, ma'am, but don't need the car's registration. I know it's an inconvenience, but with the new homeland security laws, it's what they make us do now. I'm sure you two aren't on the terrorist list, but I still have to check because of the new protocols. This'll just take a minute to log your information into my computer, and then you'll be on your way."

Dean raised his window back up after handing over their licenses to keep the pounding rain out.

The officer walked back to his vehicle. Inside he laid the licenses on the seat beside him and took pictures of them on his phone, then sent them to his tech support for verification. A few seconds later, he got a thumbs up emoji and the word GO! He pulled out his walkie-talkie and said, "I'm ready here. Are we clear?"

He got a "clear" from the guy he dropped off five miles behind him, then another "clear," from his guy five miles further up the road. Both clears meant that no vehicles were coming in either direction.

The officer hustled back to the Setlock's car and tapped on Dean's window. Dean hit the down button again. When the window was halfway down, the officer shot Dean in the face. Then he shot

Maggie in the forehead as she recoiled from Dean's organic material that splashed all over her blouse. He put another round in each of their heads and hearts, just to be sure.

He reached in and took Dean's wallet and Maggie's purse. Then he ran back to his vehicle. He put it in drive, hit the gas, and smashed the rear driver's side of the Setlock's car, breaking the taillight. He backed up, put the car in park, got out, picked up all the pieces of the broken taillight, and got back in his vehicle. He made a U-turn and drove back down the road about fifty yards, and stopped. He opened his window and threw the pieces into the same lane the Setlocks were traveling in. The real police would figure that the Setlocks were victims of a bump-and-grab robbery. Robbers bumped cars in front of them, and when both parties pull over to inspect the damage, bang. Case closed.

The cops will wrap this one up in short order and have plenty of time to relax and have some doughnuts and coffee. Lorenzo laughed to himself and called his boss. "I got 'em, Mr. Lentini. Dean and Maggie Setlock. No heirs. We scammed all their personal information a month ago and used it to alter their trust. The beneficiary of all their assets is now the Lentini Charity Foundation.

"Great. Hold on a sec, and let me pull up the trust. Ah, there it is. Perfect forgery, right down to their signatures. I'll let our friend, the Senator, know what her cut is. Good night's work, and great job, Lorenzo. See you back at the office."

"Thank you, Mr. Lentini. Enjoy the rest of your evening."

***

Nick stopped thinking about the Lentini Charity and its possible crimes. He needed to focus on what is, instead of a list of what-ifs. The "what is" he needed to concentrate on most was Juan Martin and his connection to the organization.

Modern-day criminal organizations hid their illicit incomes from gambling, prostitution, etc., behind the sanctified veils of charities. Now the latest brainchild of criminals, robo scam calls, have been added to that list and cloaked behind the same curtain. Since most people recognize a robocall for what it is and ignore it, scammers have to make huge volumes of calls to catch those susceptible to their pitch. That's why 85 billion robocalls are made worldwide each year. With that kind of volume, it's not surprising that one of those calls rang through to Mary's phone.

Getting Mary's money back from what looked like a well-established crime syndicate would be difficult but not impossible. Nick and Shawn had combined their talents many times to extract monies from some of the world's largest terrorist syndicates. Nick didn't think this would reach that level, but they had to prepare just in case.

After he looked over all the compiled information, Nick realized he had to call a team meeting right away. This was bigger and with more players than anticipated. Because of the late hour, he'd try to set it up for first thing in the morning.

He called Brody and Shawn and gave them a short synopsis, and they agreed to meet at his house at 9 a.m. They would convene to look over what he'd gleaned, and he'd see if the guys made the same conclusion.

**

Brody and Shawn pulled into Nick's driveway simultaneously, their watches and brains perfectly synchronized. You could take the man out of the military, but you couldn't take the military out of the man. The three Seals knew the value of timing. There were times when life or death literally depended on a split second one way or the other.

Inside, Nick checked his watch and clairvoyantly walked toward his front door to greet them. He wasn't at all surprised to see Brody as he stepped onto the porch, wearing a black sleeveless sweatshirt, black shorts, and Reef flip-flops. Shawn had on a light brown suit, dark brown wingtips, a white button-down dress shirt, and a tie that matched.

Mutt and Jeff, for sure.

Nick greeted them in his pajamas and a black Italian silk robe.

"Hi guys, Sofia has fresh coffee on and will keep it coming for us as long as we need. Let's go into the den and get started. From what I've uncovered so far, we have a big job ahead of us."

"Good, I've been bored out of my skull for the longest time," Shawn said, grinning.

Brody shook his head and said, "Just what the hell have I gotten us into, Nick?"

"Well, it's never been easy for us, has it?" Nick led the way into his den. He took a seat behind his custom cherry wood desk. On the desktop were three binders labeled with the mission's name—"Kill the Scammer"—not that they were actually planning to kill anyone. They just wanted Mary's money back.

Nick handed out the folders. Inside were geographical printouts of the target's location in Seattle, and copies of all the other information he obtained. Shawn and Brody sat in two leather chairs facing Nick. A light tap from the outside of the den door interrupted their thoughts.

Sofia leaned in balancing a tray of coffee mugs, and said, "Hi, Brody. Hi, Shawn. Nick told me you guys were working together to help that sweet Mary who lives next to you, Brody. I'm so sick and tired of hearing about elderly people getting ripped off. Enjoy the caffeine. Anything else you guys need, just let me know."

"Thanks, Sofia," the guys chorused in unison.

"Well, I want to help too. Also, I'm glad you have something for Nick to do. The last few months, he's been following me around the house like our dog, Beans, always underfoot."

"Oh, come now, Sofia. What would you do without your big Nickelodeon chasing you around the house? You know you like it."

"Okay, Shawn, you're right. Truth be told, I let

him catch me more times than not. But this time, I want him to concentrate on getting that guy who hurt Mary. And, well, Nick told me it's going to be a long day, so I have lunch and dinner planned. No worries there." She handed out coffee cups and left cream and sugar on Nick's desk. "I'll leave you three musketeers alone now. Good luck."

The guys thanked her again as she closed the door. Then they opened their files.

Nick filled them in on the name of their target, his location, unit number, and who was backing him. Then he got into the details.

"I'll just yack away, and you can follow along. All this information is in your binders. I did a lot of research on his condo building, including area maps, interior floor plans, pictures' of the exterior, the roof, and the surrounding grounds. I located all the hard-wired security cameras on the exterior and interior of the building. There's a room behind the greeter's desk in the lobby where the monitors are. There's a designated breaker for the cameras and for each unit's alarm inside an exterior electrical closet on the south end of the building. Throw the breaker for the cameras and the breaker for the alarm in Juan's unit, and they both go dark."

"Ridiculous design, but good for us," Shawn commented.

"Exactly," Nick agreed. "The closet has an electronic key card lock, as well as the main entrance and all the units. I'm working on a master key card for you, Brody. You'll have access to the whole building."

"How does the security system work?" Shawn wanted to know.

"The building has 24-hour access. There are no alarms in the common areas of the building, only the individual units. If one of those alarms is triggered, a horn sounds inside the unit, and an outside vendor is notified at the same time. Since we'll be able to shut off Juan's alarm, we won't have to worry about vendor interference."

"Easy pickings so far," Brody observed.

"Each unit has an alarm on the entry door, motion sensors covering the living room area, and the bedrooms. It's all activated when the keypad next to the door is armed, but like I said, it all goes off with a flip of the breaker."

Nick explained how the trash is picked up, how the mail is delivered, and where all the building's mechanicals, utilities, heat, air conditioning, gas, electric, sewer, and water are located.

Brody laughed and said, "Very impressive, but knowing you, I'm thinking there's more. Unless you've missed a step in your old age, Nick?"

"Hold on, hold on. Of course there's more. I also investigated all the occupants from the HOA records, current and past, and all paid staff. I compiled a complete dossier on each, including their family backgrounds, biographies, education, criminal histories, and current financials. I cross-referenced all that information and applied it against our perp's name and the Lentini Charity. No connection to either. So kiss my ass, Brody, sir!" Nick said, grinning.

"Better back off him, or he'll start investigating your love life. Man, I'd like to get my hands on those transcripts." Shawn barely stifled a laugh.

"Okay, boys. Let's stay on point," Nick interrupted. "The Lentini Foundation is paying all the bills for Juan's unit, including wireless phone, cable, and internet. The building was built by a well-known national developer who used both union and nonunion subcontractors. No red flags there. The city permitting and inspection processes were normal, with no signs of payoffs or corruption. So it looks like the only criminal activity coming out of that building is sponsored by the Lentini Charity, and run by our guy in unit 348."

"We'll have to peel back all the layers of the charity," Brody commented.

"Yep, and see who else is connected with it. It's a big onion, so I think we should divide up the peeling," said Nick.

"Good idea. It'll speed up the due diligence and get me into action. Let's do it this way. I'll find out when the foundation was first registered and licensed, and who the donor is. Shawn, see if you can get an organizational chart of the current leadership top to bottom, and Nick, dive into the details of the financials, tax filings, 501Cs, yearly statements, etc. Knowing you, I'm sure that's already next on your list."

"You know it. Already on it."

Nick anticipated that Brody would organize them and split the work up according to their specialties. He had workstations complete with computers and accessories for Brody and Shawn set up at two small desks in the room. They got right on their individual tasks and worked continuously, stopping only for short lunch and dinner breaks, lovingly provided by Sofia.

Each made three copies of relevant information and inserted the pages into all the mission books. At 9 p.m., they called it a day. They'd read the new information at home and write down questions for the next day's meeting. Shawn volunteered to have it at his place at 9 a.m. Positive information was coming in fast. They'd have to decipher it and analyze it just as fast to get Brody on the road to Seattle to see one Juan Martin.

Chapter 6

STOMPING GROUNDS

Shawn's condo was located in San Diego's East County in the city of Santee, just a few miles from the bordering city of Lakeside. Lakeside was a throwback to a shit-kickin' cowboy town with bar fightin', horse ranchin', and weekend rodeos. He liked that it was close so he could visit and relive his youth growing up country tough on a farm in Michigan.

He, Nick, and Brody occasionally drove the few miles to soak up vestiges of another era. One of the best places to do that was at the Lakeside Tavern in the middle of town. When you passed through its swinging café doors, it felt like entering the old west. They'd have a few beers and check out the locals.

One such night, they stood at the old wooden bar waiting for an open pool table. A group of six tattooed biker dudes sat at a table together, eyeballing them. Three got up and started walking towards them. The other three soulless thugs stayed at the table and turned their chairs around to face the bar, all smiles.

Clearly, they were anticipating a show. One with lots of blood splatter, broken bones, and three strangers at the bar getting knocked the fuck out.

The apparent leader of the hardasses walked right up to Brody. He was huge. Six foot five, three hundred plus pounds, and heavily muscled. His nose had been broken so many times, it would remain forever in the shape of a large S. His cauliflower ears said, "I've been hit over and over again, and I like it."

He didn't try to hide the multiple ragged scars appearing around both eyes, forehead, cheeks, mouth, and jaw. On the contrary, he held his head high and flaunted his damaged face like a scary Jason mask from Friday the 13th. He obviously enjoyed seeing fear in people's eyes when they looked his way, especially potential adversaries.

Scarface was flanked on each side by his two psycho pals, just slightly smaller at six foot three and two hundred fifty pounds. The three of them looked like the offensive line of the Green Bay Packers. Scarface was so close to Brody, he could smell his beer breath. He also saw several teeth missing when the ghoul opened his mouth to say,

"This is our bar, asshole. You and your girlfriends get the fuck out now while you can still wa—"

Before he finished the word walk, Scarface tried sucker punching Brody's jaw. He launched a huge right hand.

Good, Brody thought. *This makes it a clear case*

of self-defense. He easily blocked the punch with a karate kid (wax off) forearm, and then charged forward. Planting his head in the biker's chest, he pushed away from the bar with his foot. The maneuver forced the huge slug to backpedal awkwardly.

While Scarface was flailing and flying backward, Brody wrapped his arms around the biker's legs, placed a hand in the back of each knee, and pulled up. This maneuver lifted the helpless punk high off the ground so Brody could then slam the Goliath's back flat onto the floor.

His back hit first, which forced his head to whiplash and bounce off the concrete with a sickening cracking noise. The man was down and out. Instantly, he started to snore. That proved two things. One, he was in a deep unconscious state, and two, still alive as intended. However, he'd definitely have a righteous concussion to deal with.

Meanwhile, the two biker friends rushed forward to attack Nick and Shawn. The two Ex-Seals couldn't have been happier. With lightning speed and perfect technique, they each stepped into their man and threw an elbow to respective noses, breaking them. Blood gushed from all four nostrils. While the knuckle-draggers were stunned by the maneuver, Shawn and Nick followed up with uppercuts and right crosses to their jaws. The biker's eyes rolled back into their heads, and they were asleep before they hit the floor.

Brody was already walking back to stand with his

friends at the bar. They looked over at the table with the three remaining bikers, who stared back at them in disbelief. Their lips silently mouthed *W.T.F. just happened?* They looked at each other and quickly raised their hands above their heads as if they had guns pointed at them. It was a clear gesture of surrender to the alpha males—Brody and the boys. The losers had gotten their show, just not the one they thought they'd see.

Brody told them, "You should call an ambulance for your friends, especially the big guy with the cracked skull."

One of the bikers replied, "Uh, he'll be okay. Not the first time he's been knocked out. Won't be the last."

Then they held up their beers in a salute. Brody, Nick, and Shawn downed their beers and walked out of the bar.

***

In sharp contrast to Lakeside, Santee was a friendly and modern community. It suited Shawn's lifestyle perfectly. This was his home and would remain so till they planted him in the ground. His condo was a three-bedroom with an office that overlooked the pool from his third-floor perch. He had converted one of the bedrooms into a poker room that the three of them with other friends, used at least once a month. Brody, having stopped for doughnuts and coffee, (Shawn's coffee could get you drunk), arrived a second behind Nick. They sat down in Shawn's office, ready to work.

Brody started. "Here's what I have on the inception date of the charity and the identification of the original don—"

Brody's phone blasted with the *Raiders of the Last Ark* theme song. "Son of a bitch! This is the third friggin' bullshit robocall today. It's a voicemail from a female saying, 'I'm sorry to bother you. I know you're busy, but I want to let you know that the interest rate I quoted you for your business loan has changed. I can get you a better deal. Please call me right away.' Then she left a phone number. Like, if this was legit, I wouldn't know what her phone number is."

"I know what you mean. I keep getting a message about signing up for a great home warranty package," Nick said.

"The one I hate the most is a warning that it's the last day to extend the warranty on my 12-year-old truck. Bastards," Shawn griped.

"This scamming crap is out of control," Brody said with anger.

"I wanna take them all down," Nick shouted.

"Well, let's eliminate the turd that hurt Mary. Then we can decide what we want to do about all the other asshole scammers afterward. Sorry for the phone interruption, guys. My bad. It's on airplane mode now. Moving on...the Charity's application was made by Sal Lentini. He named it the Lentini Charity Foundation and designated it as a private foundation. It was recorded and made a legal entity on October 13, 2001, in Las Vegas. The application defined the foundation as a family endowment, with Sal being the sole donor. He applied for a tax-exempt license for all federal, state, and city taxes.

"The filing showed a Las Vegas commercial building, owned by the Lentini Realty Group, as the main address for the Charity. There are two subsidiary addresses. One in Seattle, and the other in Malta, near Italy. Both post office boxes. I think we might be dealing with your Godfather, eh Nick?"

"I read that in your papers last night, Brody, and wondered if we're going to butt heads with my Italian Mafia brethren."

"What do you think, Brody?" asked Shawn.

"Well, whoever it turns out to be needs to give Mary's money back. Are we all agreed on that count?"

"I was afraid you were going to say that, but nevertheless, I see it the same way you do," Nick said.

"Likewise, I'm with you my brothers. The scum bags need to pay," Shawn said.

"Well, that's what I have so far. Shawn, you left us quite a package to go through. I see there's a new guy in charge of the Lentini Foundation."

"Right. I got a ton of inside information on the charity yesterday at Nick's. A lot of it was easy, off of social media and websites. I can't believe what people post. The new player is Tony Lentini, Sal's son. He took over the Foundation when Sal stepped down two years ago. Sal retired and moved to the island of Malta where he lives with the rest of the

Lentini clan. They have a 150 acre secluded Villa on the Mediterranean Sea with a private dock and beach."

"Did you get pictures?" Brody asked.

"Oh, yeah. A ton. I included images of the whole family, with blow ups of the new boss, Tony Lentini. I also included satellite photos of their compound. A truly spectacular place, fit for kings and presidents. Stealing people's money and ruining their lives must be very profitable, at least temporarily."

"What else do we know about this Tony character," Brody wanted to know.

"He's also the current president, CEO, and CFO which means he has complete control. He's 38 years old and single with a playboy reputation. He's been splitting time between Malta and Las Vegas where he has a so called "legitimate" furniture manufacturing plant on the outskirts of Vegas, and a real estate business in the city—another perfect way to launder dirty money. Buy a property with the dirty cash, re-sell it, and get clean money in return."

Shawn paused for effect.

"Here's the best part, guys. I've been monitoring calls coming and going to Juan's unit. When I got home last night I got a big surprise. A call came into Juan, from?"

"Tony Lentini," Brody answered.

"You got it. I traced the call to a landline in Tony Lentini's name. The location is his penthouse on the top floor of his real estate building. Tony called Juan at 2300. The conversation was brief. Tony asked

Juan, 'How many today, what plays, and when will the transfers be made?' Sounds like scamming lingo to me. Now we have a direct connection between the two. We'll have to figure out how to isolate Juan to get Mary's money without involving Lentini."

"That could be hard to do since he's just an employee. I doubt he has $25,000 laying around in his condo," Brody said.

Nick said, "This is my cue, gentlemen. We may have a way of doing what you suggested, Shawn. All income for the charity is in the form of cash that's deposited into the foundation's checking account at the Bank of Malta on the 15th of each month. Money from that account is wire transferred to the Wells Fargo down the street from Juan in the name of the charity. From the bank records I hacked, it's always the same amount. $150,000. The average account balance is $180,000. Juan Martin is the primary on the account. He makes weekly withdrawals in cash. At the end of the month, the total withdrawals are close to the $150,000. That money has to be the bankroll for Tony's operation there in Seattle, and Juan must manage it for him. What do you think, Brody?"

"I agree. It adds up. Good work, Nick. I think you found our way around Lentini. I make Juan give us access to that account at Wells Fargo, then you guys do your magic and lift the money out of it. You know what, guys? That money was stolen from Mary and others. I say we take it all and throw a monkey wrench into their operations. The Lentinis would try and find out why $20 was missing, let alone $25,700, and they're not going to call the police to do it. We take it all, and compensate ourselves and whoever helps us. Once you guys have the money, you can make it disappear without a trace, right?"

"Yep, Nick and I can do that. One thing bothers me though, is Juan's role in this. If he's the manager, why did he take it upon himself to do a solo scam on Mary? Doesn't make sense to me."

"Good point, Shawn. That's a ton of money each month. There has to be a place there in Seattle where Lentini has a crew working the scams. You'd think Juan wouldn't be doing the grunt work, especially out of his home, but for some reason, he did. All we can do now is make him pay for it. We know who, where, and how to get Mary's money back. Let's meet at my house tomorrow, 9 a.m. We'll take what we have and come up with the best plan of attack so I can get up to Seattle. The sooner, the better. We can adjust the plan as more information comes in, no different than any other mission we've done. I know we'll all be thinking this through tonight and putting it together tomorrow. See you then, guys," Brody said.

***

At Brody's, the guys shared their ideas and reached a general consensus by mid-day. By early afternoon, they had finalized their plan. It included all aspects of a well-thought-out and cohesive military operation with multiple contingencies. No military mission was ever considered or approved without a plan A, B, C, and D. C being retreat, and D being surrender. However, whenever the guys put together a plan, C and D were ceremonially dismissed with, "That ain't gonna happen!"

The first part of the plan was to get Brody to Seattle. They all agreed the best way to do that was for Brody to hitch a ride with their friend and pilot, Dan Knapp. Flying there with Dan would allow Brody to take the weapons and equipment he needed for the mission. He'd never be able to get them through a security check at a civilian airport. If he couldn't get a private flight, he'd have to drive. Doable, but it would add a lot of time to the mission. Brody would call Dan, while Nick and Shawn went home and worked on their parts of the plan.

Captain Dan Knapp, Brody, Nick, and Shawn, had become lifelong friends after their shared mission in Syria when the four of them took out Aahil Aydin. Dan joined the Army under the Bill Clinton administration's "Don't ask, don't tell" military directive of 1993. That policy opened the door for gay men like him who loved America and wanted to serve in the armed services. He was always thankful for the opportunity and took full advantage of it. His lifestyle choice had remained a secret in the military, but not to his closest friends. They couldn't care less. He lived alone with his Labrador retriever, Bucky, in a high-rise apartment in Mira Mesa, San Diego.

After retiring, Dan retained full flight status as a reservist. He was required to fly a certain amount of hours each month to maintain his combat readiness. He had the freedom to file a flight plan out of Marine Corps Air Station Miramar for training anytime to meet that requirement. The Army needed reserve pilots trained and ready to fly at a moment's notice, and were extremely lenient on the flight plans they submitted. More than one of those flight exercises ended up being a round trip to Vegas.

Brody, Shawn, and Nick, hitched a couple of those rides with Dan after they all retired. Brody was pretty sure that once he explained this Mission to Dan, he'd be on board, and do his best to get a flight to Seattle for them. If he could, Brody knew Dan would also volunteer to be his back up. Regardless of how Brody got to Seattle, once he was there, the rest of their plan was solid.

"Heyyyyy!" Brody said when he heard Dan pick up.

Dan immediately replied, "Hooooo!"

This completed the personalized greeting they had used for years, but couldn't remember how it started.

"How's it going, Dan?"

"Going great, Brody. How you doing?"

"Good. I'm going to cut to the chase. Shawn, Nick, and I are working on an unsanctioned mission to help a friend. Let me explain. My elderly neighbor lady got a robocall, and unfortunately, she fell for the scam behind it. The scammer completely cleaned out her bank account, except for a few dollars. We found out who we think the scammer is."

"Where does he live?" Dan wanted to know.

"Washington State," Brady answered. "I'm going to pay him a visit and suggest he give her money back. From what we've learned, he's working for a crime family from Malta. If we manage to get the money from him, it certainly won't go unnoticed by them. He's just an employee, and the money he scams goes to them."

"They're going to want to know what happened to it, so this sounds like it could get dicey," Dan commented.

"Exactly. I want you to know that before you decide to get involved. That's the story, Dan."

"Thanks for filling me in. Sounds to me like a righteous cause. I hate it when our precious seniors get abused or taken advantage of. I'll help if I can. What are you going to need from me?"

"I'm hoping you have some flight hours available, and if so, that I could hitch a ride with you to where this guy is," Brody said.

"That's a lot of hoping, my friend," Dan said. Brody could tell by the inflection in his voice he was smiling. "I'm totally sympathetic with your mission. I get those F-in scam calls on my phone and e-mails all the F-in time too. Nothing I could ever do about them. Sounds like you're giving me an opportunity to do just that, and the stars may be lining up in our favor. I'm due to log some required hours, and I've been thinking of several flight plans. So the first part checks out. On to the second part. Where do you need to go?" Dan asked.

"Well, I know it's one of the places you fly to, because your sister lives there. It's Seattle. Is that a possibility Dan?"

"Hmmm. You know, that could work my friend. The round trip distance is more than I need, but I can roll the overage into next month's hours. By the way, if I'm able to swing this, you'll make me look like hero to my sister. She's been on my case to visit. When do you want to go?"

"Sorry for the short notice, but I'd like to leave in two days. We don't want to take the chance that our target bails."

"Whoa Brody, you are serious. I get it, can't let the trail go cold. Let me make some calls, and I'll get right back to you."

"Thanks, Dan. It would be a huge favor. I have some personal hardware I need to take with me, and the only other way I could do that is if I drive," Brody said.

"Roger, I got the picture. I'll get right on it." Dan clicked off.

A few hours later, Dan called back. "Brody, great news, buddy, the flight plan to Seattle is approved, and we leave in two days just as you wish. I logged you in as a retired Navy Seal taking a military hop. You Seals always get preferential treatment, so that was easy. We leave at 6 a.m. day after tomorrow. Also, talked with my sister, and she's thrilled that I'm coming. She told me I can use her husband's SUV while I'm there. He'll be in New York for a two week investment seminar. So, if you need backup, I'll have wheels."

"As far as the back-up goes, only if I'm in mortal danger. Otherwise, like I told Nick and Shawn, I'm doing all the fieldwork."

"Is it just the two of us in Seattle?" asked Dan.

"Affirmative."

"Okay then. I'm your backup. Mortal danger or not, fieldwork or not. Not negotiable."

"I knew you'd say that, and I'm not going to argue with you. We all know having a backup is the best way to approach any mission. I appreciate your commitment. However, I'm confident it won't be necessary. This is just one low-life scum bag that I'll isolate in his home, one on one. I should be able to take him down, convince him to give me access to his bank account, and be out of his unit in a few minutes. But, I'm glad you'll be in standby mode just in case. It's the smart thing to do. Juan will have to explain the missing funds to the organization he works for after I'm long gone. Don't think that will go over well for him though. Nick, Shawn, or I, will keep you updated on my progress, and when I make the move on Juan. When that happens, you'll be in on a live feed and be able to respond instantly if something should go sideways."

"Perfect, I'll bring my hardware, you know, just in case," Dan quipped. "I've got the days reserved, just have to pin down the times. I'll call you back as soon as I get the flight times."

"Roger that. Thanks, buddy. Also, before you go,

I want to let you know if we're successful on this mission, we're planning on compensating you."

"Whoa, don't even go there Brody. I won't hear of it. We're friends."

"I insist. Besides, the funds will be coming from the target and not me. I'm pretty sure he'll be happy to pay once I have a heart-to-heart with him."

"Okay, Brody, I'll leave that up to you and the guys. I'll call you the night before we leave with the final details. Talk to you then." Dan clicked off.

Chapter 7

PREPARATIONS

Brody got up before sunrise, anxious and energized. His mind was on the mission, and adrenaline coursed through his veins with the pressure of a firehose. He put on his jogging clothes and was out the door for a five-mile run in the cool sea breeze of San Diego. A run always mediated his heightened emotions and steadied his nerves.

When he finished, he felt his body and mind return to their usual even keel. He showered, made himself a bowl of steel-cut oatmeal with bananas, raspberries, and blueberries, and chased breakfast down with hot green tea.

After he finished filling up, he sent some back-and-forth e-mails to the guys and scheduled a face-to-face for early that afternoon at his place. That done, he decided to go next door and update Mary.

On the short walk next door, he noticed a newer Camry parked on the street in front of Mary's house and wondered who it belonged to. Standing on her porch, he ignored the doorbell and knuckle-knocked on the door. Doorbells didn't always work, and you ended up knocking anyway. In less than 15 seconds, Mary opened the door wearing a light yellow blouse, blue jeans, and a bib-style apron with all varieties of hand-painted fruits and vegetables. She greeted him with her usual welcoming smile.

"Hi Brody, come on in. There's someone here I want you to meet."

Brody stepped past her into the living room, where a stunning woman sat in a chair, holding a cup of coffee. Mary closed the door and said, "Brody, this is my niece, Jane Peltier. She flew in from Vegas to stay with me a bit."

"So that's a rental car outside," commented Brody, staring past Mary at her gorgeous niece.

"Yes, I'm so sorry she had to rent a car, but it's just too scary for me to drive to the airport with all the cars rushing around everywhere."

"Aunt Mary, don't you dare feel bad about that. I like having my own car to get around," Jane said.

She wore white shorts that emphasized the deep tan on her muscular legs, and a black tank top that contrasted nicely with her long curly red hair. What a beautiful smile, but it was her green eyes that mesmerized him.

"Jane, this is my friend and neighbor, Brody."

Jane placed her coffee cup on a side table and stood. Brody gently gripped her dainty outstretched palm, noting how much his hand dwarfed hers.

"My aunt has told me so much about you, Brody.

She's been talking nonstop about how you're trying to get her money back. I'm so very glad to meet you."

Brody was definitely stunned by her beauty, but the warmth and softness of her hand made him hold on longer than what would be considered a normal handshake. When he let go, he could still feel her touch. His blood pressure spiked and his heart rate soared, but he managed to control both and say without a shaky voice, "Mary has told me about you too, Jane. I'm very glad to meet you."

"Have a seat, Brody, I'll go and get you some coffee while you two get to know each other."

"Thank you, Mary, just a small cup, though. I can't stay long. I have a lot to do before I leave tomorrow morning and wanted to give you an update on our progress."

"Oh, that's wonderful. I can't wait to hear. Jane, more coffee?"

"No thanks, auntie, I've had my limit."

"Okay, you two, I'll be right back." Mary headed for the kitchen.

Brody sat on the couch across from Jane. He was enchanted by her physicality for sure, but he could tell there was much more to her than that. He knew he was still staring, but he couldn't help it. He used Jane's comment on her coffee limit to break his trance.

"So, what is your coffee limit anyway, and why?"

"Well, I get jittery if I have more than two cups in the morning, and I never have a cup after 2 p.m.

because it makes it hard for me to fall asleep. How about you?"

"Coffee's no problem for me. I can drink it all day and even before going to bed. It's never kept me from going right to sleep."

"I love my coffee so much and wish I could do that. It's so wonderful of you to volunteer to help my aunt. It was devastating when she told me what happened. She was so overwhelmed with emotion, she could barely get the words out. I had to tell her several times to calm down and not to stress."

"She was really being very hard on herself," said Brody, "but her generation is so decent and trusting. I explained that a lot of people are being taken advantage of these days, not just her."

"I see it all the time at my bank. People come into my office in a panic after being scammed out of their money, hoping we can fix it for them. Sometimes we can, if it's a stolen credit card, or obvious fraud on their account or card. Unfortunately, when they give up all their personal information and account numbers to scammers, there's nothing we can do."

"It's heartbreaking," Brody agreed.

"You know, when she told me what happened, I got so angry I wanted to find that criminal and punch his lights out."

"You're my kinda gal, Jane, because that's exactly what I want to do too. What happened to her is a travesty, and it needs to be straightened out."

Just then, Mary walked in with Brody's coffee and sat next to him on the couch. "I hope you two are having a good conversation."

In unison they said, "We are."

Brody and Jane turned and looked at each other and smiled over their impromptu duet. While their eyes were locked, a mysterious warmth washed over Brody's entire body. He wondered if she was feeling something too.

He reluctantly turned away from Jane to face Mary and said, "I'm happy to tell you what we've been able to find out. We know who the guy is that scammed you and where he's living right now."

"Oh my goodness Brody. How were you able to do that, and so soon?"

"Simple, really. I have very talented friends."

"Oh yes, Nick and Shawn. I was very glad to meet them. Please thank them for me."

"I will, but they're very happy to help, believe me. There's too much fraud and crime going on nowadays. I'll be leaving tomorrow to pay your scammer a visit and persuade him to do the right thing and return your money."

Jane asked, "How are you going to be able to do that, Brody? It seems to me that these kinds of people are hardcore dangerous."

"Not to worry, and that's the key here. We don't want either of you to worry about this at all. We have legal ways to force these people to give the money back, or they'll face some serious jail time." He lied only to ease their angst and give them peace of mind. "I'm not sure how long I'll be gone, but I'll keep you updated on my progress Mary. Will you be staying awhile, Jane?"

"For seven days, and then I have to get back to work."

"Great. I'm glad you two will be together, and I hope to be back before you have to leave, Jane."

"I hope you will too. I'd love to hear how it went, successful or not. You seem very confident."

"I am confident. My friends and I have dealt with these kinds of people many times. They're really the biggest cowards when they're confronted."

They stood and said their goodbyes. Mary gave him a strong hug. Jane extend her hand once again, not knowing it was the best parting gift he'd had in a long time.

***

On the short walk back to his place, all Brody could think about was Jane. He didn't know why, but he imagined her being an integral part of his life and all the different roles she would play in it. Friend, partner, companion, playmate, lover. Each individual fantasy flashed like a picture in his mind, completely absorbing his consciousness. So much so, that when he arrived at his door, it surprised him.

What is happening? He'd never been so hypnotized by a woman he just met. Yes, he'd experienced sparks before, but never a full-blown inferno. Seems like her aura fused with his, and now they were one. He looked down at his chest, expecting to see Cupid's arrow poking out. How could green eyes, red hair, and a simple handshake put him on such an emotional path?

Impossible! Ridiculous! Get it together, man. He had no time for these thoughts or feelings. He'd try to make some kind of sense out of this when he got back from Seattle.

In the living room, he took the to-do list from the lamp stand and added some new items. Then he checked off what he had already completed.

A sudden knock on his door interrupted his process. When he opened the door, Jane was standing there, smiling up at him.

"Brody...I...I." She paused, then started another "I..." Again a pause. She was struggling, and Brody thought he knew why.

"Jane, I'm feeling something magical here. Are you too?"

"Yes!"

He stepped out on the porch, wrapped his arms around her, slowly leaned down, and touched his lips to hers. The kiss was soft, warm, gentle, and timid. Jane's lips quivered. In their embrace, they both learned something very intimate about each other. As they became more familiar, the kiss gradually gained in strength and intensity, pressing harder and harder. The passion, pleasure, and heat between them grew with each passing second.

This erotic synergy made them breathe faster, as if they were racing toward something. Their bodies and souls were melding together, there was no doubt about it. The world and time itself paused to allow this moment to happen. Just for them.

Brody didn't hear the truck pull into his driveway,

but he did hear the horn. It was the guys, right on time. *Dang!* He released his hold, pulled back, and looked into Jane's eyes. He had to catch his breath before he could speak.

"We'll figure this out when I get back."

Her breathless response came quickly, "Yes, yes."

Shaking, she turned away with a shy smile. With her head down, she quickly walked past Nick and Shawn, who stood next to the truck, gawking. When she got to the sidewalk, she hurried back to Mary's.

Nick and Shawn walked up to Brody with juvenile grins and said in unison, "What the hell was that all about, bro?"

Brody, needing a five-mile run and cold shower, stared back. "Honestly, guys, I'm not sure."

He looked past them and saw Jane's eyes locked on him as she moved across Mary's porch and into the house. He could still taste her and feel the warmth of her lips and the imprint of her body. Her scent lingered and filled his senses. He was going to want a lot more of Jane Peltier.

Brody shook off the euphoric trance and ushered his delinquent friends into the kitchen. He grabbed three beers from the Fridge and sat with Shawn and Nick at the table. Both guys were staring at him with frozen smiles, like the Joker in Batman. Brody downed half his beer to relax. He knew their grins would remain and they'd get nothing done until he gave them an explanation.

"Okay, here it goes. That was Jane, Mary's niece, visiting from Las Vegas. This morning I went over to

Mary's to give her an update on what we've learned and what we're planning to do. Jane was sitting in the living room, and when Mary introduced us, it was magnetic. I guess she felt something like that too. We don't even know each other. We literally just met minutes ago. But I'm already missing her, like she's always been the best part of my life. I don't understand it, and for the first time ever, I feel a bit helpless. Like I'm treading water in the middle of the ocean, and there's no land in sight. How about throwing me a lifeline, guys?"

Nick, the frozen smile still fixed in place, said, "It's really not that complicated, Brody. Is it Shawn?"

"Nope," Shawn agreed.

"It's a cliché called love at first sight," Nick stated with a grin.

"Love? You're saying I'm in love?"

"Duh, buddy. That's what they call it when two people who just met become infatuated with each other."

"Okay, infatuation, maybe so, I don't know. I do know I can't wait to see her again. I told her we'd figure out this thing between us when I get back from Seattle, and she agreed. You guys think that's enough? Should I call her right now?"

"He's got it bad, Nick," Shawn said with a wink.

"Yeah, bad," Nick agreed, returning the wink.

Brody drained the rest of his beer, took a deep breath, and opened his mission book.

"Okay, she's agreed to see me when I get back. I have to trust that. I'm focused now; let's get to work and see what we have." Brody rubbed his temples, trying to clear the sticky cobwebs of this sudden love sickness.

Nick and Shawn winked at each other again with even goofier grins.

"Hey, come on now. Knock that shit off, and let's get serious, okay?" Brody said, almost flustered.

The guys had never seen Brody so smitten and enjoyed his vulnerability and confusion. They reluctantly agreed to quit the ribbing and move on.

They hashed over the compiled information. Nick recently added some new info on the Lentini family and organization. Turned out that Tony Lentini was designated a whale by Las Vegas insiders. Between his gambling, his businesses in Vegas, and his home in Malta, he qualified. So he had a lot of comps at several high-dollar casinos.

"We'll have to keep an eye on his movements. Don't want him showing up at Juan's unexpectedly," Nick said.

***

By the end of the day, they refined their plan and were ready to go. Their goals were simple—get Mary's money back, get compensated for their trouble, and get home. The mission was a go.

After the guys left, Brody finished packing and made one of his favorites for dinner. Tuna salad, made with sardines instead of tuna. Some years ago, he read a scientific study on the benefits of sardines. The study concluded it was the healthiest food on the planet containing every vitamin, mineral, and antioxidant the body needs. He'd been eating them on a regular basis, at least once a week, ever since. He became convinced that sardines kept him young, strong, healthy, and virile.

After he finished, he took a cup of green tea into his modest living room and sat in his favorite leather chair. Sipping the tea, he began organizing his thoughts on the mission. It was a struggle. His mind kept wandering to Jane. It was 9 p.m., and he desperately wanted to go next door to see her. What happened between them was special, and they both knew it. He was wishing the mission was over so he could find out just how special.

Just then, his phone sang out. It was Knapp.

"Heyyy!" Knapp said.

Brody returned the customary, "Hooo!"

"Brode, everything's good. The weather's perfect all the way to Seattle, and we'll get there just ahead of a major storm moving in from the west. We're cleared to depart tomorrow at 6 am as scheduled."

"Dan, that's awesome news," said Brody.

"And I have good news about our return flight. The Blackhawk we're using is due for a complete maintenance check on electronic flight systems and mechanicals. I arranged to have that work done while we're in Seattle. The Navy Captain in charge of maintenance has crews available to start the very day after we land.

"How long will that delay your layover?"

"The work will add four days to our original plan. This'll give you more flexibility with the mission's timeline. I know the original plan was three days and leave for home on the fourth. That was tight and allowed just a one-day cushion for any unforeseen problems or potential setbacks. It's better with the longer layover. What do ya think?"

"I'm thinking you're the man, Dan. We were stressing about the timeline. The guys will be thrilled to hear it."

"Tell them the truth. I got lucky. See you in the morning."

Brody was resourceful enough to make the original timeline work no matter what the circumstances. He had to do it on every mission he could remember. However, to have more time in the bank on this mission was a huge plus. Mainly because Juan Martin's movements would be the biggest variable on the timetable.

Knowing that, Shawn continuously tracked Juan through his phone, credit cards, and his car's GPS. He also attained phone records for the past three years. With both sets of information, Shawn reconstructed every movement Juan made over that entire period and transposed them onto a map of the Seattle area.

This was the critical part in putting their plan together. Obviously, they had to know Juan's movements and where he was likely to be at any given time. The information revealed most of his patterns and routines. Other than a car trip he took to an old industrial area on the outskirts of King County on the first of each month, Juan stayed within walking distance of his condo.

When Brody arrived in Seattle, he'd spend the first day surveilling Juan's location and surroundings. Barring any surprises, the plan was for Brody to make physical contact with Juan inside his condo on the second day. He'd force Juan to give up the Lentini bank account passcode so Nick could wire the funds to an offshore account. Brody would have to hit Juan fast, hard, and with the brutality necessary to make that happen. Brody liked that aspect of the mission, and couldn't wait to administer a little payback for Mary.

Brody thanked Knapp for the info and told him he'd be at the air station at 4 a.m. to assist with the preflight checks and preps. It was time to get this mission in the air.

After he hung up, it was time for a shower and bed. He thought about how he'd spent his whole career training and fighting to defeat those who committed evil deeds. It was a tall order, given the fact that everyone has the dual capacity to do good or evil. However, the majority of people lived out their lives controlling the temptations that evil presented and lived good, honest, loving, compassionate, caring, and hard-working lives, never hurting another human being.

His military job was to go after the few who took advantage of good people for their own personal gain or pleasure. Juan Martin, by his own free will, chose to be one of those people. He was going to suffer the consequences by Brody's hands now, and

God's later.

Chapter 8

SEATTLE

Brody got to Miramar Air Station at 4 a.m. and pulled into a parking space in front of the chopper hangar. He wasn't surprised to see his friend Dan Knapp already there, going over every inch of the Blackhawk. Their Blackhawk had extra fuel tanks, so they wouldn't need to stop and refuel on the 1200-mile trip.

"Hey, Dan! How you doing?"

"Great, Brody. You?"

"Ready to go. Feels like old times, eh?"

"Yeah, still saving the world."

"I'll store my gear, sign in, and get us some coffee," Brody said cheerfully.

"We'll be off on time with an ETA into Seattle of 11 a.m. I'll be staying at my sister's until we come back, but I'll be ready whenever you need me, brother."

"Thanks. We really appreciate all your help," said Brody with a handshake.

"Glad to help you take out some human trash," Dan responded.

The takeoff was smooth and uneventful, a very good start to a mission that probably would be anything but. Every mission had its drawbacks, none were ever perfect, and this one had a lot of unknowns.

As Dan piloted the Blackhawk and checked out its hundreds of instruments, Brody sat back in the co-pilot's seat and revisited the day that he, Nick, and Shawn got off the bus in Coronado, California to start their BUD/S, (Basic Underwater Demolition/Seal training).

Their class of 40 was greeted by a sadistic drill instructor with some unbelievably cruel information he couldn't wait to lay on the new plebes.

With a smug smile he said, "Attention, ladies, here's the deal. The regular Seal's barracks you would normally be using, the one with bathrooms, showers, and comfy cots, is currently being refurbished. Therefore, you lucky ladies will be upgraded to our first-class accommodations. You get to use these three smelly porta-pots you see lined up at the back of the barracks. By the way, you'll be sharing them with the construction workers. Next, you get unlimited use of our large bathtub. We even came up with a name for it. We call it the Pacific Ocean. That covers bathrooms and hygiene. Finally, we come to your sleeping quarters. Your government has erected 20 tiny tents here on the beach for you. There are 40 of you, so if you can do the math. Two of you will be sharing a tent. No Seal has ever gone through the BUD's training with such luxury. So, my associates and I have decided to make your BUD's training the hardest one yet."

The instructor walked over and put his hand on a sparkling ship's bell.

"Don't forget, if you want out, all you have to do is ring this bell. Isn't she beautiful? She can set you free. She wants to set you free. She's easy. Just ring her three times, and she'll let you go home to Mommy. Good luck, ladies."

Anyone who decided the training was too hard, or for whatever reason wanted to quit, could simply walk up to the bell and ring it three times. It had been strategically placed in plain view of all their exercises. They could see it all day long, every day. Those who succumbed and made her sing would pack their things and go back to their regular duty station...forever thinking, *What if?* At one time or another, every Seal was tempted to ring that freaking bell.

Brody, Nick, and Shawn, after listening to the drill instructor, made a pact. They would wipe that smug smile off the instructor's face. They agreed to die before they quit. That bond got them through, and when they became Seals, the three of them could never be more bonded to any other human being.

"Hey, where'd you go, bro?"

"Oh, just thinking about things."

"What's the plan to get close to the target?"

"That's Nick's idea. I'm going to impersonate a

Seattle Fire inspector to gain access to his building. Once inside, I'll be able to get into his unit. It'll be my job to make sure he's there. You'll be linked in when I make my move."

"Well, that's why you guys are the best."

The rest of the flight was uneventful. They landed at the Seattle U.S. Coast Guard hangar at 10:45 a.m., 15 minutes ahead of schedule. The Blackhawk would go through the maintenance program before the return flight home. When they exited the chopper, Dan's sister was already waiting for him. Brody went over to her car to put Dan's gear in the trunk and said hi while Dan checked in and did the paperwork. A few minutes later, Dan came out, and Brody waved goodbye as they drove away.

Brody saw the white Ford van with official SFD license plates and Seattle Fire Department inspector stenciled on the sides. It was parked right where Nick said it would be, in front of the hangar's administration office. The guys never failed to impress him. He walked to the van and knelt by the tailpipe. Hanging out was the piece of string he knew would be there. He pulled and grabbed the keys attached to the other end. Stowing his gear in the van, Brody drove off to the hotel across the street from Juan Martin, the scammer. He had arranged an early check-in.

Brody didn't know how Nick and Shawn were able to do all the things they did, and he didn't ask. He did know they were the very best at their particular jobs. They were the brains, and he was the brawn. The three of them were happy with that arrangement. Sure, Nick and Shawn didn't mind getting physical, but preferred breaking fingernails on keyboards instead of breaking bones these days.

Brody would make sure they were compensated for their expertise, and Juan was going to be the source of that compensation. He calculated an amount he thought was reasonable and figured Juan and the Lentini's owed them whatever was in their account at the Wells Fargo bank. Shawn was keeping a running account. And how to get that money was one of Shawn's parts of the plan. After Mary got her money, whatever was left, they'd split evenly between Jane, Shawn, Nick, Sofia, Dan, and himself.

Brody had no doubt Juan would spill his guts about whatever they wanted to know to save himself even the slightest pain. He would have zero loyalty to anyone but himself. His priority would be to remain whole so he'd be able to run from the Lentinis when they found out the money was gone. Secrecy and intimidation was how criminal syndicates survived. Anyone working for the organization who became compromised would "disappear" to protect that secrecy, and become an example to other employees. Brody didn't know how the Lentinis would take Juan out of the game, but he had a good idea it wouldn't be pleasant. He believed Juan knew too. He planned to use that to get his cooperation.

***

Brody pulled into the underground parking of the hotel, grabbed a couple of bags out of the van, and took the stairs up to the lobby. He checked in and again took the stairs up to the third floor—an opportunity to stay in shape. No brainer. On the third floor, he went through the stairway fire door and walked down the hall to room 331. He put the bags on the folding aluminum luggage rack by the closet.

He went in the bedroom and stripped off the bedspread, pillowcases, and sheets, and piled them in the corner. He replaced them with the new ones he'd brought. He would just leave them in the room when he left. He wasn't a total germaphobe, but he did sleep better by taking these simple precautions. He knew bed bugs, scabies, and other undesirables were notoriously prevalent these days in hotels and motels. In the bathroom, he sprayed Lysol in the sink, toilet, and tub shower combo. In the small kitchenette and sitting area, a vigorous wipe-down occurred.

Next to the only window was a round table with two chairs. Brody opened the curtains and blackout blinds. Nick was right, he had a perfect line of sight to Martin's third-floor unit, number 348. The two buildings were about 150 feet apart, separated by opposite sidewalks, parking lanes on each side of the street, and the two-way traffic lanes between.

Luckily, Juan didn't seem to mind leaving his blinds open. Brody opened one of his bags and pulled out binoculars equipped with night vision.

He'd be able to see Juan in light or darkness. Juan's unit had two windows facing Brody's. The one on the left showed a clear view of the bedroom. Brody saw a body in bed under a blanket. A scraggly mop of black hair was exposed near the headboard, and bare feet stuck out at the foot of the bed. It was 1 p.m., still early for a lazy ass criminal to get up.

The other window was to the right of the bedroom. He could see the back of a computer monitor at the lower half of the street-facing window. It was probably sitting on top of a desk. He saw a couch to the left that backed up to the bedroom wall. Beyond that, a small hallway led to the front door. To the right of the front door hallway was a small kitchen with a table and chairs in the foreground. On the wall across from the couch was a wall-mounted TV. The layout was exactly as expected.

Brody moved his table away from the window and opened one of his bags. He pulled out a roll of special transparent filament, cut it into pieces, and installed it on the inside of the window. He'd be able to clearly see out, but its unique reflective qualities wouldn't allow anyone to see in. He moved the table back in place and set up his laptop. He plugged in an external camera, aimed it at Juan's windows, and adjusted the focus. He sent the feed to the guys, and they verified by text that the signal was crystal clear. They all settled in at their own locations, eager to spy on the target.

Juan finally got up at 1:30 p.m., went to the

bathroom, put on basketball shorts and a Lakers sweatshirt, and headed for the kitchen. He poured cereal, took it over to the couch, and ate while watching TV. When he finished, he sat down at the desk and began fingering the computer keyboard like he was Harry Connick Jr. He worked the computer and his phone till 6:45 p.m., pulled a boxed frozen dinner out of the freezer, and nuked it in the microwave. Again he ate while watching TV. When he finished, he went back to the desk and continued his evil deeds.

An hour later, Brody texted Nick and Shawn.

BA: Pretty boring, eh guys?

SO: Yes, surveillance usually is.

NB: Yes, I've had enough. I'm taking Sofia out to dinner and a movie. I hope it's a go for tomorrow, and Brody, if it is, break a leg.

SO: I've seen enough for today also. From the looks of him, you'll have an easy time of it. I sort of have a date with my new neighbor I told you guys about. Remember, she's the single lady that I helped move in the other day. She just called and wants to repay me with some wine and cheese down by the pool. Says she wants to meet there because her place is still a mess.

BA: You horn dog. Be home by midnight. Ha, ha.

SO: Don't worry, guys. I'll be ready at 6:30 a.m. I'm ready for this dance to start.

BA: Roger that. Have a good evening, and we'll do a final com check in the morning. I hope you both get lucky tonight! I'm going to watch a bit more, then hit the sack.

Brody was hoping he could make his move on Juan in the morning. The guys would be able to see and hear everything in real time through the special bodycam equipment he'd be wearing. Back up would be from the camera feed from his hotel room, and everything would record on both. In addition, Brody had a piece of technology that only a handful of people in the world possessed. Being a special OPS Seal had its advantages.

On a former secret Middle East mission, two things happened. One, the Navy lost track of him when the signaling device attached to his vest was damaged in a hand-to-hand fight. Two, he lost a tooth just a second before he killed the terrorist. He was mad at himself for being a second too slow, but it turned out to be a good thing.

When he got back to the states, the Navy made sure they didn't lose track of him again. They borrowed top-secret technology from the CIA. Their techs were able to make a tracking device for their field agents from a tooth crown that they installed on a titanium dental implant. The crown that snapped onto the implant had a battery-powered tracking signal. The Navy installed one in him to replace his missing tooth. The signal could be tracked by different sources—satellites, drones, and handheld devices. They could pinpoint his location anywhere in the world.

Before he left San Diego, he snapped on a fresh crown from the four the Navy gave him while on active service.

***

It was getting late, just past 10 p.m., and Brody was about to get ready for bed when he saw Juan make a phone call. As soon as he put the phone down, Juan started running around his unit. He picked things up and put them in drawers. He went into the bathroom, brushed his hair, and used a deodorant stick. Then he went back to the kitchen, pulled a whisky bottle and two glasses out of the cupboard, and placed them on the kitchen table. He sat down and poured himself a tall glass. Looks like Juan was expecting company. After about a half hour, he finished off his drink and was about to pour another when he stopped and put the bottle down. He got up and went to the door.

When he opened it, Brody saw a tall, young, scantily dressed short-haired brunette holding a heavy coat. This told Brody it was cold outside but hot inside. He figured it was going to get much hotter soon, sweaty even. She was wearing a red short-sleeve t-shirt that fit like a layer of skin. Based on the way her nipples showed through and the swing of her breasts as she walked, she had nothing underneath but real skin. Her tight-fitting black leggings also revealed feminine nakedness underneath.

You never knew for sure these days, but there was no doubt about this girl. The clothes were simple tools of her trade, designed to be quickly removed and just as quickly put back on. Time, after all, was money. Bright red lipstick matched the color of her pumps. With no other visible accessories, her attire was complete.

She was already in the bedroom before Juan closed the door. Obviously, she'd been there before. Juan walked into the bedroom and motioned to the whisky on the table. She shook her head no so Juan pulled out his wallet and handed her some cash. Brody, curious, was disappointed he couldn't see the amount. It was a no-brainer where this was headed, but surveillance demanded he observe without interruption. It was a tough job, but it had to be done. He wasn't a voyeur, but couldn't help anticipating an exhilarating change of pace after the boring hours of watching Juan doing his scamming job.

While standing next to the foot of the bed, they quickly undressed. Stretch marks showed on the girl's belly, maybe from weight loss or perhaps a recent delivery. Probably just another young mother forced to sell her body to support her baby in a bad economy.

When will the world's males stop exploiting women by forcing them to use their bodies as means of survival? Why aren't women completely equal to men? Is it simply because they are physically weaker? Brody wondered.

Juan sat down on the bed, feet on the floor. The girl got down on her knees before him. Again, in a subservient position.

I wish she'd bite his balls, take his money, and

leave.

After a couple of minutes of touchy-feely foreplay, she reached in her purse and put a prophylactic on him. She was in a hurry to get this job over as fast as possible.

To that end, they both stood up. The girl moved forward to the foot of the bed and faced the headboard. She bent forward and lowered herself down onto her forearms, head and shoulders up off the bed, hands out front like she was preparing to read a book. The space wasn't big enough for her large and swollen breasts, so when they compressed, milk expressed. The mystery of the stretch marks was solved. *I hope someone responsible is watching her baby.*

She was in position. Head up, back arched, and legs straight to the floor. She began wiggling her rear to encourage Juan to get going. Brody noticed she held something in her hand. *A knife? A taser, just in case Juan got out of control? Wait a minute! Was that her cell phone?* He adjusted his binoculars. Unbelievably, she was playing Candy Crush. Well, he guessed technology had replaced the comic books prostitutes used to read during these sessions.

Juan stepped up behind her and began moving like he was trying to keep a hula hoop from dropping to the floor.

After maybe a whole minute, loser Juan collapsed forward onto the girl's back. *Man, what a pathetic performance. Looks like I'm not the only one who's glad it was over.* The prostitute put her cell phone back into her purse, slipped back into her clothes, walked to the front door, and let herself out.

Juan, now spent, turned out the lights and crawled under the sheets for the night.

Brody figured the guys weren't watching the fiasco; otherwise, his phone would have been pinging like a pinball machine with plenty of colorful narrations. He checked—no calls, texts, or emails, except, of course, from scammers.

It had been a long day. He was going to get a good night's rest, and tomorrow he'd get justice for Mary and Jane. He fantasized about the many different ways he'd make Juan pay, careful not to go too far, at least until he got the money. He showered, got in bed, and opened the mission binder on the night table. He was reading through it again when his phone pinged—a text message from Jane. She must have gotten his number from Mary. There wasn't time to exchange numbers before he left.

Text:

Hi Brody. Been thinking about you nonstop, actually. (: I want you to know that I've never had such a strong attraction to anyone before in my life. I make this admission with confidence that you won't think it strange, based on the way you kissed me. I'm glad we agreed to figure this out when you get back, and I can't wait for that. Until then, please be careful. Jane.

He created a new contact, saved her number, and texted back.

Jane, I can tell you that any meaningful relationship I've had took significant time before it became meaningful. With you, that's changed dramatically. From the moment we met, it's like I've known you my whole life. Strangely, I'm missing you now as if I had. I'll be careful, and please, you too. See you soon, but not soon enough. Brody.

He tried to concentrate on tomorrow's tasks and not think of Jane. That brain battle was draining him, but he pushed through and finished reading the mission files. He turned out the light, wrapped his arms and legs around an extra pillow, imagined it was Jane, and relaxed into a deep sleep.

Thick black clouds were speeding toward Seattle from the west that night. The storm was a beast, covering hundreds of miles. Once it made landfall, it would unleash howling angry tears on all of Seattle for several days.

Chapter 9
FINAL PREP FOR THE FACE TO FACE

The next morning Brody woke to a monstrous storm. He rolled out of bed naked with his usual woody and walked over to the window, knowing he wouldn't be seen from the outside. The wind and heavy rain obscured his view, but he could still see that Juan was in bed. Good start. He got dressed, went downstairs, and went out into the fray. He charged through the storm and into the café next door to his hotel.

He ordered lox on a bagel, a piece of lemon poppy seed bread, and large black coffee. Brody sat at a small high table next to a window facing the street. He looked through the liquid silvery tracers formed by the rain, and stared at Juan's windows across the street.

He knew the building housed forty identical 760 square foot units, 10 per floor, each with a small balcony overlooking the street. A possible escape route, if needed. A manned reception desk for residents and guests was in the lobby on the first floor. To the right of the desk, a long hallway led to elevators, a small gym, laundry, a gathering lounge with a fireplace, and double doors leading out to the pool and barbecue area. Another escape route.

Homeowners needed an electronic key card to access the amenity areas and their units. Shawn hacked into the building's security system, cloned a master key card, and gave it to him before he left. He'd be able to open any door. Up on the third floor was the modern-day dungeon where Juan, by stealing livelihoods and savings, conducted his mental torture and financial dismemberment of victims.

Brody's anger was building, and he knew it would hit a crescendo soon. He sipped his coffee and thought through the plan's sequence that would ultimately get him in and out of that dungeon quickly and safely.

After breakfast, he'd go back to his room and check in with Nick and Shawn. They'd go over any new information, make necessary adjustments, and completely discuss the mission's checklist. Lastly, they'd make sure all communications and video feeds were running smoothly. That done, he'd cross the street and enter Juan's building. He'd tell whoever was at the front desk that he was making a required fire department safety inspection. Dressed in a fire marshal's uniform with proper credentials (thanks to Nick), he'd have free rein of the building.

He'd take the stairs up to the third floor. If the

hallway was clear, he'd camp out in front of Juan's door, still in direct communication with Shawn. Nick and Dan would watch and listen too. Dan was on standby as physical back up, though none of them thought it would be close to necessary. Nevertheless, Dan's gear was loaded in his sister's husband's car and ready to go. He could leave her house in a second.

Brody's thoughts were interrupted when Juan stepped out of his building's lobby onto the sidewalk. Brody checked his watch—9:50 a.m. Early rise for Juan, who waited at the curb and looked straight at the café. When the traffic cleared, the powerful wind had him staggering around like a drunk all the way across the street. He pried open the café door against the blow and entered. At the counter, he ordered food to go, paid, and waited by the pick-up area.

Standing there, Juan ogled the ass of the barista. His lecherous trance broke when she moved out of his view. Then, he casually glanced around the room, unaware that his life was about to change. His criminal attire of the day was a blue long-sleeve button-down from Walmart, black Levi jeans with the red tag on the back pocket, a Seattle Seahawks ball cap, and a grey nylon insulated jacket stitched in a diamond pattern.

Just a regular Joe being inconspicuous, blending in and hiding in plain sight, confident. He had no idea he'd been caught. It would literally be a breathtaking surprise when he found out.

Some of the tattoo ink on Juan's neck was visible, and Brody was certain he recognized a partial prison tat that said Lompoc, but he could only make out the "poc." The rest was covered by the collar. *Looks like the puke got his rip-off education during his stay at Lompoc state prison.* Brody was facing away, but watched him peripherally. He estimated Juan to be about five-ten, one-sixty. A thin pretzel rod about to be snapped between Brody's powerful hands.

Brody covered his fire captain's uniform with a long tan trench coat. The collar was turned all the way up, covering his profile to just below his cheekbone. His leather-banded cowhide Indiana Jones fedora covered his head to his eyebrows, in stealth mode, concealing himself from Juan and any cameras.

The barista handed Juan his order in a brown paper bag. He enjoyed a final stare at her firm booty as she walked away. *The pig.* Then he headed for the door and stopped to look around the café before exiting. His head swiveled and locked onto Brody who was still looking out the window.

Brody was totally aware that Juan had zeroed in on him. Acting nonchalant, he could feel the laser beams emanating from Juan's eyes, and his neck began to heat up. He felt that same kind of sensation when he pushed an all-in bluff at the final table of the World Series of poker in Vegas. The pro was deciding to call or fold and stared at him, trying hard to get a "Tell". At that time, Brody felt his mind and body being probed and wondered if the pro could see one of those comic thought bubbles above his head saying, "I'm bluffing!" The pro folded. From then on, Brody was confident that no one could read him.

He was sure Juan couldn't detect danger or anything else from him, yet he continued staring. *Was he tipped off somehow?* After what seemed an eternity, Juan turned, opened the door, and jogged back across the street to his building. Brody figured Juan had a simple case of criminal paranoia, a condition shared by all ex-cons. After being released from prison, their fear of going back made them suspicious of everything, especially if they'd fallen back into the life.

Regardless, this is good timing. Even if Juan is spooked, I won't give him time to do anything about it.

Brody left the café and rushed up to his room, anxious to finally confront Juan face to face. His anger was still spiked, being that close to the scum. Close enough to squeeze the bloodsucking leach's neck. *Soon, very soon*.

Inside his room, Brody hurried over to the window in time to see Juan come through his door, grab a beer from the fridge, sit at the table, and consume his café grub. Brody unzipped a travel case, pulled out a Navy Seal standard issue Ontario MK 3 knife, and a silenced SIG Sauer p226 9mm handgun with three extra clips. He strapped the knife and leather sheath to his right ankle. The gun in a special nylon shoulder holster was slipped over his left shoulder, hidden under his armpit and covered by his fireman's overcoat.

Brody lifted out a 10-foot length of nylon rope, gorilla duck-tape, gloves, zip ties, a cell phone-sized electronic bug finder, hand-held taser, and a small biometric scanner for Juan's fingers. The fingerprints would verify Juan's true identity and if, indeed, he had been a resident of Lompoc.

Brody stuffed the pockets of his coat with the interrogation party favors and a can of spray foam and put on his body cam and mic. At the table, he sent a Facetime request to Nick, Dan, and Shawn from his iPad. In seconds he was looking at the three of them. The time was 11:00.

"D-Day, guys. I know you're watching Juan through my laptop's Zoom camera, and you'll be getting a close-up from my body gear when I get in. As you can see, he's alone, and I'm ready to go with an all-clear. What's it look like, Shawn?"

"First off, anything happen last night after Nick and I signed out?"

"You didn't miss much. Juan had a hooker stop by, and it only lasted a couple of minutes."

"I'm glad I didn't stick around for that. I had a great time with my new lady friend. Okay, down to business. New twist. Early this morning, I detected a two-way wireless signal coming from the air duct above Juan's bedroom door. It doubles by covering the main room and the bedroom. I tried to jam it but can't. Makes sense that they'd be keeping an eye on him. It's probably turned on and off from a remote location to conserve the battery because it didn't come up when I swept the unit yesterday. Just bad luck that they reactivated it, but now that we know, we can do something about it. You'll have to take it out quickly…"

"Right," said Brody. "I have the can of spray foam you gave me."

"Spray it through one of the slats and fill the vent solid from both sides. Let's hope no one is watching, but assume they are, so watch your time."

"Got it."

"I haven't detected any other wireless devices other than his phone and computer. There's good news. I checked Juan's account at Wells Fargo this morning, and there's $197,000 in it. You just need the ID and passcode so you can access it and make the transfer we set up."

"No problem."

"Okay, next. The zoom camera on your laptop is working perfectly. We're watching on our iPads in Nick's office, and Dan's watching from his sister's house. Brody, when you're in position outside Juan's door, I'll give you his exact location inside the unit. If he's in the main room, you'll have enough time to rush in, tase him, and tie him down. Let's run a com check on your body cam and earpiece."

"Okay, I'm switching on," said Brody. "I'm aiming the camera at his window."

"We can hear you clearly, and the picture is crystal." Shawn, Nick, and Dan all repeated the word "testing" into their mics.

"How do you read us, Brody?"

"Perfectly. Good job, Shawn."

"Thanks. Take it away, Nick."

"Roger. I've checked on all the Lentini passports. Tony is the only one with a flight scheduled from Malta, and it was to Vegas yesterday. There's no planned visit by the fire department to interfere with that part of our plan. No texts, phone messages, or emails indicating a visit by anyone to see Juan today, so if it happens, it'll be purely random. We're saying it's a go on our end. Good luck, bro."

"Thanks, brothers, let's do this."

Brody took the stairs down to the parking garage and got in the van. He drove over to the front of Juan's building and parked by the entrance. He left the van unlocked for a fast getaway. Being an official city vehicle, it shouldn't be bothered. As he figured, the storm had practically eliminated people out and about. He could only see one man walking in his direction, head down with a hoodie almost completely covering his face.

Confident no one would notice him, Brody exited the van and walked up to the main entrance. He scanned his key card into the reader and entered Juan's building. Carrying a clipboard, he walked to the counter and gave his inspection spiel to the thirty-something blonde in black pant suit, complete with white shirt and tie. The only other colors she exhibited were purple lipstick and a yellow flower sticking out of her lapel. A nose ring perched on one nostril and a diamond studded the other.

Why do they do that shit? Doesn't snot get hung up on those things? Definitely not appealing or sexy.

The blonde looked giddy over Brody's fireman's uniform and the hunky meat filling it out. With a come-on smile, she asked him to sign the guest log and told him to be sure to sign out when he was done. With a wink, he agreed. He walked past the elevator to the privacy of the stairs and made his way to the third floor. *Hallway empty, good.*

"You with me guys?" Brody asked. He heard a chorus of affirmatives.

He walked within a few feet of Juan's door.

"I'm in position. Give me a status on our target, Nick."

"He's still at the table sipping a beer."

"That's my cue. I'm going in."

At 12:30, Brody swiped the master key card and heard the locking mechanism release. He rushed through the 10 feet of hallway in less than a second. Hearing the front door opening, Juan stood. Too late. Brody tased him in the shoulder with 50,000 volts.

Juan did a great imitation of a standing knockout victim and fell to the floor. Lying flat on his back, he struggled to restart his stunned diaphragm, unable to utter any kind of sound or catch his breath. Brody quickly duck taped his mouth and wrapped him up in zip ties. No time to talk yet.

Brody hustled to the vent hiding the camera and shoved the plastic straw upwards, spraying foam until it oozed out of all the slats on both sides of the two rooms Shawn mentioned. Camera and mic terminated. Using his handheld scanner, he checked the unit for any other listening devices and found none. He turned on the flat-screen TV to cover any sounds that might alert neighbors.

Bending over the mummified Juan, he scanned fingerprints to a secure database, a copy of which was sent to Nick. They should get his real ID in seconds.

Juan's breathing sputtered. His terrified eyes stared up at Brody. The scanner dinged.

"Hey asshole, looks like we got a hit on your prints," Brody announced. "Look at that. What a surprise. You're Juan Aguilar, not Juan Martin. What? Too dumb to learn a new first name, shithead? Let's see, looks like I've got your life story here. Age 36, Born in Chula Vista, California, to Jorge and Lupe Aguilar. No brothers or sisters. Married a smart wife that divorced your ass in 2006. You've been in and out of jail since your first car theft at age 18. What did you do, jump one of your neighbor's cars and drive it across the border to Tijuana for a quick buck?"

Juan stared helplessly, his eyes wide.

"From there you moved up to armed robbery. That got you a 10-year vacation at Lompoc Prison, 2005 to 2015. Served your full term and released three years ago. After all that, here you are, stealing again. I know all about your organization and the misery it produces by raiding checking and savings accounts of innocent hard-working people, you piece of shit."

"Mm...no...no..." Juan struggled to say through the duct tape.

"Shut it. Don't even try to deny it. I'm here to take advantage of those accounts you've looted. You see, I'm what you'd call a human vulture. I let predators like you do the dirty work, then I move in and feast on the spoils. So, I'm going to make this simple. You give me the money you scammed, and I'll fly off to another road kill somewhere far away. You'll never see me again. I'm smart enough not to feed on someone's carcass more than once."

Only moans from Juan now, and tears dripped out of the corners of his eyes.

"You're thinking you have other options. You don't. You're lying there vulnerable, and the only way to avoid some nasty permanent disfigurement is to comply. Just concentrate on what I'm gonna say right now, and you might be smart enough to make the only move you have. Just give me the money, and I promise not to kill you. Why would I? We both know the Lentini wolves will do that for me when they find out about this. Which they will. Give me the money, and I'll let you go so you can run."

More mumbling through the duct tape.

"I'm gonna remove the tape. If you yell, you're going to lose an eye, understand?"

Juan nodded yes. Brody yanked it off and said, "Clock's ticking."

"You're making a big mistake, you stupid gringo.

There's no money here. It all goes to a bank in Switzerland. Dude, you don't know who you're messing with. They're gonna kill me and cut you up in little pieces. They'll never stop looking for you. Look, I know someone that'll take me to Mexico, I can hide there. If you leave now, you might be able to save yourself too."

Brody re-taped his mouth.

"Well, I guess you didn't pay attention in school either. Try to pay attention now."

Brody grabbed Juan's left hand and very slowly broke his pinky finger at both joints. While Juan sang a muffled serenade that sounded a lot like a scream, Brody said, "That's just the beginning. It's gonna get real bad for you and fast. I don't have time for your bullshit. I know all about the money trail."

Brody began to lay the groundwork for the cover story he and the guys devised to deflect away from the real reason he was there. Just in case.

"I did some digging after one of my street girls told me about your operation. A drunk ass scammer at your out-of-town warehouse told her all about it after they had sex. I know the money comes to you, and you pay your crew of scammers. Right now you have $197,000 in a checking account at the Wells Fargo Bank just one block from here. I'll break the rest of your fingers one at a time, then I'll start on your legs so you can't run. If you're still not cooperating, I'll leave you here for the Lentinis to finish you off. You can avoid all that by giving me your online banking ID and password. I'll transfer the money and be gone. Sound familiar? You do it to people 50 times a day, right?"

Juan's eyelids scrunched tight from the pain. Brody slapped him.

"Now listen. If you're gonna give up the codes, blink your eyes twice now."

Juan blinked twice.

"Okay, but if I don't hear ID and passcode immediately come from your mouth, I'll put the tape back on, and the next finger snaps. Blink twice again if you understand."

Again Juan blinked twice. Brody partially lifted the tape, and Juan hissed through the pain.

"Okay, okay, I'll do it. I see I have no choice. Man, you ruined my finger. I'll cooperate, I need to run. I know they're watching me."

He gave up the codes and Brody made a beeline for Juan's computer. He entered the ID and password, and saw the account balance of $197,000. He clicked on the transfer funds option, traversed through the required steps, and sent the money from Juan's account to the account number Nick gave him.

"You getting all this, guys?"

"Yeah, you did great. It went through. Now plug the stick I gave you into the USB port. It'll fry the cache and hard drive," Nick coached.

Brody plugged it in, clicked on the screen prompt, and the computer was scrubbed.

"Perfect. Now get a move on, pal. We'll handle the rest from our end. Great job, bro. We'll see you soon." Shawn said.

"Rrooogggerrrrrrrrrrrrrrrrrrrrrrrrrrrr."

That was the last sound out of Brody's mouth as he fell to the floor, unconscious. Nick, Dan, and Shawn look on in shock.

Shawn spoke. "Dan, get on your horse, we'll keep you updated."

"I'm on my way."

Chapter 10
LIBRARY OF SOULS

Brody slowly opened his eyes, squinting and blinking from the brightness. Soon his eyes adjusted and he looked around. A chair dwarfed his above-average bulk and made him look like a child. He wasn't shackled or bound; the chair was backed against a wall in the middle of a very long and wide hallway.

The incredibly tall walls on both sides of the hallway were paneled with a variety of exotic woods and ornate moldings. The ceiling was one giant skylight with blue skies and thick white clouds floating by. The floor was shiny white marble. He sat directly across from a pair of 20-foot-high iron doors that were closed.

Standing in the center of the doors and facing him was a man who might be Arab, Jewish, or Italian. Italian. Yeah, it had to be one of the Lentinis. How did they possibly outmaneuver him and his team and bring him here?

The man was dressed in a long black robe that

stopped just above his sandaled feet. He had a full black beard with long black hair that fell to the middle of his back.

Wait, he definitely looks more Muslim than Italian. Did the hit squads of the Middle East finally catch up to me? But if they did, why aren't I bound?

The man smiled with perfect bright white teeth. In the deepest voice Brody ever heard, he said, "Welcome to the library. You must be excited to make your very first selection. I'll open the doors, and we can go in and get started."

"Wait!" Brody said. Where am I, how did I get here, and who are you?"

"Well, you're in the library, of course. I'm the librarian. Trust me, and please relax. You are here of your own free will and fruition. You've earned the right to be here because of the way you lived your life. You're about to embark on a wondrous experience that will last forever."

Aha, they're gonna brainwash me, convert me to Islam, and get information about who and where my friends are so they can get them too. They will try, but it won't work. I'll die first.

Brody stood up. He looked around for an escape route and the man's bodyguards. He saw neither.

Why would they leave this one man alone? He's small, unarmed, and certainly no match for me. If the doors are an exit out of here, I could simply push him aside and flee.

"I see you're suspicious, Brody. Come, follow me. I promise you have nothing to fear."

He raised a hand, and the doors opened. "I'll explain everything once we're inside."

Brody cautiously followed him in. They stepped into another wide hallway with no visible end. Both sides of the hallway were filled with one-foot by one-foot wood lockers from the floor to an unseen ceiling. Each locker had a door with a small glass window in the middle of it. A light was flickering through the glass from the inside.

Still no armed bodyguards in sight.

The man stood next to a pedestal just inside the doors in the middle of the hallway. On the pedestal was a book. It was opened to a page that had Brody's name written at the top.

"What is this place? Are you gonna torture me to make me talk? It won't work. You're wasting your time," Brody said.

"No, no Brody. Nothing like that. Let me show you and explain at the same time," the man said.

He stepped up to one of the lockers and opened it. Floating inside appeared to be a small stone that looked anatomically similar to a human heart. It was surrounded by a burning flame. That explained the dancing light Brody saw.

"What you're looking at is a soul, Brody. All living things have one. The soul records a life from conception to its end and is indestructible. When a life ends, a copy of its soul comes here to this library. I mean any life. Human, eagle, dinosaur. From a majestic blue whale to a tiny ant. Anything that lived and died. Anyone allowed in this library can select any soul they desire and relive that life, start to finish. You will feel and experience every aspect of that life as it was lived, but you will still be aware of who you are."

"What's the catch?"

"Ah. There is a caveat. Any life you choose to experience will be lived exactly as it was. You won't be able to change anything, no matter how much you may want to. Some people think this is reincarnation, but really it's just a choice made by the ones who come here. It's easy. All you have to do is take hold of the stone in both hands and hold it next to your heart. It really is that simple."

Brody's mind was spinning. He tried to grasp what the man was saying. They must have used some kind of mind-altering drug, like LSD. He was finding it hard not to grab one of the stones, even knowing it would burn his hands.

That must be it. I grab the stone, and it sticks to me and keeps burning till I talk.

The man continued.

"Brody, it's been my experience that people choose to relive their own life as their first choice, but again, you can choose any life you want."

Brody thought about what the man was saying. Of course, he would want to relive his own life; who wouldn't? He had an idea that might make the man show his hand.

"Okay, mister. I would like to live Tony Lentini's life." *You know… the guy you work for, buddy.* He studied the man's reaction to the Lentini name, but got none.

"That choice is unavailable at this time. However, we do have your father's soul here, if you'd like."

Something snapped in Brody's mind at the mention of his father's soul. He told the man that, yes, he wanted to relive his father's life.

"Let's go to your father, then."

Somehow they traveled without any sensation of doing so and stood in front of an open locker in a different section of the library.

The man told Brody, "Here, this is your father."

Brody looked inside. "That looks exactly like the other stone you showed me. Is it really my father?"

"All the stones are identical on the outside, but on the inside is one's unique life. I assure you, this is your father. Take the stone and hold it to your heart. When you're done, you'll automatically arrive back here to make another selection if you choose to do so."

Brody succumbed. He reached in and grabbed the flaming stone, surprised that it didn't burn him. It was actually cool to the touch. Holding it in both hands, he pressed it hard against his chest. His body wrapped around it in a fetal position, and he fell asleep. He sensed that he was floating in a warm, safe, but dark sanctuary that nourished and protected him while he slept.

* * *

Brody shivered from a cold that stung his skin like aftershave. He felt a stinging slap, then another. He wanted to cry out, *Stop!* He heard a voice asking someone if he was awake. The reply was no. Brody tried to open his eyes and see who was talking. Slowly, the blackness changed to gray, then slowly to brighter shades of white. Like turning up a dimmer switch to high from low, it became so bright that Brody's eyes ached. He shut his eyelids tight and tried again to reopen them, this time more slowly. Through tiny slits in his eyelids, he saw blurry images. After a couple of deep breaths, the images became clearer.

Like in the library, he was sitting in a chair, and again a man was in front of him. He was pretty sure it was not the same man. For one thing, this man was sitting rather than standing and was facing him. Brody could see the man was securely tied to the chair. Two men with their backs to Brody stood in front of the man and looked down at him. Brody's vision was clear enough to recognize the man in the chair.

Juan.

Slowly, through his grogginess, Brody realized what happened to him. He steadied his breathing and watched the three men, straining to listen while his mind was clearing. He was sure he'd been drugged somehow at Juan's place and brought here with him. He knew Nick, Shawn, and Dan had to have seen what happened and that Dan was probably on his way here. He was smart to put in a fresh crown with a tracking device before he left and was thankful that Dan was close by for backup. He'd have to stall for time. The powerful visions of the library that seemed so real were obviously side effects of whatever drug was used on him. However, he certainly would rather be there than here. Maybe someday.

Juan was naked, and what was left of his right eye deflated on his cheek like a used rubber. His threat to Juan about losing an eye if he didn't cooperate had strangely come to fruition.

Brody looked down. He was in the same naked and tied-up condition as Juan, except he still had both eyes. The rest of his body looked intact. They hadn't started working on him... yet.

The two men hadn't noticed he was waking, so Brody feigned still being out. Again, through the smallest slits he could muster, he used his excellent peripheral vision and carefully looked around. He could tell he was in the middle of a room. It was just the four of them.

The room was square, approximately 20 x 20 feet in a basement. He knew it was a basement because he spotted a small window near the top of one of the concrete walls, just above ground level. Through the window, the wind and grass and weeds waved at him. Rain pelted the upper half, and some of it ran down on the inside of the wall because the window was tilted open. That explained the cold chill he felt while regaining consciousness. They must have cracked it to dilute the strong stench in the room. The window was about four feet wide and about 10 inches clear in height. Not an escape route for his thick body.

Two of the walls were concrete. The one he faced with the window was obviously an exterior wall. The one on his left must be too. The other two walls, one on his right, and one behind him, were wood-framed partition walls. He had to turn his head stealthily to see the wall in back of him, and he noticed it had the only door to the room.

This must be a small corner room built at the end of a larger basement. In the three corners, he saw cameras near the ceiling. There could be only one reason for them, and it was a perversion he didn't want to think about. On the framed wall without the door on his right, a wooden bench sat with a peg board above.

The bench and board held everyday tools, but they wouldn't be used for their normal purposes. No, they'd be used to destroy bodies and make people talk. Brody had seen these same tools before—blow torches, hacksaws, knives, hammers. This room had been set up entirely for one thing. Torture.

He looked back at Juan. They'd been working on him for a while. Each knee had 16 penny framing nails driven in with the heads flush to the skin. These guys weren't just doing this for answers. To their sick minds, this was fun.

Brody could tell this wasn't the first time they tortured someone by the fact that an intravenous line was fed into Juan's arm. It no doubt pumped a special cocktail of fluids to prolong their playing with him. An extra port spliced into that line. Brody knew it would be used to inject small doses of morphine to keep Juan from going into shock or dying of cardiac arrest.

Obviously, they planned to work on Juan for a very long time. They found another use for the hammers, besides putting nails in his knees. All of his toes were flattened mush piles, splattered in a large arc around the front of his chair. The smell of burnt flesh hung in the air—they cauterized the toe tips with the torch, ensuring he wouldn't bleed out before they were done with him.

Between the two men, Brody could see that Juan was a total mess. He saw the broken pinky finger that he himself had done. From that one finger, he had gotten all the information he needed to get Mary's money back.

That should have been the end of it, Juan. One broken finger. Yes, I hated you for hurting Mary, and I wanted to physically hurt you back. Even fantasized about it. But as I see you now, I only have compassion and mercy in my heart, and I feel sorry that I brought this on you.

One of the guys, or both of them, used pliers to break and mangle the rest of Juan's fingers. Some fingernails were pulled out, but not all of them. Obviously, they broke the fingers first. More painful that way. A puddle of urine mixed with the bloody mush around a floor drain under Juan's chair. Brody knew Juan would have told them everything after they broke just one finger, put one nail in his knee, or smashed one toe. What they were doing to Juan was simply for their macabre enjoyment.

One man held a pair of pliers, aka, a fingernail removal tool, and the other man held an ice pick, aka, eye pick. Their holstered Glocks hung on their hips. Mister Ice Pick must have just finished working on Juan's eye because fluid still dripped off it onto the floor.

Pliers, wearing a wife beater that smelled like garlic, was white, short, and stocky. Like a pit bull. About five eight and just over two hundred pounds. His blue jeans and Nike shoes were blood splattered, and so were his heavily muscled hairy arms that seemed way too long for his body. *He reminds me of a knuckle-dragging gorilla.*

Ice Pick was white too, but built just the opposite—tall, probably six-six and over three hundred pounds with very little fat. Bodyguard, for sure. Thick straight blond hair covered his shoulders. Probably a big hit with the ladies. He was bare-chested. That made it easier to shower off the blood, tissue, and bone fragments sticking to his skin, basketball shorts, and sandals. Those would be thrown away. He sweated profusely and reeked of a combination of BO and beer.

With their backs to him, Brody couldn't see their eyes. He guessed blue for Pick and dark brown for Pliers. Both sets would no doubt be soulless and malevolent.

Ice Pick asked Juan a question in a deep voice that didn't seem human. "So Juan, tell us again who your partner over there is, or you're gonna lose your other eye."

Juan, tears streaking just one cheek now, responded, "I told you I don't know him. I told you over and over. He broke into my place, tased me, tied me up, and forced me to give him access to the account. He knew all about it. Said one of our crew told one of his girls."

The shortness of his breath, the dryness and frigid stuttering of his words told Brody that Juan's body was going into shock from pain and loss of blood. If Juan's heart stopped, Brody would be the next object of torture.

"Honest, I've told you everything," Juan's weak and breathless words whispered out of his toothless, swollen, and bloodied mouth.

"You know, Juan, we actually believe you. We believed you about an hour ago, right, Vinny?" said Pliers.

"Yeah, but we had to make sure, eh, Horst?"

It's stupid to use real names when committing a crime, but these guys aren't worried about me or Juan leaving the room alive. Thanks to this breach, I know that Pliers is Vinny and Ice Pick is Horst. Brody wasn't sure what good it would do, but he was trained to gather any information he could in every situation.

"Yeah, it's our job, Vinny, my man." They both laughed loudly, not caring about being overheard.

"Please, I can't take any more of this. I'm so cold and I'm freeeezing." Juan spat out.

"Hey, Vinny."

"Yeah, Horst, I know. We can't let him die until Damon gets here. He was sure pissed the last time that stupid punk died on us before he got to talk to him."

Damon...who the hell is Damon? Brody wondered.

"Yeah, Damon threatened Mr. Lentini with pulling his government contract and finding another contractor if it happened again. We sure got our asses reamed over that one. We deserved it though, especially from Tony. Damon is Tony's biggest client, and he works for some big shots in the government. We were lucky they believed that guy died from a weak heart. And that we tried to revive him but couldn't," Horst added.

"Okay, Juan, I'm getting you a blanket and a little taste of morphine. You have to last three more hours till Damon gets here. You can have a little break while we work on your partner over there, then we'll get back to you. Don't go anywhere." Vinny chuckled.

"Tape up his yap while you're at it, Vinny. I can't stand his whimpering. Can you believe that these idiots thought they could get away with stealing money from the Lentinis?"

"Yeah, lucky for us. Otherwise it'd get pretty boring around here, and all these nice tools would go to waste."

"Speaking of being bored, let's wake up this big guy and have some more fun," Horst replied.

Brody saw Horst put the pick on the table. He

closed his eyelids and waited. Horst was close—
Brody could feel puffs of acrid breath on his chest.

Smack! Brody felt the sting of a huge open-
handed slap across his face.

Chapter 11
BRODY'S TURN

"Time to wake up, asshole," Horst sneered.

"The last drug we gave him should be wearing off right about now anyway," Vinny said.

Another slap. He'd love to return the slaps with his fists. Then, a plume of smelling salts stung Brody's nostrils and shocked his senses. He fought the sensations off without a flinch. He knew he has to stall for every single second. It was the only defensive weapon he had. He was sure Nick and Shawn tracked him here. Staying perfectly still, Brody braced for what might come next. He knew from experience that there are only a few things you can do to bring a drug-induced person back to consciousness. The best way is a decent dose of adrenaline.

"Hey, Vinny, get me that syringe of adrenaline."

Shit!!! Brody screamed inside his brain.

"I'll inject it into the port of his IV, and it'll wake the son of a bitch up pronto."

Vinny handed the syringe to Horst, who injected adrenaline into the line. Instantly Brody's heart went into radical fibrillation, and his breathing increased rapidly. He tried to control it but couldn't. With his eyes still closed, he groaned, pulled a little on his restraints with his arms, and moved his head slightly. He knew he couldn't fake unconsciousness any longer.

Horst said, "That's a good boy. Wake up and take your medicine, ha, ha."

"Let me slap him some, Horst. I like beating on big guys," Vinny said.

"Sure, have at it."

Two small hands slapped Brody in rapid succession, knocking his head from left to right like he was shaking his head no.

What a couple of sick moronic psychopaths. Brody had never felt so helpless. Unfortunately, he could tell by Juan's quiet breathing that the morphine put him to sleep. Temporarily. Now, Brody would be these lunatics' main focus. All his training and experience told him one thing. He needed a miracle.

Brody slowly opened his eyelids and stared at the two goons with the best groggy look he could muster. He faked semi-consciousness and lucidity.

"He's coming around, Horst. Bring the hammer. Let's start with his toes. I just love the way they explode. Reminds me of hitting rolls of caps when I was a kid. Pow!"

"Yeah, Vinny, I did that too. You're right, they do

explode but without the smoke."

Brody got another left and right slap to the face from Vinny and groaned. He tried another stalling tactic. Slurring his words he said, "Whoooa, hey, hey, where am I? Wha...sss going onn..? Whyy...y my naked? I can't movvve my arms legss..."

Vinny grabbed Brody's jaw and tilted his head so he was looking eyeball to eyeball, and said, "Shut the fuck up, asshole. We ask the questions around here not you."

Brody looked between the two guys at Juan and said, "Oh, my God, what have you done to my friend?"

Vinny fist-punched Brody in the nose. Immediately, warm blood ran from his nostrils to his upper lip, putting a salty copper taste in his mouth. Not the first time he'd tasted his own blood.

"Pay attention, ass wipe," ordered Vinny. "I told you we ask the questions. So let's get started, big guy. Tell us what you were doing at Juan's place."

"Okay, okay, I get it. You ask the questions. I'll answer, no problem. I just went over there to watch some football and have beers with him," Brody said.

"Oh really? Um, that's not what he's been telling us. Right, Horst?"

"Not even close. He said you busted into his place, forced him to give you his ID and passcode to his bank account, and then you stole all the money from it. By the way, that was a big mistake, pal. That money happens to belong to our boss."

Still stalling, Brody said, "I have no idea why he

would say that except to blame me for him stealing the money to cover his gambling debts. He told me he owed a lot of money to some bad dudes."

"Well, big guy, if that's true, I guess we should let you go. What do you think, Vinny?

"Nah. I don't think so, Horst."

"Me either."

"Mister, you must think we're stupid giving us that bullshit story. Juan was tied up with a busted finger, and you were sitting at his computer. How do you explain that?" Vinny continued.

Thinking fast, Brody realized Vinny just handed him a way to chew up some more time. Using Vinny's question, he'd create a reasonable cover story as to why he was in Juan's unit, just in case this was all being recorded.

"Well, okay, you got me there. The truth is I'm Juan's partner. I'll explain. I work for the Seattle fire department, and I met Juan while I was doing a fire inspection of his building some months ago. We struck up a conversation and discovered that we both owed a lot of money. He had a lot of gambling debts, that part is true, and I owe money to my ex. Stealing the money was all Juan's idea. He convinced me it would be easy. He knew if he stole the money outright, you'd never stop looking for him, so we made a plan that would look like a home invasion/robbery." Brody was on a roll.

"My part was to make it look like he was forced to give up his bank account. He transferred the money out of his account to my bank. Then I tied him up and broke his finger to make it look like he put up a fight," Brody continued. "After that, I was gonna leave and call the cops, pretending to be a neighbor, and report that I heard a gunshot from Juan's unit. That would help prove Juan's story to you because he'd have a police report and an ambulance ride to the hospital. I was gonna immediately pay off his gambling debts with some of the money so they wouldn't come after him. Then we'd wait till things cooled down to split the rest of the money. It was all working great. I wanted to see if the transfer was completed, and that's why you found me at his computer."

Brody was really proud of himself. The story made sense with what they found on the scene. Horst and Vinny looked at each other, shook their heads, and said bullshit at the same time.

"Nice try," Horst said. "But you're gonna tell us the real story. You only explained why you were dressed in a fire marshal's uniform, but not the part about why we found very sophisticated electronic equipment and military-issue weapons in your possession. See, what you and Juan didn't know is that we have sophisticated equipment of our own. As soon as you clicked on the transfer funds option on the account page, you automatically activated software that silently triggered a device that released an odorless gas knocking both your asses the hell out."

Horst smirked in Brody's direction. "At the same time, the software notified us, our boss Tony, and his semi-boss Damon. Good thing we were in a strip club just around the block. It only took us five minutes to get there. The gas should have worked fast enough to prevent you from completing the transfer, but it didn't. The system was put in place in case one of our managers got greedy."

Brody kept his composure, absorbing the details.

"Well, it didn't fail completely because you weren't able to escape," Horst taunted. "We tried to call our boss Tony, but he didn't answer. He was probably in a casino playing poker. That's the only time he ignores calls. But Damon called us right away and wanted to know what was going on. We told him that Juan was tied up and it looked like you stole our money. He told us to bring both of you here and get some answers before he arrived. You don't know how happy we were to get those orders. Our bosses know we love extracting information from people, and when they're satisfied that there's nothing left to extract, they let us do whatever we want with what's left. It doesn't matter if you cooperate or not, you're still gonna end up dead eventually, right Vinny?"

"You bet. And the less you cooperate, the more fun it is. Keep going. Tell him how helpless his situation is."

"Before we brought you here, we checked for trackers on you and your stuff, so don't think anybody is coming to save your ass. We boxed all your shit up for Damon. He works for a couple of Senators, so they'll find out from the military where you got the stuff. He's gonna want to know everything there is to know about your dumb ass when he gets here.

"When?" Brody asked, earning him a slap across the ear.

"That's in about an hour and a half, shithead, so we don't have much time. Since you didn't have any ID or phone, you better stop with the bullshit and start talking fast. Otherwise, you're gonna start to resemble Juan over there. Take a good look at him and make up your mind. Personally, we're hoping you keep your mouth shut, and we get to take turns smacking you around, right Vinny?"

"Right, Horst. So what's it gonna be, ass wipe?" Vinny asked.

Brody, desperate to stretch out the clock, thought of another plausible story.

"Okay, okay, you guys outsmarted me. No need to get rowdy. I don't want to end up like Juan. I'll tell you the whole story."

"Hold on," said Horst. "Just in case you think about lying to us, I'm going to give you a little incentive not to. Horst took a small triangle-shaped wood block and a ball peen hammer off the table. He knelt down and wedged the wood block between Brody's toes, isolating the small toe on Brody's left foot.

"Hey, what are you doing?" Brody said. "This isn't necessary. I told you I'm gonna tell you everything. You don't want to do this, trust me. Here's the real truth, and for your sake, you should listen close. I'm ex-military. That's why I had the stuff you found. I'm working as a mercenary for some badasses who have decided to take over your operation here in Seattle. It's gonna happen, so you might want to save yourselves and get on the right side of this. You let me go, and I can get you an in with us. We'd like to have some inside information on your whole operation. Join us. Otherwise, you'll be very sorry."

"Wow, that's really a very generous offer there, mister, but the only badasses around here is us. Right, Vinny?"

"Fuckin eh!"

"Besides, Damon and our boss Tony are gonna want to hear all about this big takeover. Damon will want you all tuned up and ready to talk when he gets here. He doesn't like to waste his time. So, sorry, pal, you ain't gonna spoil our fun," Vinny said.

Kneeling on the floor in front of Brody, Horst started singing a lame version of a nursery rhyme. "This little piggy went smash, smash, smash. Ha, Ha." With his eyes bulging and a crazed grin on his face, he raised the hammer high above his head.

Horst's smile, teeth, blood, and brains splattered all over the front of Brody's face and torso. The dead man fell forward, and what was left of his head fell in Brody's lap in a sexually provocative position.

As Brody stared down at the large hole in the back of Horst's head he was instantly hit with another warm spray on his face. He looked up just in time to see Vinny looking down at the giant smoking hole in his chest where his black heart use to be. A split second later, the light went out of Vinny's eyes, and he fell to the floor.

Brody looked up at the window in the outside wall and saw the silenced smoking end of a Sig P220 Legion. On the other end was his friend, Dan Knapp.

Dan kicked the window in and squeezed through the very tight opening backward, feet first. He lowered himself down as far as he could, then dropped a few feet to the basement floor. He turned around and looked at Brody, who signaled with his eyes for Dan to shoot out the cameras in the corners. He did with three quick bursts of the Legion. Hopefully, nobody was watching or listening in the last couple of minutes. Dan rushed over and pulled Horst off Brody, and untied him.

"My little toe is mighty glad to see you."

Dan looked down at the block between Brody's toes, then over at Juan. "I see what you mean."

"Thanks, my brother. I was out, so I don't know what day it is or what time either."

"Same day, 8:30 p.m. You were out about four hours. Thanks to Nick and Shawn's expert tracking skills, they got me here as fast as possible. The three of us were shocked when we saw you passing out at Juan's place."

Dan put his phone on speaker so all four men could communicate, then checked on Juan. He put his fingers on Juan's carotid artery.

"Hey, everyone, Juan here is dead."

"Simplifies things," Nick replied.

"Too bad," Shawn said sarcastically.

"Hey, Shawn, Nick, thanks for saving my ass again."

"That was too close. Man, we're happy to see you safe and back with us. Gotta tell you, though, we were feeling completely helpless there for a bit. Heck man, after all the battles we survived, we couldn't believe we might lose you to some chicken shit low-life scam outfit."

"Believe me, I was feeling the same way. I'll tell you what I know, then you can fill me in on what happened when I went out, and how I got here. A guy named Damon is on his way. I heard these two guys say three hours, but that was about fifteen minutes ago. He was gonna interrogate Juan and me. He gave some kind of government contract to Tony, and I think he might be a partner in his operations. We don't know who he's bringing with him. Shawn, are there any satellites in this quadrant?"

"Less than 30 minutes. A satellite with all the goodies, including penetrating infrared, will be over your location. We'll see your whole area for at least six hours. It's a military secret that some of our satellites are programmed to circle in a curly cue pattern, similar to the white frosting on a hostess cupcake. That pattern prolongs the satellite's time over an area. We're gonna get you guys outta there."

Chapter 12

RESCUE

"Dan, you can squeeze through the window, but there's no way I can. Gotta find another way outta here."

"I'm with you. We're going out the front door, wherever that is," assured Dan.

Brody went to a sink in the corner with a hose hooked to the faucet. He turned it on and began rinsing off Vinny's and Horst's gore.

"These scumbags told me that the transfer process on Juan's computer triggered software that released a knock-out gas. It was designed to stop someone from completing the transfer. I guess it malfunctioned because they were really pissed that it didn't work the way it was supposed to. Did you get the funds?" Brody asked.

"Yeah, $197,000 landed in the offshore bank account we gave you. It's an account for a bogus shell company in the Caymans. We immediately transferred the money from there to our secret

Swiss account. Then we made that Shell Company disappear. All the money in our Swiss account is untraceable, going in and out. We can transfer any amount to anywhere we want anonymously. We'll put Mary's money back into her new account tomorrow."

Nick piped up. "I'll need to get Jane's account info and yours too, Dan, so we all can get our cuts. I already have yours, Brody."

"That's great news. I can't wait to tell them. That's all I know since being knocked out."

"Right. Well, that explains why we saw you guys pass out. Scared the hell out of the three of us. Dan took off immediately and headed your way. Less than 15 minutes after you hit the floor we saw two guys with guns come into the unit. That really baffled us as to how they got there so soon," Nick said.

"Sorry, guys, I'm still a bit groggy. I can help with that. I forgot that they told me the software alerted them at the same time the gas was released, and they just happened to be close by at a strip joint."

"That explains how they got there so soon. No problem with your memory, Brode. There's always an adjustment period after being knocked out. We don't know what the gas was or if they used anything else. You need to go to the base infirmary and have some blood drawn for analysis for any residual side effects. How do you feel?" Nick asked.

"Okay, other than a little brain fog," Brody replied.

"I'll keep my eye on you, Brody, but you seem fine to me," Dan said.

"Good," Nick said, and continued. "When the two guys came in to Juan's place, they saw that you two were passed out and put their guns away. One of them turned off your body cam and stripped you of all your equipment. He put it all in a box. They were pretty smart about getting the two of you out of there without alarming anyone. While the one guy was getting your stuff packed, the other guy left the unit and came back with a wheel chair and one of those hotel luggage carts.

They tied you in the chair, put sunglasses and a hat on you, then covered you up to your neck with a blanket. They put the smaller Juan on the bottom of the cart and hid him under clothes, put the box with your stuff on top of him, and trash bags over that. We couldn't hear what they were saying since they pulled the plug on your equipment, but we still had visual from your camera across the street. When they rolled the both of you out of the unit, we temporarily lost sight of you. Take it from there, Shawn."

"Right. We picked you up again when they brought you out of the building and onto the sidewalk. They loaded you guys in the back of a white Ford panel van parked directly behind your phony fire marshal van, Brody. They drove off, and we lost visual again. However, we tracked your implant's signal. Dan was already driving, and we directed him to intersect you. Unfortunately, your movements were traveling away from him. It was about an hour later when your signal stopped moving, and we locked in on that address."

"How far away was Dan?" Brody asked.

"By that time, Dan was still about an hour from catching up to you, even though he was following as fast as he could. We kept him updated with the fastest route possible. I was able to flip red traffic lights to green. When Dan arrived, he told us that the warehouse was completely fenced with a coded and locked traffic gate. He was able to park in an adjacent lot, climb the fence, and get to the window where your signal was the strongest. You know what happened after that. Thank God the timing was good, and Dan is such an excellent shot. Good job, Dan. I knew you were more than the best chopper jockey," Shawn said.

"No problem. Sorry about the mess I made on you, Brody, but I had no choice. I got to the window just in time to see the big guy raising a hammer above your head."

"No worries, better their mess on me than the other way around. You're my hero," Brody said.

While Shawn had been talking, Brody had toweled off, got dressed, and loaded up with all his gear from the box that Vinny had pointed to. He had a backup body cam set up and gave it to Dan.

"Hey Shawn, let me stop you for a sec. Dan and I have our com equipment on. Let's do a quick check so we can get off Dan's phone."

"Sure thing."

Brody and Dan's equipment checked out, and Nick was the first to comment.

"Wow, that whole room is a nasty mess."

"It'll have to stay that way. Right now, we have to get out of the building. Any ideas what we're dealing with here?" Brody asked Shawn and Nick.

"The live Satellite is almost there, but we do have a satellite image of the building and the surrounding area. It's out in the sticks in a rundown industrial area that looks like it had been deserted many years ago. There are several other smaller buildings around, but all are vacant and boarded up," Shawn said.

"As soon as your tracker stopped, I zeroed in on the address," Nick said. "I researched the city archives for any information on the building and property. It's a medium-sized warehouse built in 1947 for the purpose of repairing, maintaining, and supplying boats with parts and accessories."

"How long was it operational?" Brody asked.

"It was closed down and abandoned about thirty years ago," Shawn answered. "Lentini's corporation bought the property at auction five years ago. The upstairs main floor may still have some old boat parts, but we don't know what they've done to the inside, or in the basement. Other than that horror room you're in, you'll have to see for yourself what's there and find your way out," Nick said.

"Thanks, guys. I'd like to wait for the satellite but don't think we can. Dan and I will start clearing the basement, then find our way up and out. Don't want to be stuck down here when Damon shows up."

"Brody, think we should call in the local cops?" Nick asked.

"Not yet. Damon and Tony Lentini might have the local authorities in their pockets," said Brody. "And this guy Damon has some kind of government connection. We may have to find out what that is for all of our safety and security going forward."

"Okay. We'll be monitoring and recording your every move," Nick said.

"You ready, Dan?'

"Ready."

Brody slowly opened the torture room's door just enough to get one eye in the crack and peer through. To his left was an empty hallway about 10 feet wide and 80 feet long, dimly lit by fluorescent lights attached to the middle of the ceiling. About 10 feet to his right was a solid wall. The torture room was obviously at the end of the building's foundation wall.

Looking back to his left and down to the end of the long hallway, a wide stairway appeared that must lead up to the main floor. The four doors on both sides of the hallway mirrored each other, then another room on Brody's side down by the stairway. So, nine rooms in the basement.

Two choices. They could make a run for the stairs and try to ambush Damon outside the gate. Or, he and Dan would have to clear and secure the eight remaining rooms in the basement, then ambush Damon upstairs inside the building.

Brody closed the door and whispered the options to Dan. They both agreed that they'd have a better chance of controlling the situation inside after they cleared the basement and the upstairs. They didn't want to be surprised by an attack on their six's. Brody let Shawn and Nick know their plan.

Brody reopened the door and signaled all clear to Dan. They slowly move into the hallway, guns drawn. Sounds from the intense storm still raged outside and helped cover their stealthy movements. Not anticipating a trap, they moved to the first door directly across and positioned themselves on each side. Brody on the lock side and Dan on the hinge side.

Brody gripped the levered door handle and slowly pushed down. No resistance. He hand signaled Dan that it wasn't locked and to cover the left side of the room. Brody took the right. One, two, three, Brody pushed in the door and moved two steps to his right. Then he stopped, taking a knee to shrink himself. Dan did the same to the left.

The room was totally dark and quiet. Brody searched the wall by the door and found a light switch. He flipped it on, ready to shoot anything that moved. Light exploded, illuminating a storage area.

Shelves on three of the walls held boxes of canned food, bottled water, snacks, and various paper goods. A large sorting table sat in the center of the room. In the back corner stood a large refrigerator and large chest-style freezer. Unfortunately, Brody and Dan both spotted a camera in the opposite corner covering the whole room.

Brody whispered to Shawn, "Hey, we got a camera here like the one we took out in the torture room."

"Not to worry. As soon as I knew where you were, I used a communications satellite and detected several continuous signals from various points in and around the building. Obviously, from wireless cameras. The signals were bundled together and transmitted to four locations. Two inside the building, probably offices. One to Juan's condo, and one to Lentini's office in Vegas. I blocked all the signals as fast as I could," Shawn assured.

"That's why you guys are the best. Two rooms down, six to go," said Brody.

Dan turned off the light and closed the door behind them as they stepped back into the hall. Using the same tactics, they opened the next door on that same side of the hall.

This room was different. Still dark, except for a table on the back wall with a small night light plugged underneath. It gave off just enough light for them to survey the whole room. On the left where Dan was positioned were metal lockers, like the ones in schools or gyms. On Brody's side were three small cots, each occupied by a sleeping male. They looked Hispanic in their early 20s.

Brody quietly stepped over to the bed closest to him. The man was asleep on his back. Brody put his large hand over the gaping mouth. The man awoke with such fear in his eyes that Brody had to calm him down quickly before he tried to rabbit.

Holding the index finger of his gun hand to his mouth, Brody indicated to the man to be quiet. He removed his hand and motioned him to follow them out of the room. The man quietly got up in his underwear. The three snuck out into the hall and closed the door.

Whispering, Brody asked the man if he spoke English.

"Si," he said. Then, "Yes. I'm sorry, when I'm nervous, I sometimes mess up my English."

"That's okay, don't be nervous. We're not gonna hurt you. Did you see when I was brought here with the other man?"

"Yes, everybody saw, and we all got scared. Especially the way they were treating Juan. He was the other man, and he's our boss."

Not wanting to frighten the man any more than he already was, Brody put his hand on his back and nudged him down the hall toward the storage room across from the torture room. Brody saw the man stare at the torture room as they passed by it, and he started to shiver.

"You don't have to worry, nobody is coming out of that room. They're all dead," Brody told him.

Brody opened the storage room door and told the man to sit on one of the boxes on the floor.

"What's your name?" Brody asked.

"My name is Carlos."

"Do you know the two men who brought Juan

and me here?"

"Yes, very bad men. The tall one, his name is Horst, and the shorter one is Vinny."

"Are there any more guys like them here?" Asked Brody.

"No," Carlos said.

"Look, Carlos, we're not gonna hurt you. Let me tell you what happened."

Brody wanted to keep the robbery narrative as cover just in case Carlos was questioned later on.

"Well, Carlos, Juan and I were working together to steal some money, and we got caught. That's why they brought us here. My friend here helped me escape, but it was too late for Juan. We're not gonna hurt anybody, we just wanted money, understand?"

"Yes," he said.

"Is there any money here?"

"No, señor, only a few dollars. They never keep any big money here."

"Okay, fine, Carlos, I believe you. Now tell us how many people are in this building, where they are, and what you all are doing here," Brody said.

"We are 15, nine men and six girls. We sleep down here. The men on this side of the hall and the girls on the other. Three men to a room, and two girls to a room. The last room on the other side of the hallway is a bathroom. It's just to the left of the stairway. At the top of the stairs is a door that's locked by Horst and Vinny when we come down here to sleep. They lived upstairs. They each had their own apartment at the back of the building."

When Carlos used the past tense for Horst and Vinny, that meant he understood they weren't coming back.

"We work for Juan, but his boss is a mean rich man who brought us here illegally. He promised to get citizenship for us if we worked for him for five years. Then he said he'll let us go free. I've been here four years now. We all know he's lying and will never let us go, but what can we do? The only other room down here is this storage room and the punishment room over there. His hand shook as he pointed to the room across from them.

"You know about that room?" Brody asked.

"Yes. Six months ago, one of our guys escaped with one of the girls through a window in the bathroom. They put iron bars over the window after that, but none of us would even try to escape after we saw what they did to the man and the girl. The day after they escaped, the police brought them back here. The two men that brought you here, took the man and girl from the police and put them in that room."

"Then what happened?"

"They made all of us come in and watch the horrible things they did to them. It went on for hours. It was so terrible, none of us can forget what we saw or the horrible screams that came from the man and girl. They pleaded for mercy and begged them to stop, but they just laughed. We all silently prayed for God to take mercy on them. We think he heard us because both of their heads dropped at the same time, and they died."

"And?"

"They made us clean up and bury them in the trees behind the building. I pray to God to help me forget what I saw and heard. We are so afraid of them and the police."

"Well, you won't have to be afraid anymore, and just maybe we can get you all out of here so you won't have to worry about someone taking their place," Brody told him.

"That would be a miracle, señor. It seems impossible. The police are in it together with these bad men. The girls here have to do sex with them and with other men the police bring here. They are diablos. The girls also have to do all the cleaning and cooking."

"What do the men do, Carlos?" Brody asked.

"Upstairs, there's a room with computers and phones where we are trained to call and scam people. I feel so bad about it, but what can I do? I have to protect myself and my family in Mexico. They say if I don't do what they say, they'll kill my whole family in Guadalajara. So I do what they say."

"How does the scam work?"

"After we get people's personal information, we use that to get money from their accounts. Then we transfer it to a special account. We do the scams in English and Spanish. That's why they snuck us across the border because we know both languages. They send out voice calls, emails, and texts to people in English and Spanish, and the people call us worried.

That's it, señor. That's who is here and what we do."

"Thank you, Carlos. Who else comes here?"

"Just the rich boss man. He comes once a month with another bad man. He looks around, talks to Juan in the office upstairs then leaves after a couple of hours," Carlos said.

"Do you know the rich boss's name?" Brody asked.

"Damon," Carlos replied.

***

"You were right about the local cops, Brody," Nick said into Brody and Dan's earpieces.

"Yeah, unfortunately. Guys, we have to get these people out of here. Dan, go see if you can find any keys or money on the dead guys."

"You got it," he said as he hurried back to the bloody room.

"Carlos, if we can get you all out of here, does everyone have someplace to go?" Brody asked.

"Oh, yes. Most of us have some family living in this country, that's why we tried so hard to get here. The ones who don't, would feel lucky to get out of here and go back home to Mexico, Honduras, Venezuela, or El Salvador."

Dan rushed back into the storage room.

"Jackpot! I found two identical sets of key rings on each of them, probably for this warehouse. The other sets are car keys for two different vehicles. I also found over $2,200 in cash between the two," Dan said.

"Good. Come on, Carlos, let's get everyone up

and dressed as fast as we can, but quietly, just in case there are bad guys upstairs. How many of you can drive?"

"I can, and so can most of the men, but none of the girls," Carlos replied.

Brody and Dan helped Carlos open each room, one at a time. Brody and Dan cleared each room first, then Carlos entered and got the people up. Carlos quietly told them to get dressed, not to worry, and that they were going to be set free. Brody worked with Carlos imploring the people to hurry, while Dan went up the stairs to try the keys on the locked door.

"Good news," Shawn piped in. "The satellite will be over you in less than five minutes, and then we'll be able to see everything around you."

"Perfect. We'll hold our position down here till then."

Dan tiptoed down the stairs and told Brody that he got the door unlocked, but didn't chance opening it without cover. They both organized the men and girls into two groups, with the men at the foot of the stairs. The girls lined up behind them. Most everyone had full backpacks. The rest carried shopping bags or pillowcases stuffed with their belongings.

They were all dressed in various sports clothes, pants, shirts, skirts, and hats. The good news is that they all had some kind of overgarment for protection from the cold wind and rain outside.

The men looked anxious. The girls' faces showed

fear. All of them stared hard at the guns Brody and Dan held. Brody quietly talked to the whole group to calm them down.

"Look, we came here just to steal money. We're not gonna hurt any of you, I promise," he told them in English.

Carlos interpreted for those who might not understand much English. Brody noticed that a couple of the very young girls just stared at the floor. He'd seen that same stare and melancholy before, from girls who had been enslaved and oppressed by men over a long period of time in the Middle East and other places. That kind of mental torture always resulted in the girls losing hope and the will to resist. Sometimes, they lost the will to live.

Whispering, Brody told them not to worry, that he and Dan were going to help them. They moved their heads in the direction of his words, but there wasn't the slightest change in their stoic expressions. He realized they'd heard those very same words before from the men who ended up abusing them. Brody knew he had to show them he was speaking the truth through actions, not words. That action would be to get them out of there, and soon.

He told the group to move in closer. They all crowded behind him. He, Carlos, and Dan waited in front of the group at the bottom of the stairs.

"Brody, we have your heat signatures from the satellite," Nick's voice cracked into Brody's earpiece. "Your group in the basement has the only signatures inside or outside the building. You're good to go."

Brody and Dan led the way up the stairs and out onto the main floor of the warehouse. They were in the front part of the building. Carlos showed them a side door that opened to a parking lot on the right side of the building. It was locked from the inside. Dan quickly found the right key on one of the key rings, and they all rushed out of the building. Carlos told Brody that Horst and Vinny had their SUV's around to the rear, where their apartments were. Everyone hurried in that direction.

When they got there, the two cars were parked next to each other. Dan located the right keys and started them up. The men and the girls decided amongst themselves who they wanted to leave with, and filed toward the SUVs. Carlos and another man were the drivers. Carlos, as their leader, told them to hurry. He was the last one standing outside, and before he jumped in, he wrapped his arms around Brody and said, "God bless you," in Spanish.

"You're welcome. By the way, Damon should be here in about 40 minutes. Anything you want me to tell him?"

"No, but I wouldn't mind if you kicked him in the balls," Carlos said with a big smile.

"Will do."

The SUVs were high off the ground and had stepping boards on each side. Brody stepped up and motioned for Carlos to roll down his window. Dan did the same on the other SUV, and the two headed for the gate with Carlos in the lead. The gate automatically opened from inside the compound as the vehicles pulled up close. Brody and Dan jumped off, and Carlos and his people drove away to freedom.

The gate was closing as Brody and Dan ran back into the building to wait for Damon.

Chapter 13
VEGAS CASINO

Sitting at a Texas Holdem cash table in Vegas, Tony Lentini heard his cell phone ring. He fingered it out of the inside breast pocket of his immaculately tailored $10,000 Brioni wool suit. He was surprised to see who the call was from. Intrigued, he hit accept and put the phone to his ear.

Immediately the dealer said, "Sir, I know you're in the hand, but if he you're gonna take the call, you gotta step away from the table."

Furious with the dealer's order, he shouted, "Do you know who I am?

"I'm sorry, sir. House rules, not mine. You can cancel the call, or you'll have to step away."

Steaming, but because the call was highly unusual, Tony stood and walked away to take the call, leaving his pocket aces face down on the table, pre-flop.

"What's up, Carlos? Why are you calling me and not Juan? This better be real important."

"I'm so sorry to call you, Mr. Tony, but Juan gave me your number and told me if anything ever happened to him to call you. I think he might be dead."

"What the hell happened, Carlos? Why do you think he's dead? Tell me everything."

"Yes sir, Mr. Tony. Earlier today, I saw Horst and Vinny bring Juan and another guy here. They put them in the punishment room and told all of us to go to our rooms and stay there. My room is right across the hall, so for a long time, I heard some terrible screaming. Then it stopped, and I didn't hear anything for about twenty minutes. I was surprised that after all the screaming, I went to sleep."

"Do you know who was doing the screaming?"

"I'm very sure it was Juan. I know his voice, and when they brought him in, I saw that his little finger was broken in many places like they already started torturing him on the way here."

"Go on, Carlos."

"After a while, I don't know how long, the other guy they brought here and a new guy I didn't see before came to my room. The big guy woke me up and took me to the storage room. He told me that he and Juan were gonna steal money from you, Mr. Tony. He asked me if there was any money here in the building. I told him there wasn't. He asked me what I do here. I was very scared, so I just told him that we only make the girls have sex," Carlos lied.

"You didn't say anything about the scamming business, did you?"

"No, señor. Then he made me wake everyone up. They took all of us out of the building, gave us Horst and Vinny's SUVs, and told us we were free to go. The big guy told me he knew Damon was coming, and they were gonna wait for him to get money. I waited till we were out of sight of the complex to pull over and call you. You're not gonna punish me, are you, Mr. Tony?"

"No, no, of course not, Carlos. You did the right thing to call me. Have you ever seen those two new guys before?"

"No, señor. You want me to tell you what they look like, Mr. Tony?"

"No, that won't be necessary, I'll take care of them before they leave the complex."

"What do I do now, Mr. Tony?"

"I want you to get everyone down here to Vegas. I'll have a similar complex set up for you and your people at my furniture shop out in the desert by the time you get here. And Carlos..."

"Yes, Mr. Tony."

"I'm putting you in charge of the girls and the scamming operation when you get here. You've handled yourself and the situation there perfectly. You've also proven your loyalty to me. To show everyone that you are now part of the Lentini family, when you get here, I'm gonna have our tattoo artist put one of our Ls on your neck."

"Thank you, thank you so much, Mr. Lentini. I'll do anything for you. I'll make you proud, I promise."

"I know you will, Carlos. Listen, we hide a loaded

40 caliber Glock handgun in each one of our vehicles. Do you know how to use them?"

"Yes, Mr. Tony. My father taught me to shoot guns in Mexico."

"Great. You'll find them hidden in the spare tire compartment under the tire. Get one, and show everyone that you are now their new boss. Tell them they must all stay with you, or I will send people to kill them and their families. Let them know they must do whatever you say, especially the girls, if you know what I mean." Tony laughed.

"I'll do it right now, boss. Do you want me to go back and kill those two guys at the warehouse for trying to steal from you?"

"Thank you for the offer, Carlos, but I have other plans for them and Damon. I'll text you the address of the plant here in Las Vegas. Get back on the road and get here as soon as you can. I'll take care of those guys back at the complex. See you soon, Carlos."

"Yes sir," Carlos said.

Tony hung up and called the Senator's emergency number. While waiting for the Senator to pick up, he told one of his bodyguards to cash him out of the game and bring his car around. He was going to clean up after Damon for the last freakin time and show the Senator that he should have been in charge all along, and not Damon.

The Senator finally answered. "This better be an emergency, Tony."

"It is, Senator. Damon screwed up again, and

because of that, our operation at the warehouse has been breached. Two guys broke in and killed our Seattle manager and two of our security guards. After that, they freed all our whores and scammers by letting them drive away in our vehicles. They're still at the warehouse waiting to ambush Damon, who's on his way there now. Senator, I don't have anyone I can send to the warehouse in time to take out those guys or intercept Damon. Do you want me to call Damon and warn him?"

"Shit! How the hell did this happen, Tony? Never mind, we'll talk about that later. Don't call Damon. I don't want him to spook those guys. I'll handle this situation. You'll be hearing from me soon." Tony heard the line go dead.

Just then, Shawn's voice chirped through Brody and Dan's earpieces.

"Brody, I'm getting clear pictures and video from the whole area there. There's a highway about 20 minutes north that has an exit to a road that leads right in your direction. Right now there are no cars on that road, except the two SUVs the workers drove away in. They're almost to the highway now. Since there isn't anything out where you are, our guess is that any vehicle that takes that exit and heads your way will be Damon."

"Okay, that gives us at least 20 minutes to prepare, plus whatever time it is till you see Damon's vehicle," Brody said.

He and Dan went back into the warehouse from the side door they exited from. They scoped out the main floor's kitchen and laundry on one side, and a small office at the front of the building that must have been Juan's. The office, next to the large roll-up entrance door, had a large window with opened louvered blinds. Obviously, the window was so Juan could keep an eye on his workers.

The office had a small desk with a desktop computer, one metal file cabinet, and three cheap metal folding chairs. Two doors opened into the office, one from the outside, and one to the main floor. On the same side of the building as the office, Brody saw an old broken-down boat that never got repaired. Brody had an idea of how to use it. On the wall next to the boat were racks lined with boat parts that Nick suspected would be there. Next to that area was obviously where all the criminal activity took place. The large area had 10 small desks, each with a computer and two landline phones.

"I guess they didn't want to take the chance on missing a call from one of their victims," Brody determined.

"I got something, guys," Nick shouted. "A Cadillac Escalade that took the exit off the highway is heading your way on that single road I told you about. They must not be expecting any trouble because if they were, I'm sure there'd be more than just one vehicle. We have a large heat signature for the driver and a smaller one for the lone passenger. They're traveling very fast, so the ETA is probably less than 20 minutes," Nick said.

"What's the play?" Dan asked Brody.

"I see an accumulation of tire marks in one spot here on the concrete floor just inside the roll-up door. It measures approximately where the front tires of a decent size vehicle would stop after it drives in. The cars must drive in and brake to that spot each time," Brody speculated.

"Makes sense to me. Much easier than parking outside and going through two office doors. So, I assume that you think Damon will drive in and stop approximately where these marks are," Dan said.

"Yes, and the stern section of that old boat lines up with where the driver's side door should be when it stops. Also, that large refrigerator behind you, Dan, on the other side in the kitchen, lines up with the passenger's door. I'll lay down on the floor of the boat, and you hide on the backside of the refrigerator. We should be able to take them by surprise and without a firefight," Brody said.

"Sounds like a good plan. Let's take up positions and see what it looks like," Dan said.

While Dan stood behind the refrigerator, Brody found a ten-foot piece of rope on the floor. He calculated the distance from the front edge of tire marks to approximately where the SUV's front doors should be. He laid down the rope parallel to the marks. That way, both he and Dan could see where the driver and passenger should exit the car.

Brody climbed into the boat. Given where the boat was, the best position he could manage inside the stern was about three feet back from his end of the rope, which would be closer to the rear passenger door.

"Dan, can you see your end of the rope?"

"Yeah. I'm a couple of feet back toward the overhead door."

"Perfect. That lays out well for two reasons. One, we won't be shooting at each other, and two, when they get out, they'll both be facing our direction. As soon as they exit, let's show them our guns and tell them to stop where they are. We'll have the drop on them, so if they're smart, they'll give it up. If they do, we'll move in on them, zip-tie their hands and take them down to their torture room. They should be willing to talk once they see all the carnage down there," Brody said.

"For a fast and impromptu analysis of the situation, I think you've got it nailed," Shawn concurred after overhearing Brody's plan.

Nick and Dan agreed. Nick told them there was no doubt that the car was heading for them fast and without any other vehicles in tow. "Get ready, guys, they're just a few minutes from you," he said.

Brody and Dan hid in their sniper blinds and waited for their prey.

When Brody was a kid and played hide and seek with his friends, time moved with the seeker but stood still for the hidden. This was the case now. What seemed like an eternity in limbo was actually just a few minutes. The noisy door opener started to pull up the garage door for Damon's car to enter. Only the dingy light of the opener illuminated the space inside the warehouse. But it would be enough to see their target's every move.

He heard the outside gate sliding closed behind the SUV. The harsh cold and rain rushed in ahead of the metal crypt on four wheels. Brody could only think of the evil men inside as two dead souls. The SUV's engine revved up, pulled into the building and stopped very close to where Brody had predicted. The engine turned off, and both front doors opened simultaneously, and the men stepped out.

***

Dan moved out from his hiding spot and told the passenger to stop. He immediately complied when he saw Dan's gun pointing at him. At the same time, Brody told the driver to stop. Instead, in a flash, the driver/bodyguard reacted automatically to his training. He reached for a gun holstered inside his jacket.

Brody yelled, "Don't do it!"

The man crouched down and swung his gun in Brody's direction. Without hesitation, Brody took the idiot down with a headshot. No body mass shot for Brody. He didn't want to take a chance that the man had a vest on. From what exited the man's skull onto the car, there was no need for a follow-up shot. The guy was dead before he slumped down into a sitting position with his back against the car. He sat there with his eyes open, staring into another realm. Brody wondered if he was getting his life's evaluation from the other side.

He snapped out of the thought when he heard

the passenger yell out, "Don't shoot, don't shoot!

Brody climbed out of the boat and took a giant step over the red river leaking out of the driver's huge body. He headed over to help tie up the passenger and heard Nick's voice in his earpiece. It always sounded like an old drive-in movie speaker.

"Guys, there's still no other vehicles in sight. Your six is clear."

"Thanks, Nick," Brody said.

"You okay?" Dan asked Brody.

"Yeah."

While Dan had the guy covered, Brody zip-tied his hands behind his back and removed his cell phone and wallet. He wasn't carrying a gun.

"You're not gonna be stupid like your driver, are you?" Brody asked.

"Absolutely not. I'll cooperate completely. You're the ones in a whole lot of trouble here, not me."

"Really?" Brody quipped.

"Yeah. I know if you wanted to kill me, I'd be dead right now. That tells me you want information. So, when I tell you what you've got yourselves into, you'll understand what I mean."

"You're right about the information. Let's start with your name. It's Damon, right?"

Brody showed him he was holding some cards of his own.

"Yes, it is, but whatever you think you know won't be anything close to the reality of the situation you're in."

Dan hit the button on the interior wall to close

the rollup door. As it noisily rolled back down, the three of them took the stairs to the basement and to the bloody torture room. Brody shoved Damon down hard into the very same chair that he had recently occupied. Damon's ass made a wet squishing sound as it displaced Horst and Vinny's puddles of blood and goo still coating the seat.

When Damon realized what he sat in, he angrily said, "Really, that was totally unnecessary, you assholes. I told you I'd cooperate, and you didn't have to ruin my suit."

Brody ignored him and secured his arms and legs to the chair. He wanted to make him feel as helpless as possible. If people think there's a chance for escape, they hold back information.

Damon looked around at the three bloody corpses, shook his head, and said, "Quite a mess you've made here." He paused. "Okay, pay attention. I know you guys took $197,000 out of our account using Juan's computer. Let me guess. Somehow you learned Juan was in control of that money. You figured with or without his help, you were gonna take it. Either way, it's backfired on you."

"How so?" asked Brody to keep the asshole talking.

"All you've done is get yourselves in deep shit, and you're sinking deeper by the minute. You might as well know that I won't be able to help you. Here's your best option, and I strongly recommend you take it. Leave me tied up and make a run for it. I left a message for the owner of this warehouse. I told him I was coming here to interrogate his manager and an accomplice who compromised his organization. I told him I'd give him an update by 10 p.m."

"Thirty minutes from now," said Brody.

"Yes, and when I don't contact him, and he can't get a hold of me, he'll send some guys here to look for me. That'll give you a few hours head start before they catch up to you and kill you. Oh, and don't think if you return the money that will save your asses because it won't. That's about the best you got, boys."

This isn't making sense, thought Brody. *Instead of pleading for his life, Damon is acting like he's in control. So I'll just play another card to keep him talking.*

"We know you work for Tony Lentini," he told Damon.

"Lentini?" Damon laughed. "He works for me, and he does a lot more than simple run-of-the-mill scams. Well, since you and whoever else is working with you will be dead soon, it doesn't matter what I tell you. When I say us, I mean the U.S. government, and other governments."

Brody and Dan looked at each other, puzzled.

Damon noticed and said, "That's right. Good old Uncle Sam. I'm part of a secret organization of Washington insiders run by a woman Senator. I think the bitch has bigger balls than most guys. She's so evil, she even scares me. She devised a simple plan that Lentini executes. It stops the payouts of Social Security and Medicare to a specific group of recipients. The money saved rebuilds the slush fund, and at the same time, she gets an immediate dividend from Lentini. Let me give you a little history lesson on how all this got started."

I know people who love to hear themselves talk, thought Brody, *but Damon takes the gold. That spec of white powder under his nose is no doubt fueling him on too. How could anyone trust him to manage anything?*

"When Roosevelt signed the Social Security Act into law, it was the biggest scam ever perpetrated on the American people," stated Damon. "It was so good that all the other industrial countries followed suit shortly after. It was a brilliant plan to steal money from the masses and keep it for themselves. Lawmakers around the world told their people that they would be taxed a few dollars each week, and it would be kept for them in a savings account. Then, when they retired, their government would pay them a portion from that account each month for as long as they live. Sound familiar?"

"Sure does," said Brody.

"That was the very first Ponzi scheme, but better because politicians never intended to pay anyone out of those funds. In 1935 when the Social Security law was passed, they knew people wouldn't live long enough to collect. The bill set benefits to start at age 65, but at the time, the average life expectancy was 61. All that money kept piling up in accounts year after year, and the politicians had complete control over it. They created their own personal slush fund on the backs of hard-working Americans. Worked great for a while until something happened that they didn't expect. People started living longer, and suddenly all those slush funds began to shrink," Damon explained.

Are the people running the world really that depraved, that evil? Brody wondered. He turned back to Damon's dissertation.

"Well, losing any of that money was unacceptable to them," Damon continued. "So the world leaders secretly got together to figure out how to decrease the payouts. Several natural phenomena, like wars, diseases, drugs, alcohol, and even cigarettes, helped stem the losses, but the over-65 demographic continued to grow and collect.

"Then what happened?" Brody asked.

"That's where I came in. The Senator hired me to implement a plan to stop people from collecting their Social Security benefits. Her plan was a temporary stopgap until she and other world leaders could find a better and more permanent way of eliminating people 65 and over. From what I hear, there's an Asian leader in the Far East who found a way of doing just that. But for now, I hire contractors like Lentini to do the Senator's bidding. She gives me a list of people on Social Security who don't have any heirs. I give that list to Lentini, and he runs scams on their wills and trusts and changes the beneficiaries of all their assets to the Lentini

Charity Foundation after they die. Which happens very shortly after all the phony, but legal, documents are in order."

Damon saw Brody and Dan look at each other with *Can you believe this bullshit?* Expressions.

"That's right, guys, it's the truth. But you'll never be able to prove it for two reasons. One, no one would believe you, and two, you're gonna be dead soon."

"So how does this benefit the Senator?" Brody asked.

"The Senator gets a kickback from Lentini, and the S.S. slush fund she controls bleeds a little less. Lentini just turned a fender bender into a robbery-homicide that netted his charity over $7.6 million in assets from a Las Vegas couple."

"What is this permanent solution you talk about?" Dan asked.

"Something that eliminates the need for geriatric hit squads like the Lentinis and makes me find another line of work. Apparently, this man has convinced all the world leaders that what he developed will eliminate people in their targeted age range of 65 and up without suspicion. There will be no retirement payouts for the elderly after that, except for the leaders and other elites that have the antidote. That's all I know about it, except that it won't harm anyone under 65. Have to have all those people contributing to the slush fund, right?" He laughed.

Brody motioned to Dan to go out into the hall.

"Hey guys, can you believe this shit? That's Soylent Green he's talking about."

"Yeah, I definitely see the correlation," Nick said.

Dan being the youngest of the guys, asked, "What's Soylent Green?"

Nick being the oldest, explained. "This movie in the early seventies showed an overpopulated world running out of resources, mainly food. Charles Heston played a cop, and Robinson is his aging father. To keep people from panicking and rioting, world governments banded together to supply free food in the form of green wafers called Soylent Green. It turned out to be made from dead people, in particular older dead people. The leaders of the world passed laws approving voluntary euthanasia and bribed older people to do it to keep the supply of food coming," Nick explained.

"So you're saying you think this new plan is to turn people into food?" Dan asked.

"No, this is clearly about turning old people into money."

"Damon doesn't seem like a conspiracy theorist or a crazy. So, if he's telling the truth, our mission could change from getting Mary's money to possibly saving the world. It's incredible, I know, but he's talking about killing maybe a billion people. We can't unhear that, so we're stuck. This is too serious. I think we have to assume he's being truthful since he truly believes we're dead men anyway. We have to prove to ourselves that he's lying," Brody said.

Nick, Dan, and Shawn all agreed.

"One thing I can do right now is to look into the deaths of that couple in Vegas he talked about. It's a daunting task, but it could prove some of what he said," Nick said.

"Come on, Dan, let's go back in and see what else we can get out of Damon."

As soon as they stepped back into the room, Shawn yelled out to them.

"Hold up, guys."

"What the hell? Nick! You see this?"

"Whoa! Yeah, I can't believe it."

Chapter 14

RUN

"Brody, Dan, you guys get out of there right now. There's a military chopper flying low and headed straight for you. It's coming in from the south, about thirty miles out, and traveling fast. Four rockets designed for Napalm-B. Configuration is unmistakable. Enough Napalm in just two of those rockets to melt an entire city block. Maybe five minutes to get out of range. Haul ass, now!" Shawn shouted.

Damon overheard the conversation and pleaded, "Don't leave me, don't leave me. Cut me loose..."

Without a second to spare, Brody and Dan sprinted to the stairs with Damon's screaming plea ringing in their ears. Outside of the building, Dan led the way to the spot in the fence where he climbed over, and they scaled it. Dan rushed to his car with Brody tight to his six. Dan jumped in the driver's seat, and Brody hopped in the passenger side. They sped into the stormy night with the car lights off.

The next thing they heard was Nick's voice.

"Guys, there's a small bridge with a culvert about two miles north. Drive down to the right, turn left under the bridge, and stop. If that chopper does what we all think it's gonna do, they'll be looking around for any witnesses after they blow up the warehouse."

Dan floored the gas pedal to put as much distance between them and the complex as possible and hoped he could get to the bridge before the chopper spotted them. A few minutes later, the dark night lit into huge yellow and orange fireball from behind, so massive the concussion rocked the car like a California earthquake. Intense heat penetrated the rear window like a blowtorch. Brody knew Napalm-B would turn the cinder block building they just left into dust and literally melt the concrete foundation. Nothing left but a smoldering crater for days.

A second after the blast, Dan was already pulling off the road and down into the culvert. At the bottom, he turned left under the bridge and turned off the engine.

"Shawn, what's the status on the chopper?" Brody asked.

"They fired all four rockets from about three miles out. They're doing a wide circle around the explosion, obviously assessing the damage. Hold on. They've completed a second pass and are heading up the road toward you."

"It's a very small bridge and Dan's SUV barely fits

under it, but it's surrounded by tons of foliage. Hopefully, it covers us from the air. We're lucky it was here," Brody said.

"You should be able to hear them. They're flying over you right now."

"Yep," Brody said as he heard the flat rotor blades slap the air above them, making loud woop-woop sounds above them.

"They're not slowing down. That's a good sign," Shawn said. A minute later, he continued. "They went about a mile further down the road and made a sharp 180 bank heading back your way, flying due south. They must be satisfied no one got away or saw them. Stay put till we're sure. We'll monitor their heading and distance for the next 10 minutes. At their rate of speed, they should be 30 miles from you by then, and you'll be good to head north."

"Agreed. Obviously, someone got tipped off that we took over the warehouse and ordered it vaporized to take us out. But how? How did they get that kind of firepower here so fast?" Brody asked.

"Doesn't make sense. All electronics were shut down in the warehouse, so it had to be from outside, but by who? And when?" Nick asked.

"Couldn't have been Damon. He drove right in and was completely surprised," Dan said.

"So there's only one way they could have known. It's hard to believe, but it had to be someone in the group we helped escape," Brody surmised.

"Yeah, you must be right. Bastard, whoever it was. But still, the timing is amazing. I don't think we were ever that good," Nick said.

Brody chimed in. "Damon wasn't bullshitting us. These guys have some serious clout with contingency plans in place to handle every conceivable situation. Think about it. That chopper had to be in constant stand-by mode, ready to take off and nuke that place at a moment's notice. That could only happen with someone high up in our government pulling the strings and providing the right equipment. God help us if I'm right. All right, guys, here's what we do. Dan and I will head back to the hotel, and I'll clear out of my room. You guys still have eyes on Juan's place, right?"

"Yes, and we'll keep watching till you get there," Shawn assured.

"Perfect. When I leave the hotel, I'll take the van back to the hangar, and Dan will head back to his sister's. I'll bunk down at the base until our chopper is ready to fly back to Diego. We'll all meet up at my place when Dan and I get back, and we'll figure out what to do after that."

"Solid plan. Hey, by the way, the chopper is 30-plus miles away and still heading due south. We'll still be watching, but you're good to go."

"Okay, we're pulling onto the road now," Dan replied.

"How far are we to the hotel, Dan?" Brody asked.

"About 90 minutes."

"Sorry you got so involved. That wasn't the plan."

"I know. No worries. We're doing the right thing by canceling some of the evil in the world. I'm always good with that. Why don't you lay the seat back and get some winks? You've been drugged and beat on. It'll do you good to recharge for a few minutes. I got this, bro."

"Thanks. I'll admit I'm a little tired and probably still shaking off some side effects of the drugs." Brody pulled the lever and laid back down as far as the seat would go, and stretched out. He closed his eyes and listened to the tires hit the expansion joints spaced out evenly on the concrete road. The sound was like a galloping horse. Ka Plop, Ka Plop, Ka Plop. He focused on the rhythm, and his body began to relax. A few seconds later, he drifted off to a peaceful sleep and much-needed rest. Even with everything that happened to him today, he was able to slumber with ease.

It wasn't always that way. He used to lay in bed with his mind racing. He'd analyze his problems, responsibilities, relationships, and decisions from the past, present, and especially short term. He tried to turn it off by tossing and turning but to no avail. Finally, exhaustion would set in, and he'd pass out for a couple of hours and wake up tired. The vicious cycle had no end.

The irony, of course, was that to make good decisions and solve the problems of tomorrow, a person had to rejuvenate with restful sleep the night before.

Eventually, to prosper, and for his health, he had to figure out how to free his mind from all those thoughts and second-guessing when he bedded down each night. One morning after another long and restless night, he went to one of his favorite places in San Diego, the serene rock jetty at the end of Mission Beach. He sat on the rocks and watched the boats go out to the ocean in the morning and return to Mission Bay later in the day.

Sitting in the sun, he listened to the rolling waves splash against the rocks, watched the pelicans fly in formation inches above the water, and the surfers ride their boards. He breathed in the clean, salty sea air and cleared his mind. He decided to attack his sleeping problem philosophically and started by asking himself the hardest question of all. What is the meaning of life?

If he could figure that out, he'd have a roadmap, a plan, for living his days instead of just winging it. Humans have always pondered the reason for their existence. Great minds philosophized over that question for centuries without coming up with one definitive answer.

However, all that brainpower did produce several possibilities derived from ideas based on religion, atheism, reincarnation, evolution, etc. While he was mulling over these choices, Brody looked to his right and saw a fishing boat returning from a half-day excursion. As it slowly passed by, he watched a crewman on the fantail lift a live fish out of a bucket. Its glistening body was squirming to get free, fighting to stay alive. He wondered about that.

Why did that dumb fish have such a will to live? Who instilled that into its DNA? The crewman placed the fish on a wood block, held down its convulsing body, and chopped off the head, ending its life.

Ending its life, ending its life. That was it!

How can anyone figure out the meaning of their life if they don't know the meaning of the end of their life? The death of that fish gave him the answer to the question he'd been searching for consciously and subconsciously his whole life. *The answer to the meaning of life is that we DIE. Of course! If we didn't die, we would simply EXIST! There'd be no need for a meaning.*

So, because he was one day going to die, Brody had to figure out what his death meant to him, and that would be his meaning of life. Everyone else's would be uniquely their own.

The first question he asked was *what do I believe happens when I die?* To know that, he had to determine what he thought about his life and the universe that surrounded him. He knew there were two prominent theories of life. First, the universe was created by a big bang. That explosion forced molecules to randomly stick together by the unexplained existence of gravity. Then over time, those stuck-together molecules somehow changed and evolved into all the different things we see. Evolution.

Second theory. The universe was a thoughtful creation, designed and built by an intelligent being.

Brody never believed in theory one. It came down to simple logic for him. Man and all the other creatures of the world needed food, oxygen, sunlight, and water (all easily available) to survive. Perhaps molecules could have randomly formed to make a human, but since all humans start life as helpless infants and are unable to sustain themselves with food, water, and air. That theory failed in his mind.

Only a highly intelligent and powerful architect of all creation would know that an adult human would have to exist first to take care of a baby. *That's a plan, not an accident. Common sense.*

If the earth was just one mile closer to the sun, or one mile further away, life couldn't exist on Earth. *Intelligent design, not an accident. Common sense.*

He unequivocally believed in an intelligent force behind creation, and his Christian faith taught him who that intelligent force was. God. *Okay, knowing and believing that God has the power and intelligence to create the universe, what can I do if God chose to interfere with my life?*

Not a thing.

So what power then, do I really have over my own life?

The answer was simple. Just two things. One. Learn and educate himself the best he could. Two. With that knowledge, make all his decisions based on logic, reason, and morality.

That's it. Two things. Simple. Nothing else to think about. God trumps everything else. Immediately, he felt relief and a calmness that drained the tension and anxiety from his body. It was like his mind just experienced a relaxing massage. Just one day, with no distractions and timeless contemplation, allowed him to discover a living formula that would change his life forever.

He'd do his best and let God handle the rest. His only regret was that it took him 33 years to figure that out, but he was still thankful that he finally had a resolution. From that day onward, he felt he'd been reborn into a life of contentment, serenity, peace, and fearlessness.

"Brody, wake up, buddy. We're about 15 minutes out. Thought I'd give you time to come back to the living. Man, I don't know how you can do that. You were asleep about a minute after you laid back in your seat," Dan stated.

"It's really easy, Dan. I'll tell you about it on our way back to Diego," Brody promised.

"Thanks, I'd like to know the secret."

Brody's phone rang just as they approached the hotel. He looked at the screen and saw that it was Nick.

"Hey, what's up?"

"A couple of minutes ago, a truck pulled in front of your fire department van and parked. Two thick guys in black suits went into the main entrance of Juan's building. They're probably just following simple orders because they didn't even look at the van. A couple of minutes later, from your hotel room camera, we saw them enter Juan's unit and close all the blinds," reported Nick. "Obviously, someone still wants to know how and why Juan got compromised.

I'm sure they'll clean the place out. Makes sense after everything that's happened. We can't see what they're doing, but we're gonna keep watching."

"We're coming up on the van right now and see the truck in front of it. You should see us any second," Dan said.

"We were tracking you by satellite, but the camera gives us a clearer view," Nick added.

Dan drove slowly past the faux fire marshal's van and Ford truck. Both he and Brody eyeballed the two vehicles as they passed. The van looked to be secure, and the truck was empty.

"We don't see anyone in the truck or the van."

Good news," Nick said.

Brody and Dan looked up and down both sides of the street. It was now 10:15 p.m. With the combination of the storm, although it was easing up, and the late hour, the streets were deserted.

"All clear. Pull around the corner and out of sight and stop," Brody said.

"What you got in mind?" Dan asked

"I get where he's going. He's gonna put one of the trackers I packed for him on that truck, right Brody?" Shawn asked.

"Yep. Yell at me if I don't have time to place it before they come back out."

"Go for it."

Brody pulled a tracker out of his bag and walked back to the truck. He pretended to slip on the wet street and fall next to the front wheel. As he grabbed hold of the truck's bumper to pull himself up, he attached the tracker above the driver's wheel well. He stood up, brushed his pant leg off, and faked a limp back to Dan's car.

"Great job, Brody. No one was looking, as far as we can tell, and the tracker is working. We can track them anywhere."

"Great. We're going to my room to get my stuff packed up. We'll have to wait till those guys leave before we try getting the van," Brody said.

"Roger that. We'll let you know if they come back out," Nick said.

Dan drove into the underground parking and stopped in a guest-designated space. He and Brody took the elevator to Brody's floor. While in the elevator, Dan reminded Brody to get his blood checked at the base just for peace of mind. Brody promised he would. In the hall outside his room, they took up the same positions they did in the basement of the Lentini warehouse complex earlier. Guns in hand, they charged in.

The main room and bedroom were just as Brody left them. They went over to the window and looked down at Juan's condo. The blinds were indeed closed on both windows, but the lights from inside still filtered through. Every few seconds, they saw movement in the form of shadows passing by the windows. They packed all Brody's gear and took it down to Dan's car.

While they were loading up, they heard, "Hold on, Brody and Dan. The same two guys are coming out of the building now. One is carrying a shopping bag. They're walking past the van, again without a glance, and getting in the truck. The lights are on. The exhaust is blowing. They're pulling away from the curb and heading north. We got 'em on our iPad, and the tracking signal is strong. We'll be able to monitor their every move," Shawn reported.

"Perfect. We'll wait 15 minutes just in case they circle back," Brody said.

"Good idea," Shawn replied. He gave them the all-clear 15 minutes later.

Dan drove onto the street and turned left to drive around the block. He approached the van from the rear again and pulled up on the driver's side, then stopped. Still no cars on the street or anyone in sight. Brody slid out of the passenger side and entered the van. He surveilled the inside and gave Dan a thumbs up. Dan acknowledged the all-clear with a single yes bob of his head and a cowboy two-finger salute, then drove off to his sister's place. Brody started the Van and headed to the Coast Guard base.

Brody rolled up to the guard shack 20 minutes later at the main gate. The guard squinted at his creds and gave him a crisp snap to salute every Seal deserved. Brody asked for a billet number and directions to the TDY barracks as well as the infirmary. Professionally getting both, Brody returned the guard's salute and drove straight to the infirmary. He told the on-duty medical corpsman that he suspected the girl he picked up at a bar slipped him a mickey at a motel and tried to rob him.

All he remembered was passing out, and when he woke up she was gone. The corpsman said he heard that one before, and took samples.

Sure enough, after a couple of tests, the corpsman said there was a trace of Liquid Ecstasy in Brody's blood. He said it would be completely out of his system in another hour or two. Brody thanked him then drove away to bunk down for the night, with peace of mind. A parking space was open right in front of the billet number and he was happy to see it was a single accommodation. He definitely needed some alone time.

With bags in hand, he entered a super clean king-sized bed unit that mirrored a Marriott property. Small kitchenette, TV, eating table, and a sterile bathroom with smells of antibacterial cleaning agents lingering in the air. He smiled when he saw that the shower tub combo had one of those curtain rods that curved out away from the tub. It would give his big body more room to move. *Gotta hand it to the military for paying attention to detail and being so squared away.*

He stripped and stepped in the shower. Looking down, he spotted a white something stuck in the skin of his chest. He pulled it out and examined it more closely. *A piece of one of Horst's shattered teeth.* He flicked it into the toilet, thinking it was an appropriate burial plot for Horst. Except an eternity in a dark smelly sewer was too good for the bastard.

He turned the shower valve and let hot spray massage his muscles, nerves, and tendons. The massaging effect loosened the tightness in his body. He soaped up, then rinsed with cold water. He knew that heat, although relaxing, tended to increase inflammation. Cold water reverses the effect. He dried off and got into bed between clean crisp sheets and was sound asleep in seconds.

***

The next morning, Brody chowed down at the base mess hall and returned to his unit. He wanted to check in with the guys, but not until he called Jane. She answered on the first ring.

"Brody!"

"Hi, Jane. It's wonderful to hear your voice."

"Yours is making me warm, trending to hot, if you know what I mean."

"Funny, listening to your voice is heating me up too. I guess we've been away from each other too long." They both laughed. "How are you and Mary?"

"We're just fine. She's at church right now. She's been going to morning Mass every day to pray for you and your team and for a safe return. I've been going with her, but today I had to stay for a conference call for work. I really wanted to go since we saw on the news last night about a huge explosion in Seattle. Silly, I know."

"Thanks for thinking of me," said Brody softly.

"Well, just because you're in Seattle doesn't mean that had anything to do with you. But it still made us worry, thinking that maybe you were accidentally nearby. The video clip from a news helicopter showed a huge crater with fire boiling up hundreds of feet. It looked like an entire city block was devastated."

"Sounds awful."

"Truly awful. Thankfully it was an old abandoned building in an industrial area that closed many years ago. A police captain on the scene told a reporter that there was absolutely no evidence of anyone in the building or anywhere near the explosion. A spokesman from the fire department said the cause was a deteriorated gas line that completely filled the warehouse and got ignited by a lightning strike."

"Haven't really had a chance to listen to the news this morning. Thanks for filling me in. Glad nobody got hurt."

Someone at the Seattle police department is orchestrating a cover-up of the missile strike on the warehouse, thought Brody. *Corroborating evidence that Damon was telling the truth and why he felt he was in charge even though he was tied up. Obviously, the Lentini scamming operation is just a small single tributary flowing into a larger cesspool of evil. For what purpose? To take control of the world? Many have tried only to fail and leave a legacy of death and devastation behind. Is this really another one of those ominous endeavors? I have to find out before we end up in World War Three. The good news is that the players who destroyed the warehouse think they killed off all their loose ends. They won't see me coming.*

"So how are you, Brody, and how's it going? Any progress?"

"I'm good, and I'm very happy to tell you that we got Mary's money back. It should be in her new account sometime today."

"Oh, my God, really?"

"Really."

"She'll be so happy. She's really been down and regretting that she got you and your friends involved in her problem. She's been so worried about the whole situation. You're a miracle worker, Brody."

"Well, I had a whole lot of help. Couldn't have done it without my guys."

"You're lucky to have such good friends. When will you be back?"

"I'm waiting for the mechanical service on my ride. I'll check the status today and let you know. You'll still be at Mary's for a while, right?"

"Yes, I'll be here for five more days."

"Good. I should be back before you leave. By the way, Jane, I have some more good news just for you."

"Really? What is it?"

"Well, when we planned this mission, our only goal was to get Mary's money back without any repercussions to her or us. We all agreed to do it pro bono. However, the guy was a criminal, and he decided to pay us so he could stay out of jail. We used some of that money to shut down his operation and deport him to the south."

That's partially true. Juan went as far south as you can go. Hell. I hate lying to Jane, but it's only temporary. Someday I'll tell her the whole truth, but for now, it's best she didn't know all the gory details.

"Long story shorter, we had quite a bit of money left over. Enough for everyone to get the same share as Mary. $25,000, and that includes you."

"Seriously? That's amazing and I appreciate the gesture Brody, but I didn't do a thing. That thief didn't steal any money from me. You and your team did all the work, and should keep it."

In a gentle yet stern voice, Brody said, "I talked with the team, and we all agreed that you get an equal share. When Mary called you about being scammed, you became part of it. I know you were hurting emotionally for your aunt and probably suffered as much anguish over the assault as she did. And you showed up when she needed you. You deserve to be compensated. End of discussion."

Silence on Jane's end.

With a much softer tone, Brody said, "These scammers need to learn that they're not just hurting the person they take the money from, but the family and friends of that person too. Once they realize they have to pay all the people connected to their scams, maybe they'll find a legitimate job."

"I get what you're saying, but it doesn't feel right to get a windfall from my aunt's misfortune."

"I knew you'd feel that way, and I'm happy my instincts about you are right, but I want you to look at it like this. By taking their assets away, it'll make it harder for them to continue scamming other people, number one. Number two, I know you'll do something good with the money."

"Well, all right. I accept your explanation and will graciously accept, and I'll do something good with it. Thank you, Brody, and your team."

"You're welcome, and I'll let my team know. Nick will need some information from you to direct deposit the money into your account. He'll call you and walk you through it. By the way, I'd like to thank you and Mary for your prayers. I believe in its power as well. I have an uncanny feeling that the more we unveil ourselves to each other, the more we'll discover we have a whole lot in common."

"Well, we'll just have to put your theory to the test. Of course, that'll take some significant time for the two of us to spend together," Jane said.

"Ah yes, the test of time, and I'm committing to that time right now. On that note, I'm gonna make some calls and find out how soon I can get back to San Diego and you."

"Hurry home!"

"I will. Bye, Jane."

"Ah, Brody."

"Yes?"

"I have a request. I hope you won't laugh or think it's silly."

"That won't happen. Fire away."

"Instead of saying goodbye, we could sign off with, 'See you soon.' It's just that I've never liked goodbyes. So final, so ending."

"Well, there you go. I hate goodbyes too. Let me be the first to solidify our unique bond. See you soon, Jane. That's my sign-off," Brody said, smiling.

"See you soon, Brody." Jane hung up, smiling.

Emotionally fired up, Brody called Dan to see if he'd heard anything from the maintenance crew working on the chopper. He hit send on his phone and waited. Nothing. He looked at the screen and verified that, indeed, he was calling Dan. He put the phone back up to his ear. Nothing. He tried to figure out what was going on when he heard "Hello?"

"Dan, is that you?"

"Yeah, I was just trying to call you."

"Well, talk about being synchronized. We must have hit send at exactly the same time," Brody said.

"Weird. I was calling to let you know the chopper is ready. We can saddle up and get out of here tomorrow at 9 a.m. if you're up to it."

"Music to my ears."

"Good. After what we've been through, it'll be a relief to be home. Hook up with me at the chopper at 7:30, and we'll get everything squared away."

"You got it, brother. See you there."

Brody hung up and immediately sent a text to Jane with a head's up for tomorrow night and included a smiley emoji with hearts for eyes. Then he texted Nick and Shawn with the same message and the same emoji, knowing they were all secure in their manhood and would get the humor. He included a meeting time of 9 a.m. at his place the day after tomorrow. Exhausted and elated, he switched off the light and was dreaming in minutes.

The next morning, once they were cruising home at 8,000 feet, Brody fulfilled his promise to Dan and told him why it was so easy for him to fall asleep after all of the chaos at Juan and Lentinis' warehouse. He explained how his belief in God and God's power allowed him to delegate things out of his control to him. It was simple as that, and it worked.

Dan listened intently, and when Brody finished, he looked at him over the top of his aviators and said with a grin, "So Brody, you had this secret all these years and waited till now to share it with me? I've agonized over a million things, and now you're telling me I didn't have to? What a pal."

"Geez, Dan, just because I believe in something doesn't mean you would, right?"

"Yeah, I see your point. Have to admit that what you've said makes real sense. I believe in God also, but lived my life relying solely on myself. Like he couldn't change my plans if he wanted to. Thank you for your wisdom and insights. You've made me see my limitations. I'll do my best each today, plan for the tomorrows, and sleep soundly every night, knowing that's all I can do."

"That's my formula. I can assure you it works for me. I truly believe that it'll work for you too, Dan. The daily challenges we face are overwhelming. The formula has helped me make decisions without second-guessing. I leave all that up to the ultimate wingman, God. I'm glad you're on board. Sorry I didn't share this with you before, bro."

"No problem. Never too late to find a way to make life easier. I'm feeling less stressed already, even with a ton of mechanical updates to do. Probably take me a few hours, so you're on your own for a while."

"Works for me. I'll start a report on the mission before I forget any details and will finish it at home."

Brody held on to a pencil and pad and stared out the window to his right. He looked down and watched the world go by far below. Being high above what happened on the ground in Seattle helped him see those events with a detached perspective. It made it easier for him to just write about the facts and put everything into proper military context.

Yes, there were negatives, the biggest being he would have been tortured and probably killed if Dan hadn't been there to back him up. He made the fatal mistake of underestimating his enemy. Retirement had dulled him in ways he was not yet aware. He did think about the positives. They got Mary's money back, and the bad guys think they're dead. Case closed. He and Dan also freed a large group of human slaves who were being used and abused by the bad guys.

At the same time he was wrapping up his review of the mission, there was a knock on an office door in Las Vegas, Nevada.

Chapter 15

LORENZO

Tony Lentini told the door knocker to come in. The door opened, and a man with ridiculously large, steroid-produced muscles scraped both sides of the 48-inch wide opening as he squeezed through the door. His quadruple X short sleeve polo shirt stretched over his body mass and was a prime candidate to split apart from just the weakest of coughs. His jeans were so tight around his abnormally thick thighs that bullets would probably bounce off the tempered and hardened flesh.

Daylight filtered through the window behind Tony and cast shadows on the deep scars that lined the monster's face. Meandering rivers traveled to even deeper scars on one side of his neck. The other side was inked with a large cursive capital L tattoo. The man sat down in a chair across from Tony.

"Give me everything you have, and be quick, Lorenzo. I have a private Zoom call with a pissed-off client in 30 minutes."

"Sure, boss. We cleaned out Juan's unit. Found some pretty large bundles of cash, drugs, two handguns, a personal cell phone, and an iPad under his mattress of all places, the moron. Unfortunately, Horst and Vinny had Juan's company cell phone at the warehouse when it was destroyed, so we're working to get records of his calls from the provider.

"What about Juan's personal phone?"

"The idiot didn't have it pass protected. We found numbers for a couple of hookers and some online gambling sites. Other than that, no connection to the mystery guy who ripped us off. We took the company's computer and the iPad to one of our techie guys, and had him check them out. He said the company's computer was deliberately scrubbed, and there wasn't a thing he could retrieve."

"What about the iPad?"

"He found some real interesting stuff. Somehow, Juan transferred our encryption codes from the company computer to his iPad, and he was using that protection along with our list of scam protocols to moonlight for himself. Raked in some serious coin over the past couple of years. About six months ago, he stopped completely. We don't know why unless he was worried he was pushing it. He was a moron, but he knew what would happen to him if we caught him."

"According to Carlos, Juan found out the hard way. By the way, I'm getting Carlos set up at the furniture plant. He'll be up and running it tomorrow.

Okay, back to Juan."

"Yes sir. For whatever reason, he started moonlighting again and recently pulled off a decent one. He scammed $25,700 from the account of one Mary Charbenau. Transferred the money into a personal off-shore account under an alias. Transferred that to the Banco Santander De Mexico in an account under his real name, Juan Aguilar. I guess he picked up some pointers on how to do all this from us."

"Figlio di puttana. The son of a bitch is lucky he's dead. Keep going," Tony said.

"We checked out Mary Charbenau. All we know right now is that she's an old lady who lives alone in San Diego. Husband passed away several years ago, and she's making it on social security and some small pensions. We passed her name onto some of our government resources for more detailed information, and told them to rush it. That's all we got, boss."

"Good work. You know I don't believe in coincidences, so my gut tells me she's the key to what happened at Juan's and the warehouse. I need more answers and fast. Lorenzo, get Aldo and take him with you on the company plane to San Diego and find out everything you can from this Mary Charbenau. If she hesitates at all, let Aldo go to work on her, but make sure he doesn't kill the old lady before she talks. Got it?"

"Got it. On my way, boss."

Lorenzo walked out of the office just as the Zoom

call pinged on Tony's computer.

***

Brody and Dan were just starting to fly over the northern part of Los Angeles. It wouldn't be long now before they landed at Marine Corps Air Station Miramar. Brody bubbled with excitement, thinking about seeing Jane again. He couldn't believe how quickly his psyche had been captured by her persona, but he figured if it was right, then time didn't really matter.

Physically, his male hormones were also raging with the thought of holding her in his arms. So much so that he thought he was going to explode if that didn't happen very soon.

"You okay, Brody?" Dan asked.

"Yeah, why?"

"You've been in a trance, staring straight ahead for the last half hour. You haven't moved an inch, not even to adjust your balls, which I've had to do at least every ten minutes. So something is occupying your mind completely. It's Jane, right?

"You know me well, Dan. I can't stop thinking about her. I miss her so much."

"Hang in there, buddy. Won't be long now. When we land, I'll do all the post-flight checks and check-in paperwork so you can load up your stuff and get on over to see her."

"That wouldn't be right. I'll help with all that."

"No thanks. You're useless in the state you're in. I'd end up having to do everything twice. Honestly, after what you've been through, just be with her as soon as you can."

"Like I said, you know me well. Thanks, Dan, I owe you another one. You better start collecting soon before I forget I owe you at all," Brody said with a laugh.

"Don't worry, I won't let you forget." Dan lightly punched Brody in the arm.

Brody had most of his report on the mission done during the flight. The pure volume of recalling everything taxed his brain. He was tired and ready to relax. Besides, there'd be more to do than finish the report when he got home. He wanted to re-energize himself before he saw Jane. With that in mind, he put the report away, laid back, closed his eyes, and wasn't surprised that the only thing he saw in his mind was Jane's smiling face.

***

Tony hated Zoom calls. He was old school and preferred to talk in person. He'd been left out of the loop with his agreement with the Bitch Senator. Only Damon knew who she was, and now that he was dead, maybe she'd reveal herself. His monitor clicked off all the verbiage, and he could see the Senator.

She sat at a table hiding her identity behind that same ridiculous Halloween mask she always wore. To her left was a strange scene. A man sat next to her, his small legs visible below the tabletop. His hands laid palms up. The insides of his arms had horrible red scars in the shape of dragons. The rest of his upper half was hidden behind a mirror that faced Tony.

That must have hurt like hell. Why didn't he just get tattoos? Tony mused.

Tony was sure it was a two-way mirror so the man could see him, but he couldn't see the man. Through a mechanically generated voice, the senator took control and started the conversation.

"Tony, under the circumstances, this won't be one of our typical update and review meetings. Serious issues concerning that fiasco in Seattle must be addressed and resolved immediately."

There she goes, leading with the polite bullshit. Fuckin typical politician.

"As you can see, I have a special guest with me. I'll tell you that he's not only my employer but in reality, yours too. You and I will refer to him by his alias, Mr. Kain. Mr. Kain is concerned that our anonymity may be in jeopardy due to our connection with your organization and this catastrophic event. He'll be observing you behind this glass shield. I'm warning you that he is very discerning when it comes to liars, Tony. So be forthright, candid, and truthful."

"I intend to, Senator, as I always have."

"Good. Now that all the parties are present and the hierarchy set, let's get to it. We need to know why and how your team and facility were compromised. But first, I want you to know that I had to jump through a lot of hoops to get that air strike in the short window you gave me."

"Yes, I know, Senator. It couldn't be helped.

When my man on the ground told me the warehouse had been taken over, I knew it had to be destroyed quickly to prevent those responsible from leaving. I would have taken care of it myself, but unfortunately, at that time, I didn't have the means to do it. If you recall, Senator, you told me if I ever needed to abort the warehouse, you had the resources to wipe it out at a moment's notice, and you weren't kidding. The strike was quick and devastating. Not only that, you provided an immediate official media cover-up to boot. Beyond impressive."

I'm such a kiss ass, thought Tony.

As Lentini and the Senator were talking, Kain was thinking about the real reason for the attack on the warehouse.

Although my puppet Senator took credit for it, in reality, the Senator already knew that a strike on the warehouse had been planned by me weeks before the actual attack. I had everyone connected to the Senator watched to protect my secret plans to take over the world. My agents uncovered a leak of classified information that was coming out of the Senator's office through a woman named Jill who was sleeping with the Senator's personal assistant Max. Jill was hired by Damon in order to glean information he could use as leverage against the Senator should he need to. Damon knew how cutthroat politicians were.

Max was clueless about Jill's connection to Damon, and mostly through pillow talk, he was telling her everything he overheard in meetings and phone conversations with the Senator. The more information she got from Max and passed on to Damon, the more money she made. She passed on enough pieces of information to Damon that even he might be able to figure out the scam on the masses that the world leaders were planning—with my help.

The most damaging piece of information Jill told Damon was that according to Max, there would be big changes to the arrangements Damon had with the Lentinis. When Damon heard that, he actually told Tony Lentini that some of his services might not be needed going forward. Stupid. Lentini would certainly want to know why.

That was the last straw. I couldn't afford to have anyone asking questions that might jeopardize my plans. I decided then to take out Damon and the whole Lentini warehouse operation in Seattle the next time Damon made a visit to the warehouse. I would've killed the Senator, too, if I didn't need her. Unfortunately it was too late in the game to replace her.

I had my agents install a tracking device on Damon's vehicle to alert my phone whenever it was moving. So when the Bitch Senator called to tell me Damon was on the move, I was already watching Damon's SUV as it sped toward the warehouse.

When I saw that Damon arrived at the warehouse, I ordered the helicopter to take off and get within striking range, then wait for my order to fire. About 45 minutes later, the chopper pilot notified me that he was holding position a few miles from the warehouse. I could see on my phone that Damon's car was still stationary inside the warehouse and was convinced that anyone else in there would be trapped inside with him. I then ordered the chopper to move in and fire all its rockets.

After the massive eruption, the chopper flew over the devastation to check for survivors or anyone that might have escaped. After a thorough search, the chopper confirmed to me that no one survived. I ordered the chopper back to base and told the Senator to handle the authorities and the media.

As for Max and Jill, I told the Senator that I'd take care of them at the same time I was going to take out Damon so Jill couldn't warn him. So, as warehouse was being blown-up, my top commander, Zimo, was taking them out too. The police would find both Jill and Max dead in Max's bed. The official cause would be a double drug overdose.

Kain tuned back in to listen to the conversation between the two idiots, Tony and the Senator.

"You know, Tony, those resources were meant to be used as a last resort, a failsafe to keep our operations secret. The fact that you allowed someone to penetrate that secrecy and I had to expend those resources, at great expense and exposure to me by the way, is most egregious and unconscionable. I'll never allow that to happen again. Understand?"

"Yes, ma'am," Tony responded contritely. *But inside his head were a series of expletives he wished she could hear.*

"Fortunately, we were able to cover up the real reason for the destruction of the warehouse by having the local authorities who you know are on our payroll, verify that it was due to a lightning strike on a gas line. Because of me, and only because of me, that incident is now officially closed.

Why, you egotistical, narcissistic, bitch.

However, loose ends have to be accounted for and eliminated. To that end, tell us what you've found out about this breach, Tony, and what you're doing about it."

"Absolutely, Senator. I have all the information right here."

***

When Brody stepped off the chopper onto the tarmac, he breathed in that cool, humid, and salty air with aroma unique to San Diego. He knew he was home. Before going their separate ways, he and Dan confirmed their plan to meet up the next day with Nick and Shawn at Brody's—9 a.m. sharp.

Brody got home at 4:30 that afternoon, excited to see both Mary and Jane's cars in front of Mary's house. He parked right behind Jane's rental on the street. He unloaded his bags and went inside, placed some things in the closet, and left the rest next to the bed. He'd put them away later. At that moment, he had a bigger priority. He sat in his chair and called Jane.

"Hey you," she said.

"Hey, I just got in. I'm wondering if I could take you and Mary out to dinner to celebrate. I know a great Italian restaurant near downtown in little Italy. What do you say?"

"Are you sure you're up to it?"

"Yes, 100 percent!"

"Okay, I'd love to, and I'll check with Mary. But first I have to tell you something that I'm very sad about. I have to go back home tomorrow afternoon for work. They called me late yesterday in a panic and need me to put out a couple of major fires. Mary overheard me trying to get out of it and signaled to put them on hold. She said that this whole ordeal really took a toll on her, and if I didn't mind, she would love very much to go with me to Vegas. Clear her head. Have a change of scenery. I couldn't turn her down, so I told my boss I'd be there Monday. Mary will be staying with me till she's back to her old self."

"Whoa, I didn't want to hear that, but I understand."

Jane could hear the disappointment in Brody's voice, and it hurt her heart. "I can honestly say this is the biggest sacrifice I've ever made in my life, and I know you're feeling the weight of it too."

"You're right about that. I was really looking forward to spending some carefree timelessness with you."

"That does sound so wonderful. Is there any way you could come and stay with us in Vegas?"

"Well, I have invoices, payments, and a detailed report to do. Even though this wasn't an official military operation, there are military materials and resources that I have to account for. Also, I'll be submitting some reports anonymously to military intelligence. Scamming and hacking affects the military too. It's gonna take me a few days, but then I'll be free."

"Then it's settled. As soon as you're done, you'll come be with me. I'll have everything ready. Oh, Brody, I can't wait!"

"Me too. These new plans make me even more anxious to be with you tonight, Jane."

"Oh yeah, I almost forgot. I'll go outside and ask Mary. She's pruning her rose bushes in the backyard. Hold on."

Brody could hear Jane call out "Mary, Brody's back and wants to treat us to an Italian dinner to celebrate. Let me give you the phone."

"Hi, Brody, welcome home. I'm so happy you're back. But I should be the one taking you out. You got all my money back. I don't know how to thank you and the guys."

"You do owe us a pie, remember. But please, Mary, let me do this. I really want to, and there's nothing like dinner down by San Diego Bay to make me feel at home."

"Okay, I love Italian, as you know. Sounds like fun."

"Wonderful. I know the owner of Filippi's, and even though it's Saturday, their busiest night, he'll get us in. What time would you gals like to go?"

"Just a sec...okay, Jane says she can be ready to go by 7 p.m."

"Perfect, I'll make the reservation for 7:45 and pick you ladies up at 7. See you then."

As Brody headed to the bathroom to shower, his thoughts turned uncharacteristically to what he'd wear. After all, this *was* a special occasion, and he didn't want to simply put on his usual jeans and sport shirt. A few minutes later, looking sharp in his black dress pants and a long-sleeve button-down powder blue shirt, he felt his excitement building with each passing minute.

***

Tony continued. "Senator and Mr. Kain, initially, we thought this was a simple robbery. As you know, our software and hardware blocker didn't prevent the money from being transferred out of our account like it was designed to. We are working to correct that as we speak. The transfer was made on our Seattle manager's computer inside his condo by who we believe is an unknown accomplice."

"Did you get a name," asked the Senator.

"Yes, Juan Martin. He perished in the explosion. Even though our equipment didn't stop the transfer, it did gas the two and render them unconscious. Two of my guys got there within minutes and took them to the warehouse. My men were interrogating them when someone on the outside killed my guys and set the two thieves free. Unfortunately, all my electronic surveillance equipment was compromised at the time—"

"So there's no video?" Kain asked.

"No, I'm sorry to say. All this and what happened next was reported to me by one of my workers. Juan's accomplice and the man who was the outside help were the only ones to come out of the interrogation room alive. They gathered up all my whores and scammers and let them leave in two of my SUVS. My worker, pulled off the road just a short distance from the warehouse and called to tell me what happened. That's when I called you, Senator. The fact…"

The Senator held up a hand to stop Tony and leaned toward Kain.

"Tony, Mr. Kain wants to know where the escapees are now."

"I told them to get here to Vegas as fast as they could. I'm setting them up here to continue their work. They know I still own them, and they're scared to death of me. Don't worry, they'll do whatever I say," Tony assured.

Kain thought to himself, *this is good, they'll all be in just two places. Tony Lentini along with all his illegal workers in Vegas, and the rest of the Lentini family in Malta. Nice of him to make it convenient for me to eliminate them so efficiently. I'll set that in motion as soon as this meeting is over. Knowing Damon hinted to Tony that some of his services might not be need anymore, I'll have to put Tony's mind at ease and reassure him. I don't want Tony to get suspicious about what's coming his way.*

"Tony, Kain says that he's very pleased you are rebuilding your Seattle operation there in Vegas," said the Senator. "He doesn't want any disruption in the revenue streams. He said he should have had you in charge out there instead of Damon. He was thinking about making some changes, but sees now that won't be necessary. What else have you found out about the break-in?"

"Sure, Senator. Thank you, Mr. Kain. I really appreciate your confidence in me. Well, as soon as I got off the phone with the employee that tipped me off, I went to work to find out who the guy was that got to Juan and whoever came to help him. I spread the word around that anyone with information about the theft should contact me immediately. The response was fast. Within hours, I learned that the two strangers weren't from any rival and absolutely no one had any information at all about who they were. I knew nobody would be stupid enough to lie to me, so I had to move on and dig deeper on my own."

They can't see it on my face, but I'm smiling. What I'm gonna tell them next will definitely impress the crap out of them. I'm gonna be moving up, up, up, thought Tony.

"The fact that those guys were organized and used sophisticated means to pull this off, told me that they weren't simple robbers. I sent two of my best guys to Juan's place to turn it inside out. I believed there had to be some clues there as to how all this transpired, and I was right. They found a large stash of cash, drugs, a personal cell phone, and an iPad, all of which Juan attempted to hide."

"Huge red flag," observed the Senator.

"Yes, I believe the information I extracted from his iPad explains how and why we were attacked. Juan, my supposedly loyal worker, downloaded hundreds of our encrypted phone numbers to his iPad, then deleted them from our list so he wouldn't be detected using them. For a long time, he secretly used those numbers in conjunction with our guarded scam techniques for his own profit. For some reason, about six months ago, he stopped his personal scamming.

"Perhaps he was worried you'd find out," commented the Senator.

"Yes, we've made it clear to everyone what would happen if they crossed us. Or maybe he just took a break, who knows? Whatever. What he did do, however, is recently start up again. He used one of our best scams and cleaned out a bank account from an elderly woman we believe was behind the infiltration of our organization. Somehow, she was able to discover that Juan was the one who scammed her and then tracked him to Seattle."

"How?"

"I promise you, we'll find out how she did that. She obviously wanted to get her money back and leave Juan with a little pain to remember her by. He did have a severely broken finger when we got to him at his condo."

"Wait a minute," the Senator broke in. "You're

telling us that some old lady managed to circumvent our elaborate security systems, then nullified them with superior tracking technology and advanced electronic forensics? She couldn't possibly have the capabilities to do that, no way. Who is this woman?"

"Her name is Mary Charbenau, 75. She lives in San Diego. And you're absolutely right. This intrusion into our operation was too sophisticated for this woman, or anyone for that matter, to accomplish on their own. How this started appears to be a simple case of bad luck. We think Juan unfortunately scammed the wrong person at the wrong time."

"Give us the facts."

"Certainly. She was the first and last person he scammed for himself after a lengthy layoff. Then shortly after that, a very skilled stranger shows up at Juan's place to steal money from him. Just those two facts alone make it hard to believe that that was a coincidence."

Shit, another hand up in my face and more whispering between the two clowns. I'll never get done at this rate.

"Oddly, Tony, we are both in agreement and believe that you may be on the right track with this woman. Continue," said the Senator.

"Yeah, sure. Like I was saying, we think she knew of or randomly hired an ex-military guy with special ops training. If you look at the whole picture, it's the only thing that makes sense. The good news is, by your quick response and total devastation of the area, her guy and his compadre got fried along with Damon. I have people tracking down the money that got transferred out of our account. So far, we know it went to an offshore business in the Caymans, and we are working to pick up the scent from there."

"You're sure it will lead back to her?"

"Yes. So for now, we're working on confirming our theory and cleaning up what should be the last loose end. I have people at this very minute in route to pick up Charbenau and bring her to me. I guarantee I'll be able to answer all your questions and wrap this up completely in a couple of days."

The inscrutable Kain had thoughts of his own which he quietly shared with the Senator.

"Hold on a minute, Tony." The senator leaned toward Kain, half of her head disappearing behind the mirror.

"I actually agree with Tony that this was a credible lead," said Kain. "I'll give Mary Charbenau's information to my lead field man, Zimo, and send him to San Diego. If he can grab her ahead of Tony's guys, I'll use her for bait to get to Lentini. I could care less that she infiltrated Tony's scamming operation and robbed him. I want to know how she did it, and what else she might know about Tony's connection to you, me, or my upcoming plans. It's time to start cleaning house, starting with the Lentinis."

Tony could hear some whispering but couldn't make out the words. He could see the Senator nod her head before she turned back to face Tony.

"Okay, Tony. Mr. Kain has agreed to your

timeline of two days, but <u>only</u> two days. It's critical to clear this up so we can move forward. Things are scheduled, and he won't allow this to delay his plans, understand?"

"Yes, ma'am."

"Besides, this has to be the simplest task you've ever had. Two days seems more than enough time to get hold of the old lady and make her talk. We'll expect a full report on how she was able to pull this off and everything else she knows. By the way, if she turns out to be a dead end and not the one who did this, make sure she becomes a permanent dead end."

"Understood, Senator."

"And, of course, if that turns out to be the case, you'll have to pursue the real culprit, or culprits. Kain said he'll give you all the assistance you'll need to find them and resolve this issue."

"Yes, ma'am. Understood. Considerate it done. I'm confident that you and Mr. Kain will be completely satisfied with how I handle this issue. You can trust me."

Some more whispering came from behind the mirror.

"Tony, Mr. Kain wants you to know that the trust you seek from us will be graciously given via one thing and one thing only."

"What's that, Senator?" Tony asked.

"Results." Instantly his computer screen went blank.

Angry didn't begin to cover how Tony felt.

Mamma cazzo bastards! They don't know me. If they did, they would never talk to me like that. He thought about sending them some of his private videos made at the Seattle warehouse. That would show them what he was capable of and what happens to people who cross him. He'd think about it some more, later. But for now, he had to get hold of that Charbenau woman, and fast.

Chapter 16

CELEBRATION

At 6:55 p.m., Brody walked over to Mary's and hesitated at the door. He knew women didn't like it when a man showed up too early, and he wanted to start the evening off right. To his surprise, the door opened as soon as his feet stopped at the door. Jane rushed right out and smothered him with an urgent, passionate kiss. She pulled back just as both of them were getting their "hot" on.

She looked up at him and said, "Welcome home, sailor."

"Wow. If I knew I was gonna get this kind of greeting, I would have come back sooner. By the way, you look absolutely beautiful in that dress. Red is my favorite color, and I love the way it clings to your curves."

Just then Mary stepped out from behind Jane and closed the door. She wasted no time stepping up to Brody and giving him a big hug and a kiss on the cheek. Brody could tell Mary had chosen a very special outfit for the evening too. She looked elegant in a fitted purple dress with pumps to match.

He offered them each an arm and escorted them over to his Ford Raptor, declaring he would be the envy of all the men at Filippi's. He opened the passenger door and he stood there feeling awkward. He didn't know which one to offer the front seat. Jane saved the situation by insisting that Mary sit in the front with Brody and she'd take the back seat. As Brody started to drive, Mary told Brody how much she liked his truck. Brody explained he wanted to support American manufacturing and ingenuity by buying a Ford.

"These days, my Raptor was probably made in Mexico instead of Detroit," he said. "But it still has a Ford emblem on the front and back, and the whole world knows that's an American story."

Mary and Jane both agreed with his loyalties to try and buy American.

Dinner, wine, and joyful conversation were just what Brody needed, and he got his fill. Mary was thrilled to have her money back, and that was all he needed to confirm that he and the guys were justified in doing what they did. Brody told them a scaled-down version of the trip and that his team considered the incident closed. However, he added, the guys decided to monitor other scamming operations and robocalls to see if they could assist the authorities in shutting them down.

On the way home, Brody was thinking this was

one of the best nights of his life. Yet, he couldn't have guessed what was still to come.

When they got out of the car, Mary decided to give Jane and Brody some time together.

"What a wonderful evening, Brody. Thank you so much. I'm a little tired and think I'll get to bed, but that's no reason you two kids can't continue the evening. The night is still young, after all."

"Sounds good to me Mary. Jane, would you like to come over to my house for a while?"

"I'd love to."

"Jane, do you have your key with you?"

"Yes, I do, Auntie."

"Good, then you just come home when you want to. I'm a sound sleeper, so don't worry about waking me. Good night, you two."

They say good night to Mary, and Brody and Jane walked to his house holding hands.

Jane sat on the loveseat in the living room, while Brody went into the kitchen to get them both a glass of wine. He handed her a glass, then he sat in his chair facing her. He wanted to see her face as they talked seriously about things for the first time. Over the next two hours, they took turns telling each other about themselves. Their upbringings, beliefs, philosophies, hopes, dreams, and some of the significant events that formed who they were here in the present.

When Jane finished her final turn, she said, "That was a ton of past years to catch up on, huh?"

"Yes, but there's still a lot more sand in the

bottom of my hourglass, and a lot less in the top."

"What's that supposed to mean?"

"What I mean is, I'm much older than you, and maybe you should consider that."

"Wow, Brody, that's deep, but you're not that much older than me. No matter how many grains you have left trickling down to the bottom, I can say right now that I want to share every single one of them with you."

"So, I guess you're also saying you want to share your grains with me too?" Brody said with a wink.

"Yes, I am."

"You don't know how happy I am to hear that, Jane. Wanna hear another deep thought?"

"I'm intrigued to the edge of my seat. I didn't expect you to be such an enigma."

"One grain of sand equaling one year of life isn't how I see life lived. In increments of years, I mean. I know couples mark their lives by how many years they've lived together, and people mark how long they have lived by birthdays. I disagree. I believe that life is lived in 16-hour segments, not years. Think about it. On average, people sleep eight hours. Sleep can arguably be described as a state of suspended animation that closely mimics death."

"What?" Jane said, shocked.

"I'll explain. If you analyze what sleep is, it's a state in which people are unaware that they are alive. A deep dark state of timeless unconsciousness. What's the first thing people say when they wake up and learn they've been in a coma? How long have I been out, right? That's because they were unaware of time or living. They wouldn't be surprised if you told them it was days, months, or even years. They were literally dead to the world in that period of time."

"And?" nudged Jane.

"Sleep is no different. When a person wakes up, they really don't know how long they've been out until they check the clock. So when I wake up, I'm aware of living until I go to sleep again. Usually, a span of sixteen hours. When I think of it that way, it helps me see how precious that segment of time is and not take it for granted. Because one day, we'll all have our last 16 hours of life.

"Oh, my God, Brody, you've given me way too much to think about."

Brody laughed. "Your right. I've gone on quite enough for tonight." He noticed their glasses were empty and asked Jane if she'd like another.

"No, thank you, but I can't leave without telling you how much I missed you."

***

While Tony was having his meltdown after the zoom call with the Senator and Kain they continued the meeting without him.

"Senator, the fraud and larceny against Lentini's business by one of his own employees went undetected by Damon or him. It turned into this unmitigated disaster. Therefore, I'm forced to make some drastic changes," Kain began. "From what I just observed, I can tell Tony Lentini is a common thug and as incompetent as Damon. We've been watching the Lentinis very closely for a long time. We won't let them jeopardize the plan we put in place so many years ago. He, along with his organization and family must be eliminated, and I have already taken steps to do just that. My best troops are ready to take them out here in the states and back in Malta. You will have no further contact with the Lentinis. Is that clear?"

"Yes," the Senator said with no further comment. She felt it best to bury that failure under silence.

Kain paused to sip his iced coffee. "I have world-changing work for you to do, Senator. You are well aware of how we've arrived at this moment and why all the contractors like Lentini have become obsolete. The First and Second World Wars resulted in the deaths of more than 150 million people within a 10-year span. Since then, the relative peace in the world has allowed people to prosper, become healthier, procreate freely, and live longer. This has resulted in the world becoming overpopulated which has put a huge strain on basic resources such as food, water, and clean air."

"Countries are scrambling to keep up with the demand," agreed the Senator. Yours and all the world's retirement slush funds, are dwindling," continued Kain. "This is the only planet we have. Scientists agree that it will be at least 150 to 200 years before we have the technology to reach the Alpha Centauri star system, where the habitable planet called Proxima Centauri B exists. We must act now for our survival and that of our planet. We must give ourselves the time we'll need to reach another Earth. As you know, the largest growing population demographic is the 65 and up segment."

"Yes," said the Senator.

"So, my scientists have been working for years to find the best way to thin the growing herd without another world war. Yes, a war would achieve the goal of reducing the world's population, but it would also destroy cities, critical infrastructures, mineral deposits, food sources, etc.," stated Kain.

"It would also contaminate the air, agricultural land, oceans, and clean water sources," added the Senator.

"Precisely. There are nearly two billion people without clean drinking water right now. But Senator, I have good news. We have the solution. My scientists have developed a protein that will alter human DNA and reduce the world's population in the least invasive way possible. It's already been tried and tested on a very large sample group, and it works perfectly. I have all the video, audio, and written documentation to prove it."

Kain's straight face concealed the fact he was lying. *The documentation has all been expertly fabricated to look real. No one can tell the difference, especially these political fools.* "I'll give you all the test results so you can see for yourselves," Kain spoke aloud. "Here's how it works. In layman's terms. When the protein enters the body, it seeks out the current status of the body's genetic code and determines if it has reached the physical age of 65. Of course, some people will reach that threshold earlier or later, depending on heredity, immunity, and lifestyle choices. Regardless, at that point, the protein will trigger the aging process of all the internal organs to accelerate by a factor of 25X. Let me explain what that means."

The Senator listened with intrigue, as Kain took another sip before continuing.

"When a person reaches their DNA age of 65, the protein will start to work on their internal organs, and in just one year, their body will have accelerated to the age of a 90-year-old person. The shock to the body will cause the organs to shut down, and death will come within a month of their 65-year anniversary. "

The truth is, the protein will actually kill everyone who ingest it in 10 to 12 months due to a massive buildup of calcium throughout their bodies. Only the antidote will prevent this from happening and stop the process, and only if it is taken within the first 30 days of ingestion. Fools. Their greed and corruption will be their demise and my triumph.

"This will eliminate the older non-producing demographic from the world's population, ages 65 and up, without harming the younger productive population. Just think of all the money and resources you and the other leaders will acquire for yourselves. This will also reverse the damage that overpopulation has caused to our climate. You will be able to enjoy your spoils without fear of the planet burning up," Kain said.

"How will the protein be distributed, and when?" the witch asked with the excitement in her voice that only greed can produce. The fact that millions would perish for her profit and pleasure obviously meant nothing to her.

"This is where you and all the leaders of the world come in. I need everyone's cooperation. Remember I said that nearly 2 billion people don't have clean drinking water as we speak? Well, that turned out to be the obvious solution to the problem of how to distribute the protein to the world's populations. Drinking water. As you know, my country supplies all the chemicals, mostly chlorine and ammonia, or chloramine, to purify water. The protein we developed survives and actually multiplies perfectly in water with these chemicals. The protein does this one task of eliminating people 65 and older, like I said, and is otherwise harmless."

"Brilliant," said the Senator.

"My people will need access and clearance around the security protocols for all the water treatment facilities throughout the world. That includes all city water and bottled water plants everywhere. You can do this under a health emergency declaration due to rising bacteria rates in drinking water all over the world. That will be the easiest way to get those approvals, and to stop people from asking questions. If anyone tries to object, we'll call them out as wanting to make people sick. They won't be able to defend that. The people in charge of the facilities will be told that our chemical engineers are adding the protein as an additive to reduce bacteria counts."

"Mr. Kain, again, it's a brilliant plan, well thought out and doable, but how will we and all the world leaders be protected?" the vile and iniquitous creature asked.

"Not to worry, Senator. Hasn't my country been protecting you and the leaders of the world for almost three quarters of a century? We've been supplying all of you the immune system serum we developed some 75 years ago that has increased all of your longevities well into the 90s and even longer."

"Yes, and that's why we could never repay you for the gift of, shall we say, the fountain of youth, you have given to the elite class. Other than we all defer to your leadership, Kain."

"You know, it has always surprised me that no one has ever asked why it is that presidents, kings, queens, senators, congressmen, etc., and all their families seem to live longer than the regular population does."

"Our unquestioning sheep, not fit for power or longevity…"

"Yes. Anyway, we'll provide the elite with all the protein-free clean drinking water needed. Meanwhile, we've calculated that it will only take three to six months for the protein to reach the elderly. Everyone needs water. After six months, we'll stop putting the protein in the water and restore all the facilities and plants back to normal operation. I need you to get on this right away and make all the calls needed so that I can start distribution in 60 days. Is that clear?"

"Very clear, sir, and that will be plenty of time to get the clearances you need. I guarantee it."

Kain couldn't help but look at the Senator with her bulging eyes, red mouth, and botoxed forehead, and see a female praying mantis. An appropriate comparison all around. The mantis was one of life's mysteries to him. He knew that after they mated, the female ate the male alive to sustain herself and her offspring. He had no doubt this female Senator would gladly do that to keep herself going without a second thought for her mate or anyone else.

"Good. You'll be hearing from me on a daily basis from now on. Goodbye, Senator."

Kain walked out of their secret office in Washington DC, took the elevator down to the street, and got into the back of his waiting Limo. He stretched out in the spacious back seat. The windows were completely blacked out. He unzipped his pants. A large glass of his favorite drink, a mixture of ginger ale, ginger beer and lime juice, called the gunner, stood in an ice bucket on the custom bar he designed. Sitting next to him was the American blond who had been waiting for him, monetarily speaking. He sipped his drink as the blond performed.

She'll demand her measly 250 U.S dollars and walk away, for now. Soon, he'll demand a different payment from her and the rest of the world—they'll pay him with their lives, or else.

When the blond finished and money was exchanged, he told her to get out. He spoke to his driver over the intercom in their native language.

"Take me to the Four Seasons, my hotel," he said.

He thought about what he just said, and laughed uncontrollably, harder and harder, until tears ran down his cheeks. His stomach cramped from the hysterics. *Yes, my hotel. It will all belong to me and my people. Soon the whole world will be ours and ours alone. The human sheep will climb over each other and rush to the slaughter, believing they'll save themselves. Fools. If they had just left us alone.*

For centuries, Kain's people lived happily from one generation to the next. Their blood line was pure. That's all they ever wanted, to be left alone and enjoy their culture without any outside influence or intrusions. That was all, just leave them the fuck alone. They built a mighty barrier with the idea of keeping the world out, and their happiness in, forever. That all changed the day they were invaded.

Kain's ancestral cities were burned and his people murdered for bayonet practice. When that happened, their culture, happiness, and sanctuary, along with their isolationist contentment, safety, and security changed forever. After they beat back the invasion, they would never allow themselves to be assaulted like that again.

Their wise leaders at the time knew what had to

be done. They had to change their attitudes and philosophies. Instead of planning our future centuries in advance, they were forced to plan the modern way. Short term, no longer ignoring the greed, selfishness, and constant desire for instant gratification that the world had grown accustomed to.

To ensure his own bloodline's protection and survival, all the other cultures of the world must eventually be eliminated. Kain hated the people who took the virtue of patience and serenity away from his culture. Their greed would make them fall for the world's last and deadliest scam, which they'll pay for with their extinction.

Kain reached for the car phone and called his General to check on the status of the weapon he would use to conquer the world.

***

Brody said nothing to Jane's confession that she missed him. It was time to show her how much he had missed her. He got up from his chair and sat next to her, leaned over and gently wrapped his arms around her. They kissed and stayed that way for the longest time, neither wanting it to end.

Eventually, hands went exploring, squeezing, rubbing, caressing. Brody's palm gently traveled up from the back of Jane's bare calf, causing her to gasp for breath. Both were uninhibited now, free to explore and make ready for the next inevitable step. Brody with one swift move, lifted Jane into his arms and carried her to the bedroom. He kicked the door closed behind him and gently laid her down on his bed. The fuse they lit an hour ago had ignited an explosion that resulted in mutual climaxes. Not just once, but three times.

Totally exhausted, Brody pivoted off Jane and laid by her side.

"That was unbelievable," Jane said.

"Perfect description. Totally unbelievable for me. I've never experienced anything like that before. Multiple orgasms. I didn't think it was possible for guys." Brody responded.

"Extreme euphoria. I never understood what it meant, until now. That was incredible," Jane agreed.

As they laid there, bodies bonded in a warm loving embrace, Brody's mind wandered back to what he had seen between Juan and the prostitute. He realized that was just one thing, sex. Two people simply fulfilling their animalistic desire driven by libido and hormones, mostly for the satisfaction of one of them. What happened between him and Jane was completely opposite and couldn't have happened without that one special, sincere, real, and unconditional ingredient—love. They must have been thinking the same thing, because their words hit the air at the very same time...

"I love you!"

They smiled at each other knowing they understood the deeper meaning of those words. Brody felt he needed to say something to emphasize this whole extraordinary event. There was only one word that qualified. He served it up first to Jane, and she returned it right back to him. They kept the volley going for a while, repeating that one word over and over to each other.

"Wow!"

"Wow!"

"Wow!"

After a few minutes, Jane went to the bathroom and came back to bed, molding her body around Brody's backside.

"Brody, is it really over with the scammer?"

He twisted out of her fleshy cocoon and turned to face her.

"For me, no. Let me explain why I just can't let it go. Our mission was to get Mary's money back. We completed that mission and I couldn't be happier. However, it got very personal when I saw how the scams worked. Bosses forced innocent and oppressed people under their control, to scam and steal from other innocent people, like Mary. When I thought about how people on both sides of that equation were being victimized, it did something to me."

"Tell me more."

"I can only explain it this way. The Japanese Admiral, Isoroku Yamamoto made a statement on the day his planes returned to his carrier after bombing Pearl Harbor on December 7, 1941. It's always stuck with me. His commanding officer was standing next to him as their triumphant planes were landing and cheerfully said to him, 'What a great victory, Admiral.' Yamamoto turned to that officer and famously said, 'I fear all we have done is awakened a sleeping giant and filled him with a great resolve.' I've been asleep on this issue, and the scammers have filled me with a resolve to fight back. That's why I told you that we were gonna keep looking into it."

"Couldn't that be dangerous?"

"We'll be very careful and smart about how we help. Several law enforcement agencies will take the lead on this, and our role would be to aid them with information."

"Okay, as long as you promise me to be safe."

"I promise."

Jane rolled out of bed and said, "I'd love to stay, but I should go. Mary's certainly no prude and I know she wouldn't mind if I stayed the night. It's just that I have all my girly stuff at her house, and I have to finish packing."

"I would love for you to stay too, but I understand," Brody said as he got up.

"What are you doing?"

"Hey, I can't let my girl walk home alone."

"Really, my girl?"

"Yeah, really."

"You don't know how happy that makes me. My guy!"

They hugged, kissed, and got dressed. Brody walked Jane to Mary's, and they kissed good night at the door.

"See you soon, Jane."

"See you soon, Brody."

***

The next morning, after an early workout, Brody was ready for the guys' 9 a.m. arrival. While he waited, he called Jane.

"How's my girl?"

"How's my guy?"

"Never felt so right to me, Jane."

"Me too."

"What time do you have to leave for the airport?"

"The flight takes off at 3 p.m., so we're leaving the house at noon. I added up the time to get to the airport, return the rental, take the shuttle over to our airlines, get through security, and have a little time to recoup before we board our flight. I left my car in long term parking at McCarran, so it'll be easy to get home from there."

Brody was quiet, prompting Jane to ask, "What?"

"I would have planned it out exactly the same way. Score another one to our theory of things we have in common. You amaze me."

"You're amazing too, in so many different ways." She giggled.

"My meeting with the guys starts in an hour and will probably go most of the day, but I'd like to take a break and come over to kiss you before you leave."

"I'll be all ready to go by 11:30, so please get here while we have enough time for a real kiss. I'll tell Mary you have to come to my room and help me close my suitcase. That won't be a lie. I always pack more than I need, and had to sit on my suitcase to zip it up to come here."

"I won't be able to get rid of this smile for the rest of the day. The guys will be merciless with their ribbing, but I don't care. It can't come soon enough. I'll be there at 11:30 sharp or a touch earlier. See you soon."

As soon as Brody hung up, he started planning. *Its 8:15 a.m., and according to the clock on the wall, the guys will arrive in 45 minutes. Two and a half hours into it, I'll call an early lunch break. While the guys are eating, I'll tell them I have to go over to Mary's to say goodbye. Then I'll get that kiss from Jane.*

But shake it off, Brody; there are serious things you need to talk over with the guys.

I need to use my Waterpik before I go over. I wonder what she'll be wearing.

Stop it, Brody! Stop.

He busied himself by getting coffee ready and cleaning up a bit. He deliberately called for a 9 a.m. meeting so he wouldn't have to provide a full breakfast. He knew the guy's habit of eating bacon and eggs at 6 a.m. every day. There was coffee and a fruit tray to snack on, and for lunch, their favorite Subway sandwiches were in the fridge. Turkey for Shawn, and the Philly for Nick.

He was just putting the vacuum away when the doorbell rang. All three pals were right on time, and congregated in the kitchen for the snacks and coffee. Brody explained that Jane and Mary were going to Vegas that afternoon for a little R&R, and he'd be going over at lunch to see them off.

"Brody..." Dan paused with a sly smile, "you sure you'll be coming back? With all we have to go over, we wouldn't want you to end up laying down on the job." Dan laughed and Nick and Shawn joined him.

"Don't you guys worry. I have a lot of self-control."

"Not with Jane you don't. Don't forget we saw you two going at it on your porch," Nick said.

"Okay, okay. I promise a quick goodbye and I'll be right back before you finish your beers."

"Did you just say you were going over there for a quickie, Brody? Dan asked.

They all had to laugh at that one. When it was over, they got down to business. Each took a turn talking about different aspects of the mission, but mainly how it grew into something totally unexpected.

Shawn and Nick had been monitoring news surrounding the warehouse explosion even before Brody told them what Jane and Mary saw on TV. After Damon's spiel, none of them were surprised by the official media statement that a vacant warehouse explosion was caused by a lightning strike near a leaking gas line. The sophisticated attack and cover up proved Damon was probably telling the truth about working for a powerful rogue faction of the government. It also gave some credence to his crazy allegations about world governments killing off old people to save money and resources.

"If Damon was truthful about one, why lie about

the other?" said Brody.

"Exactly. Who else but a corrupt government had that kind of power, scope, and unlimited resources?" Sean agreed.

They had to come to a reasonable conclusion about two things regarding the mission. Things that could come back to bite them in the ass.

"Does anyone foresee any ramifications or retaliation stemming from our mission, considering it resulted in poking a big, but yet, unknown governmental bear?" Nick asked.

"And, will the bear investigate Damon's claims about a worldwide conspiracy to scam people out of their very lives?" asked Dan.

"And if they prove it to be true, what can we do about it?" Brody chimed in.

On the first count, none of them thought there'd be any consequences from the mission. Whoever was behind the attack on the warehouse had to think that Brody and Dan were dead. The attack happened so quickly, and it was clear that someone they freed had ratted them out upon leaving.

However, the he-or-she rat could only have passed on what they knew—that Brody and Dan tried to steal from the Lentinis, got caught, escaped, killed Horst and Vinny, set the workers free, and stayed behind to rob Damon when he got there. Whoever the rat told this story to, made the decision to destroy the warehouse to kill them and Damon.

One thing about that decision didn't make sense.

Why was killing Damon okay? After all, he was one of them, wasn't he? Whatever the reason, it proved these people were ruthless, evil, and unscrupulous in killing their own.

After the attack, the chopper pilot likely reported it a success as there were no survivors. They were fairly certain no one would be trying to find out who a couple of dead robbers were. The consensus was that there'd be no ramifications and that they were in the clear. That was a wrap on the main part of the mission.

Lunch time at 11:25. They'd discuss what to do about Damon's conspiracy theory afterward.

Brody arranged the spread of sandwiches, dill pickles, beer, and chips and excused himself to go next door and kiss Jane and say goodbye to her and Mary. To keep his mouth sweet and fresh, he'd eat when he got back. The guys were too busy stuffing their mouths to make any wise cracks as he made his way next door. Not that he cared; he enjoyed the ribbing. It always made him feel more endeared by his friends.

Chapter 17
HEARTBREAK

Jane greeted him at the door, and from behind her inside, Mary let out a very delightful, "Hi, Brody," as she sat in her chair draped with a colorful homemade afghan.

"Hi, Mary," he said just as cheerfully. He couldn't remember the last time he was so happy. As planned, Jane asked him if he could help her close the overstuffed suitcase in her room.

"Of course, I'm happy to," he said. "How about you, Mary? Need any help with yours? I know how you gals can fill up a suitcase."

"Thank you, but I managed getting it zipped up just fine."

Okay, please excuse us while I perform one of my many manly chores."

"Sure, you two go ahead. I'll be right here working on my crossword puzzle."

Jane led the way and as Brody followed, he glanced back to see Mary smiling up at him with an all-knowing wink to boot. He winked back, letting her know that he knew she wasn't fooled by all the innocent banter. He also felt a sense of pride that maybe he had helped her be more aware, and that nobody was ever going to fool or scam her again.

When he closed Jane's bedroom door, she spun around and stuck to him like a magnet. She pushed into him with such force he could feel bone on bone. However, her kiss was soft, warm, and sexy. The pleasure took them to a different time-space continuum, and they didn't snap out of it until Mary knocked on Janes' door and said she thought it was time to go. Then, like a seasoned couple, Brody grabbed Jane's suitcase and carry-on and followed her into the living room. Brody, with his free hand, also picked up Mary's suitcase and carry-on. Jane held the door open, and he went out to pack the car.

At the curb, he gave Mary a hug and told her he'd keep a watch on her house. He opened the passenger door, and she kissed him on the cheek before getting in. He walked Jane around to the driver's side and kissed her goodbye before opening the door for her. They both mouthed *See you soon* through the driver's side window, and the car began to roll away.

He stood frozen in the street as he watched the car slowly disappear, holding his Jane captive. The sense of loss and dread broke down his usually rock-hard sensibilities, making him feel sick and weak. He tried to fill the emptiness in his chest by taking deep breaths. When that didn't work, he reluctantly turned to walk home, then stopped. He turned back and looked down the street, hoping to see Jane's car coming back. It wasn't. With love sick loneliness in his heart, he went home.

Back in his kitchen, the guys were impressed with the swiftness of his return, but decided not to make any comments. They all could see the somberness in his face. Brody got his food and took a bite. The guys had finished, but were working on their second beers. The bullshit circled the table several times until they all finished, and then Brody kicked off the real discussion.

"All right, gentlemen, second item to consider, and it's a big one. Beyond going after more scammers, do *we* investigate the extraordinary allegations made by Damon? I think this needs a vote and I also think it should be unanimous. But before we do, I'd like to say a couple of things. If the allegations are true, this could potentially be the most serious and dangerous undertaking we've ever done together. Our lives and the lives of our families will likely be at risk."

"Yeah, we know whoever's behind this won't hesitate to torture or kill all of us," said Dan.

"True," Brody agreed. "Our enemy could even include members of a secret group in our own government as well as groups in other governments around the world. We certainly won't know who to trust, so we'll be exclusively on our own. Having the deck stacked that high against us probably means a pretty small chance for success. The last negative I see is the obvious size, scale, and scope of the investigation."

"It'll consume huge amounts of our personal time, if not all of it," commented Shawn. "Got any good news?"

"Yes. On the positive side, we could save millions of lives, and at the same time prevent the entire world's population from living under tyrannical rule. I'd like to hear everyone's thoughts. Nick, why don't you start?"

"I think you laid out how daunting and serious this decision will be. We all originally signed on to go after Mary's robo caller. Thankfully, we succeeded without anyone getting seriously hurt, but it was a close call. We all agreed that the low life scammers should be held accountable, and we were going to talk about continuing to do that. But I think it takes a back seat to what we're talking about now."

"Good point," said Brody. "What else?"

"Shawn and I were technical backup, while you and Dan were on the frontlines. This new mission could put us all on the frontlines, and like you said, our families too. I'm assuming by the desperate and drastic actions we've recently seen, we're up against a tight clock and have to decide soon. I'll have to talk this over with Sofia. If you can give me till the day after tomorrow, I'll be ready to give my vote."

"Absolutely, my friend. Understandably there's a lot to consider, and I think your timeline is very generous," Brody said.

Dan and Shawn agreed with Nick's summation,

and wanted the time to think about it too.

"Okay, let's meet here at 4 p.m. the day after tomorrow. I'll supply the pizzas and beer."

With that, the guys left.

Brody sat down in his chair and looked out through the front windows at the daylight slowly disappearing with the setting sun. The myriad of recent events replayed over and over, capturing his reality and time. Like when he kissed Jane. Brody blinked, looked around, and realized he was sitting in total darkness.

He'd been so deep in thought he didn't notice the transition from dusk to dark. He relived and analyzed every minute since the day Mary told him her tragic story. From that moment, his simple life changed in ways he couldn't believe. He'd taken on the role of an avenger for her, and would possibly do so for others. But the biggest change was meeting Jane and falling in love with her.

She had changed his life forever. There was no going back.

He looked at the Seals watch on his left wrist. No way, it was 10:30 p.m.

His stomach growled at him, demanding food. Brody agreed wholeheartedly. He turned on the lamp next to his chair and headed for the kitchen. He reached for the light switch on the wall then froze just as the tip of his index finger touched it. A line of red light came through the sink window and stung his right eye like a flash bulb as it moved across his kitchen. He knew immediately what it was.

A lasered gun site.

It came from inside Mary's kitchen window, which faced his. A second laser lit up her bedroom window at the back of her house. At least two heavily armed persons were moving around inside her home. Knowing the girls were gone kept him calm. His mind quickly sifted through the possibilities.

Breaking and entering for robbery? No, don't need sophisticated weapons for that, and this isn't a wealthy neighborhood. Also, 10:30 at night is an odd hour for a home invasion. Most people are still up at that hour. It's a well-known fact that most B&Es happen after midnight between two and four am. Attempted kidnapping for ransom? Again, not that kind of money here. An ex-boyfriend of Jane's with a restraining order, seeking what, revenge? Could be, but why would he need an accomplice? That doesn't make sense. Besides, Jane wouldn't have kept that a secret.

This break-in was happening too close after the end of their mission in Seattle. This wasn't a coincidence, he could feel it. That left the most likely explanation. The Lentinis discovered that Mary was connected to Juan, the break-in to his condo, and the theft of the $197,000.

But how? He wiped Juan's computer completely clean of everything—contacts, all transactions, storage, emails, searches, even the cache on the hard-drive. Somehow he'd made a mistake, and now that mistake has put Mary and Jane in harm's way.

The Lentinis, or whoever else was next door, just made a bigger mistake. Brody was about to unleash a wrath upon them that would make them regret ever coming after Mary. He couldn't help but think what would have happened if they hadn't gone to Vegas, or if he wasn't here to see what was happening in her house.

Time to find out who was next door and what they wanted, although he was pretty sure he already knew—the money. He quickly backed out of the kitchen, turned the living room light out, and looked out the front window. No unfamiliar vehicles on the street. The alley behind their houses opened onto side streets at each end of the block.

Makes sense they parked on one of those streets and used the alley as cover for their ingress and planned egress. Strategically, they'd have a driver stay in the vehicle and be in constant contact for back-up and a quick getaway. This was a well-planned attack.

No time to call the guys. Brody had to get next door before they realized no one was there and left. He rushed to his bedroom to get his duffle bag with the gear still packed from the mission. Already wearing black cargo pants, he pulled on a black long sleeved Under Armour shirt and a black knit ski mask. He'd easily blend into the darkness outside.

With his K-Bar knife to the side of his right calf, he capped his head with night vision just in case and strapped on his level IIIA bullet-proof vest with a custom-made ball protector.

Finally, he slipped into his shoulder holster, stuffed it with his loaded silenced sig, and put four extra clips in pant leg pouches. His military mind would meet any challenge with adaptability, resourcefulness, creativity, and ingenuity. *Thank you, Navy*. He opened his bedroom window to the backyard and removed the screen. The bush at the corner of his house next to the window would shield him from view from Mary's house and yard. He crawled out, and dropped to the ground.

Next he went over to the fence and peered into Mary's yard with a clear view of the back door. It was splintered at the lock and standing wide open, unguarded. By boldly busting their way, they must have been confident they could quickly overwhelm anyone in the house and secure the premises without opposition.

And why wouldn't they be confident? Their target was a little old lady. He figured after they found the house empty, they'd put their guns away and simply leave the way they came. His plan was to surprise them before they reached the alley. He hoped there'd be no more than two, but no matter, he'd incapacitate all but one of them for answers. He'd force the last one standing back into the house and quietly interrogate him without alarming the neighbors.

Brody saw the perfect hiding place in the rear corner of Mary's yard, about five feet away from her back gate—a row of five tall Cyprus trees along the fence line. The branches had grown together, creating a thick green wall. He'd squeeze inside the middle and be perfectly camouflaged. He needed this plan to work because he had to find out what kind of danger the girls were in and who was behind the threat.

He ran to his back gate, crouched low, and eased into the alley. Clear, both ways. He went through Mary's gate left open by the invaders and knifed his way between the Cyprus stand without having to crouch. He stood, completely concealed, and watched the back door. The yard was about 80 feet wide and 50 feet deep from the house to the rear fence. He'd have that 50 feet to make his move.

They must've cleared the house and put their guns down because he didn't see any more lasers dancing around inside. His anxiety was building by the second. He knew that capturing one of these guys was the key to protecting the girls. Standing there, he felt that time had stopped. It was torture waiting for it to start again.

Suddenly, a faint sound made him switch his gaze from the back door to the alley. It was the sound of gravel crunching under heavy boots and it got louder with each step. Two different tones to the crunching. Two people of different size and weight.

Were these the guys in the car parked on the side street coming to hurry up the ones in the house? And if so, how did little old Mary require a four-man team? This wasn't making sense. Hopefully, it would, and soon.

Brody focused on the direction of the footfalls, but still kept an eye on Mary's back door. The crunching was on top of him now, and he saw two shadowy male figures angling straight for Mary's gate.

As the first man got closer and closer, he grew in size like a hot air balloon being inflated at lift off, and was almost as big. The monster stopped at Mary's gate in the alley. He stared at the opened back door and reached behind him, stopping the smaller man in his tracks with a light backhand that covered the little guy's whole chest. The move didn't look like much, but it almost knocked the little guy on his ass by his superhuman strength.

They were both surprised by the opened door and busted frame. Obviously, they expected to do the breaking in themselves. They were definitely not working with whoever was inside. *Could these be good guys, or are the good guys in the house, or are they all bad guys?* All Brody could do now is see how this played out. He hated being a spectator and not a player. This was getting more confusing by the second.

Mr. Big whispered something to Mr. Small, then slowly turned sideways so he could squeeze through the 42-inch-wide gate. When he did, Brody spotted a large L tattoo on the side of his neck. The giant wore black Adidas stretch pants and a matching jacket with the three reflective white trademark lines running down both arms. Not smart. Even with what little light there was, he stood out like a night rocket launch at Cape Canaveral. He held a gun with a silencer in his left hand.

Dang, huge and a south paw too, always the hardest for a right hander to fight if it got down to hand to hand.

The second guy, with a matching L tattoo on his neck, was a scrawny looking mouse, dressed in dark jeans and a black pull-over. He had a black backpack double strapped to his back so his hands were free. No gun in either hand. He must be confident in his monster friend's ability to handle any potential problem for the both of them. No doubt he witnessed the giant crushing men with his huge bare hands in the past.

Well, per the law of gravity, distance, speed, and impact, the bigger they are the harder they fall. Brody hoped he didn't have to try and prove that theory on this guy.

They hustled to the back door and it was amazing to see how agile Mr. Big was and how quickly he got there. Light years ahead of the runt. The big guy took up position behind the door and flattened his back up against the house. Even though it was a wide and solid door, it barely concealed him. He placed Mr. Small next to him and whispered something, then Mr. Small pulled off his pack and took something out.

Brody had to strain his eyes to see through the tiny slits in the heavy foliage, but the object was a syringe. Mr. Big stood ready as Mr. Small cowered next to him. He didn't have to wait long.

Just seconds later, two Asian-looking guys both dressed in black pants and black short-sleeve T-shirts, came out of the house single file. Brody noticed the lead guy had a tattoo of a rat bearing its teeth on his forearm. As Brody predicted, both their guns were holstered in the belts around their waists. They casually walked toward the back gate.

Big waited a couple of beats to be sure there was just the two of them, then stepped out from behind the door and raced up behind the trailing guy who was putting a phone to his ear.

Big raised his giant right hand and hammered it down on top of the guy's head, breaking his neck. The sound of the snapped vertebrae echoed through the night like the crack of a home run ball off a bat. The guy died so fast he froze in place like a statue. Big had to push him out of the way to grab the lead guy, which he did in a blink.

Those three moves were so fast it was hard for Brody to see them as more than a single move. Amazing. While Big held the lead guy's motionless body in a bear hug, small came over and injected whatever was in the syringe into their captive's neck. Immediately, the guy slumped into unconsciousness. The action was so close to Brody now, he could hear and see everything clearly.

Big let the guy drop to the ground, and told Small to go check inside the house. Then he told him to come back and search the dead guy. Brody was shocked by the high-pitched squeal of Big's voice. It just didn't fit the huge man he was looking at. Not necessarily a weakness but a weird anomaly.

While Big waited, he looked around the yard and his gaze paused at the cypress stand where Brody hid. Brody sensed that the guy knew he was there. If Big made a move towards him, he would empty the sig into him and hope it put him down. He just saw the man kill a guy with one fist. The guy was a bear, and when bears get shot, it just pissed them off enough to tear apart their shooter.

If he was successful in killing Big, he'd just have to get his answers from Small. Luckily, that confrontation wouldn't be necessary, because Big turned and moved away. Also luckily for Brody, Big had his back to him when he unzipped his pants and took a leak in the yard. Sometimes it was the little things in life that made one the most thankful. A smile, a word, a look, a leak facing the other way.

Small came out of the house and knelt down by the dead guy. He searched through his clothes and put the guy's lasered handgun in his backpack. Then he pried the cell phone out of the dead guy's hand.

Zipping up, Big said, "Find anything in the house or on the dead guy?"

"The dead guy is clean except for his weapon and cell phone. I have both. The house is clear. No dead bodies. Looks like it was empty when they broke in. I found a notepad with flight information next to the landline," said Small. He handed it to Big. "Can you believe it, Lorenzo? A freaking landline."

Lorenzo, alias Mr. Big's real name. I won't forget

it.

Lorenzo read the pad while finger tapping the lit screen on his phone, illuminating his face and deep horrible scars. Average people would see that, cringe, look away, and have frightening nightmares of him chasing after them.

Brody heard a ringtone.

"Boss, the old lady wasn't here, but a couple of Asian guys were in the house. Yeah, Asian. I killed one of them, and Aldo drugged the other.

Okay, Small, got your name now too. Aldo.

I figured you'd want to talk to him when he woke up," Lorenzo told his boss.

Taking the credit from Aldo, he continued.

"I found a notepad in the house. Flight information for a Jane Peltier and our Mary Charbenau. They both took the same flight out of the San Diego airport this morning to Las Vegas. Can you believe it boss? They're coming right to you..........ah, yes sir, Mr. Lentini."

Lentini. How the hell did he find out about Mary?

"Okay, we'll get back to Gillespie Field airport right now and back to Vegas as fast as we can. When we get there, I'll have Aldo take the Asian to the cold room at the plant and hold off on going to work on him till you get there. I'll go straight from the airport to this Jane Peltier's address. Yes sir, I'll get them both and bring them to you. Aldo will be happy to show you his best work. You'll have all your questions answered, I guarantee it, sir."

He put the phone in his back pocket, then

reached down and clamped one massive hand on the chest of the drugged guy like the jaws-of-life and flung him up over his opposite shoulder. He walked through the gate and down the alley the same way they came with a grinning Aldo in tow. Aldo overheard that he was going to be able to do some of his work. Brody didn't want to think about it.

As soon as they were out of ear shot, Brody squeezed out from the bush, leaped over the dead guy, and ran into Mary's house. He closed the broken door so no one could hear him from outside. He looked through the house, made sure it was clear, and called Jane. As he pushed send, he telepathically pleaded with the powers of the universe for one thing, and one thing only. *Jane, answer! Answer! Answerrrr!*

"Hi Brody, we got ho….." Brody broke in with a tone that Jane immediately recognized as urgent and serious.

"Jane, listen to me very carefully. You and Mary have to get out of your house right now.

"Brody, you're scaring me. What's going on?"

"You have to trust me. I was in my kitchen when I saw people moving around inside Mary's house."

Jane gasped loudly. "Why? Robbery? But Mary is poor."

"No. It can only be one thing. Somehow they connected our mission in Seattle to her, and I'm so sorry about that. We did everything we could to prevent it, but we can't worry about that now. I promise the guys, and I will take care of this," Brody said.

"I know you will, Brody."

"When I saw the people in her house, I went into her yard and hid in her bushes. I was gonna find out what was going on when suddenly, two more men came into the yard from the alley. Long story short, these are very bad people, and they're hell-bent on finding Mary. Unfortunately, now you too. They found your flight information and they're gonna be on their way to Vegas in a few hours. Here's what you have to do."

Brody instructed Jane to take all the cash she had and avoid using debit or credit cards for anything. He told her to take the lid off the toilet tank and put her cell phones in the water, and put the lid back on.

"Do you have a desktop computer or laptop?"

"Laptop."

"Good, take it with you. Have any duct tape?"

"Yes, my dad said you can fix anything with it and always insisted I have some."

"Good, tape over the license plates on your car and the VIN number on your dashboard. The street cameras today can see and identify you by both of those numbers. Do you know where the VIN is?"

"Yes."

"Good. Don't waste another second trying to take anything else with you. Use cash for whatever you'll need later. Go to a Walmart or BestBuy and tell them you want a burner phone, they'll know what you mean. Remember to pay in cash. I know I'm repeating that, but the easiest way to find people these days is with credit cards or checks. Then go right to your car and call me. Get moving. I'll explain everything else when you call me."

"Okay, I trust you. We're leaving now."

"Jane, I love you, and I'm not gonna let anyone hurt you or Mary."

Brody rushed back to his house. Keeping the house dark, he began gathering up his gear when he heard a vehicle approaching in the alley. He looked through the blinds of his bedroom window he saw a black Klassen Mercedes-Benz V 300 D van stop behind Mary's house. It approached from the opposite direction that Lorenzo and Aldo had come from.

Three Asian men dressed in black combat gear and wireless cameras on their helmets poured out of a side sliding door and ran into the yard. They carried Uzi Pros. Someone, somewhere, was watching and recording their every move.

One of the guys stopped at the dead guy, and the other two rushed into the house. The guy in the yard quickly checked the corpse, then covered the rear of Mary's house with his submachine gun. A couple of minutes later, the two in the house came out and signaled the all clear. The three of them picked up the body and piled into the van's side door like it was a Vietnam Huey at an LZ, and then took off in the same direction Lorenzo and Aldo had gone.

Neither Lorenzo nor the Asians paid any attention to Brody's house. Obviously, they hadn't made the connection between him and Mary. If they had, they would have busted down his door too.

He finished packing the same military gear he'd taken with him to Seattle, but added a Barrett M82 anti-material sniper rifle he had hidden in the floor. He wanted to be prepared for any possible scenario. He could take out a large SUV, or man hiding behind a wall with the M82.

He stripped off his casual clothes and put on his camos, combat boots and grabbed a go-bag in the closet. He always kept a go-bag throughout his military career, out of habit. The bag had clothes, $10,000 in ones, fives, tens, and twenties, burner phones, batteries, an iPad, chargers, toiletries, false IDs, dried food packs, and a med kit. He loaded everything in the back of the Ford. He got behind the wheel, plugged his phone into the charger, and double-checked the gas gauge. That was another habit. He topped off the tank if it dropped down to three-quarters. He had enough to make it all the way to Vegas without stopping.

It was 11:30 p.m. as he headed for the 15 North freeway.

***

Brody pressed a code into his phone and group-called Dan, Shawn, and Nick. Shawn had set their phones up with this feature and it triggered an alarm like an amber alert. It let them know that one of them had an emergency. In this case it was Brody. Shawn and Nick answered right away and Dan a second later.

"Thanks, guys, for answering so fast. Let me fill

you in."

He explained in detail everything that went down at Mary's and the names of two new players that worked for Tony Lentini. Lorenzo, and Aldo. He emphasized how concerned he was that there was now another unknown group looking for Mary. He told them that he was in route to Vegas.

"I called Jane and told her to get herself and Mary out of her Condo immediately. I went through all the standard security precautions—burners, cash purchases, etc."

"Brody, Sofia's been listening to everything you've said, and as far as voting on what we should do now about the scammers and their world domination plans, she wants you to know that we're both all in on getting the bastards."

"Ditto" said Shawn.

"Me too," Dan confirmed.

"Thanks, everyone, I really appreciate it. Okay, first things first. Let's get Mary and Jane safe, then we'll take it from there. Here's some things I need right away. Nick, see if you can find out through your FAA contacts who owns the plane that's flying out of Gillespie tonight to Vegas. I think we all know who it is, but there's at least one other player involved, probably whoever's pulling Lentini's strings. Next, I'm gonna need a safe house in Vegas for Mary and Jane. Anyone got any ideas?"

Dan chimed right in. "I'll have to check first, but I have an old friend that lives in Vegas. His name is Oscar. It's been about six months since we've talked.

He has a huge house his parents left him when they passed. They also left him millions in inheritance."

"He lives alone?" asked Brody.

"Yep, and paranoid about getting robbed and for his overall safety. He's been upgrading security on his home, but he didn't go into the details. It would be perfect, Brody."

"Any other details on his place that you know of Dan?"

"There's a large detached casita in the rear yard, and it rarely gets used. He actually deals poker at the Bellagio for fun. A lot of big name poker players and Hollywood celebs play there, and he loves to hear all the latest gossip.

"Sounds promising," Brody said hopefully.

"Yep. He's a night owl and won't be there most nights. He'll sleep late into the day. The house backs up to Red Rock Mountain. It's in a gated community with onsite security too. I'll use my other phone to call him right now. I'll still be listening in though."

"Excellent, Dan." The relief in Brody's voice after hearing about a lead on a potential safe house was reassuring, and it calmed the situation for all of them. "The way I see it, there's only one way to keep Mary and Jane safe for now and in the future, and that's for me to cut the head off the snake."

"Exactly Brody." Shawn agreed.

"And if the snake has a two heads, which this one appears to have, well then, I'll lop both of them off. Again guys, I'm lead on this, and I'll keep you all out of it as much as I can. I know you're all in, but when it comes down to any hand-to-hand, I need to be the one to take that on. I'm gonna need a lot of tech support and information, Nick and Shawn, and you two can give me all I'll need right where you are."

"We're both here for whatever you need, including hand-to- hand," Shawn said.

Dan chimed in. "I heard that, Brody. Listen, pal, you're gonna have to know the gals are safe so you can be free to do what you have to do to resolve this. No argument about it, I'm saddling up and will be on my way to Vegas about three hours or so behind you."

"Thank you, brother."

"Besides that, I have great news. I got a hold of Oscar at the casino on the first ring. He was in a dealer rotation and I caught him on his break. I explained that some goons were looking to get their hands on two of our lady friends and asked if he could help us by letting us use his place. I emphasized the possible danger, but he immediately blew it off and insisted that we use his whole place if needed. He's been anti-goon for a very long time."

"How come?" Brody asked.

"He's endured endless bullying throughout his life just because he's gay, as I have," answered Dan. "He sprung right into action, Brody. He put me on hold and called the main gate. He told the security guard that his sister Sylvia, his grandma Betty, and his cousins Frank—that's you Brody—and Pete— that's me—will be coming to stay with him for a while and to let us pass when we get there."

"Got it."

"And even though we're supposed to be his relatives, he knows not to tell anyone that we'll be staying there. I'm gonna text you the address and four code numbers. One for the gate at his driveway, one for the front door lock on the three bedroom casita where Mary and Jane will stay, one for the alarm code on the wall inside the casita, and the last for the main house if we need to get in there. He said just in case, he always keeps the casita fully stocked with food and anything else guests might need."

"Anything else?"

"Yes, the guard will give the girls a map to get to Oscar's address. When they go through the gate at his house, they'll take the driveway straight past the main house on their left and end up at the casita directly behind it."

"Fantastic, Dan, this couldn't be better. Great call on the aliases."

"That's not even the best part. Wait till you hear this. Remember he told me he added some security stuff? Well, he added a panic room in the main house, and the casita. He's gonna go over how it works with me when I get there. I think our luck is changing for the better."

"Thank God for paranoid friends. This is great news. Give Oscar our undying gratitude."

"Will do. I told Oscar that I'll be heading straight to his house and that I'm texting everyone his picture so we don't accidentally shoot him. He thought that was a great idea."

Brody chuckled.

"He said to make ourselves at home and he'll see us tomorrow. Jane and Mary will get there fairly soon. You and I will get there early morning and Oscar late morning. Let's rest when we get there, then figure out our next moves," Dan said.

"Solid plan. I'm on board. Have to stay sharp," Brody agreed.

"Great. I'm hitting the road. See you soon." Dan signed off.

Brody's heart leaped at the "See you soon" phrase and immediately thought of Jane, and how much he loved her.

"Nick, Shawn, we know one person's out to get Mary and why. It's Tony Lentini, but we don't know who's behind those mysterious Asians that showed up. My guess is it's the person who ordered the hit on Lentini's warehouse. What we know right now is that Tony's guy, Lorenzo, is taking a kidnapped Asian to Vegas to extract information. We need to know where they take him when they get there."

Nick cut in. "Brody, you were right. There's a Gulfstream at Gillespie, and yes, it's owned by the Lentini Corporation. No big surprise there. I have the flight number and flight plan. That was pretty easy, but there's a slight twist that no one at Gillespie will talk about. Here's the thing that's strange. The plane is scheduled to fly out at 5:30 a.m."

"Why's that strange?" Brody asked.

"Because the airport has a flight ban between the hours of 10:30 p.m. and 7:30 a.m. due to a noise restriction law. The law is strictly enforced after an incident that happened some years ago. A big shot celeb flew his private jet out during the restricted hours, and the airport got sued by local residents the next day. They won a big settlement, and it's never happened again since."

"So there's no explanation on how Lentini swung that flight time, Shawn?

"Right, Brody" Shawn confirmed. "He must have paid someone off or seriously threatened them. Again, we see the powers we're up against. We're talking about getting to an FAA official. They're scheduled to land at Henderson Executive Airport in Vegas at 9:15 am."

"Can you track and record the flight all the way there?'

"Yeah, I'm using a series of satellites that overlap and circle the Equator. They give me a continuous view of a swath that covers the Equator north to Canada and south to Argentina."

"So after they land in Vegas, you'll be able to see where they go from there," said Brody.

"Exactly. Once I get that location, Nick will get all the information on it and pass it to you. I'm also tracking you right now as long as your tooth stays charged," Shawn assured.

"Roger that. I tested it the day I got back, and it's still at 97%, so we're a go. I should get to Vegas proper around 5 a.m., and I'll be going straight to

Jane. Great work, guys. Thanks."

Brody's phone rang.

"Have to go. Got an unknown caller. Must be Jane. I'll get back to you as soon as I can."

Chapter 18

PROTECT THEM FROM TONY

"Jane?"

"Yes, Brody, it's me. I'm sorry. Mary and I are trying to be strong, but we're really scared."

"I totally understand. The fastest way for me to get there is by car, so I'm driving to you as we speak. I should be there around 5 am. I have your burner phone in my contacts now so we'll be able to stay connected. I've got some very good news that I hope will calm you and Mary. First though, did you do everything I asked you to do?"

"Yes, phones in the toilet tank, no credit cards, cash purchases only, took my laptop, taped over my license plates and VIN number, and got this burner phone. Also, I sent an email to my boss telling him that I have a fever and I'm probably contagious, so I'll have to do the office meeting tomorrow at home via zoom, which is my car right now, and that I'll let him know when I'm over the bug."

"Very smart. We definitely don't want people

from your work looking for you right now. You did everything right. I'm so proud of you. Now, the good news. I have a safe place for you and Mary to stay and it's ready for you right now. I'm gonna text you the address along with four separate four-digit code numbers you'll need to get into the property. It's a gated community, so when you pull up to the gatehouse, tell the guard that you're Oscar's sister Sylvia and Mary is Grandma Betty, and he'll let you through."

"Sylvia and Betty," Jane repeated.

"Don't worry, Oscar is a friend of a friend, and he's cool with you staying there. I'll be sending his picture to your phone so you'll know who he is. He'll be at work when you get there, so don't worry about disturbing him."

"Got it."

"The guard has been instructed to give you a map to get to Oscar's house since this is supposedly your first visit to his new home. You'll have one code for the gate at his home, second one for the front door of a three bedroom casita that you and Mary will be using, third one for the security alarm on the inside of the casita, and the fourth one is for the front door of the main house, just in case you have to get in there.

"Home gate, front door of the casita, casita security alarm, main house alarm. Got it."

When you drive through the gate, take the driveway till you pass the main house on your left, and drive straight to the guest casita in the rear of the property. Get going, honey, and if you run into any problems, call me. As soon as you're inside the casita, call so I'll know you gals are safe, okay?"

"Okay. The wait for 5 a.m. has just changed my perception of eternity."

"I know what you mean. I wish I was there with you right now. It's frustrating me to no end staying at the speed limit, and I'm starving, but I don't want to get pulled over and lose even one microsecond from getting to you."

"Stop for food. You're running on empty."

"I'll find an all-night drive-thru. And I know it won't be easy, but both of you need to get some sleep. I will too when I get there. I have the codes too, so don't worry if you hear me around 5 a.m. I'll find a piece of furniture to crash on, and I'll set the alarm on my phone for 8:30 a.m. We're all gonna have to stay as fresh and alert as we can. Okay?"

"Okay, we'll try. I love you."

"I love you too with all my heart and soul...and Jane?"

"Yes?"

"See you soon."

***

Brody set the cruise control for exactly seven miles over the posted speed limit. He knew that police used ten-plus miles as their ticket target. It was more lucrative to pull over the ten-plus speeders. He was so desperate to get to the girls before they were harmed in any way the tension and anxiety had given him a migraine. The pain was hindering his ability to come up with a plan to keep them safe once he got there. He had to grab food and push through the pain.

Think, Brody, think. Mary's their target and Jane, unfortunately, is collateral damage. It's too late to separate Jane from the equation because Mary's pursuers already know they're traveling together. They'll believe that whatever Mary knows, Jane most likely knows, too.

Desperate times require desperate measures, and Brody's health food regime defaulted to a junk food fix. He spotted a burger joint and pulled through, ordering a double with cheese, fries, three apple pies, a large Sprite, and a side salad to clear his conscience somewhat, and lots of napkins.

As the miles rolled by, he immediately felt better as the calories filled his belly and defeated his headache.

Lorenzo works for Tony Lentini, his thoughts continued, *and he was likely sent to get Mary for two reasons. To get his money back, and to find out how she was able to infiltrate his organization. Those were the most logical motives. What I don't know is why the Asians are after Mary too, and who they work for. I need to find out. It's the only way I can completely save Mary and Jane from this nightmare and give them their lives back.*

Since Lorenzo killed one of the Asians and took the other for questioning, Tony Lentini obviously wants to know what the hell they were doing in Mary's house too. I wish I could've questioned the

Asian before Lorenzo and Aldo went to work on him. There will be nothing left to interrogate once they're done.

Brody lowered his window to let the crisp night air hit him in the face. The heavy food and lack of sleep worked against his adrenaline, and he needed to revitalize and organize his thoughts.

Come on, Brody, keep thinking this through. You can't let what happens next turn into a wing and a prayer. Find a way to protect them from Tony. To do that, solve the problem of why the Asians are involved. That's the key. Find that out and end this. Somehow, the guys will help. No qualms about doing whatever I have to do, including killing whoever I have to kill, in order to keep the girls safe. Not for just this moment in time, but for the rest of time. I'll make sure they won't have to live in fear or worry about their safety when this is over.

The seconds ticked by so slowly, he wished he could teleport himself straight to Oscar's place. The drive was long and torturous, not just because he was in a hurry to get to Vegas, but because it was a Sunday night and a constant stream of headlights faced him, all heading back to LA from Vegas for work on Monday. It burned his eyes. To makes things worse, rain, which rarely ever happens in southern California, started pounding his windshield, adding extra tension in his mind and body. He looked down and noticed he had a white-knuckled grip on the steering and released it a bit. His fingers were stiff like rigor. The blood cells in them must have been treading water for some time fighting to stay alive. *Relax Brody, relax. You need your fingers.*

***

At the Gillespie Field airport, no one dared to ask Lorenzo why he was carrying an unconscious guy onto the plane. The flight crew worked exclusively for the Lentini Corporation, and over the years they learned to turn a blind eye to whatever went on inside the plane. Lorenzo had to toss the Asian inside first before he could squeeze through the door of the Gulfstream G-650. He picked the guy up off the floor and strapped him into a luxury seat that doubled as a full layout bed. He hated having to bend over in the tight (for his body) fuselage and quickly dropped his 375 muscled pounds in the chair across from the Asian.

Aldo came in a minute later with their bags and stowed everything away except his backpack. He sat in a chair facing Lorenzo.

"Aldo, you didn't overdose your play thing, did you?"

"No, no. I would never do that. His body mass was a tad under the specs, so it'll take a little longer for him to revive. Don't worry, I won't let anything happen to him. It's been awhile since I've had such a young and healthy subject to work on. He should last a long, long time."

Aldo said this with such enthusiasm and excitement, it sent a sharp twinge of fear through Lorenzo's chest. He'd seen Aldo's work many times, and even though he had saved Aldo's life more than once, he knew the psychopath wouldn't hesitate to cut him to pieces given the chance. Little Aldo was truly the only human on earth that he feared. Lorenzo laid his seat all the way back to get some rest, but only closed one eye. The other eye he kept on the small and deadly sadist.

**

Kain got the bad news call from the leader of his San Diego extraction team. One team member dead, another missing. The leader was a 36-year-old captain in Kain's elite special-forces by the name of Zimo Chang. Until now, Zimo had never failed to execute a mission to absolute perfection. So this news was very disturbing to Kain. Especially since this mission should have been one of the easiest for Zimo, ever. He simply had to snatch an old lady out of her home and bring her to him.

"Zimo, what the hell happened?" Kain demanded.

Zimo knew by the tone of Kain's voice he was in big trouble, but he wasn't going to leave any detail out. He knew Kain would see through any attempt to sugarcoat the situation, and he'd be in even bigger trouble. Zimo explained that he dropped two men off in the alley behind Mary Charbenau's home, then drove around the block and parked the getaway van out of sight of the neighbors. The men were to break in, wrap her up, and search the house. When they were done, they'd call him for extraction.

It took his men longer than anticipated and when Zimo couldn't make contact with them, he hurried back to the house and found one of his men dead in the yard, the other presumed captured, and no sign of the lady.

Kain was angry and disappointed in Zimo, especially about the capture of one of his men, but he wasn't worried. He had prepared and planned in advance for the possibility of any of his missions going sideways, and even for the capture of any of his people. Everyone who worked for Kain in or out of the field, had a tiny tracking chip installed inside the base of their skull.

The chip not only pinpointed the location of every employee, it had a second and very special feature that gave Kain complete control over his people. The chip could be detonated by a cell phone signal, obliterating the person's cortex and killing them. Every employee was told if they tried to remove the chip, it would automatically detonate. This was Kain's way to insure the unconditional loyalty of his people, and the ultimate nondisclosure protection if they should try to leave his employ. Talk and you'll die.

"The rest of it, Zimo!" Kain demanded.

"Yes, sir. I tracked our captured soldier through his implant to the Gillespie airport. I got there in time to see a very large man carry him inside the Lentini Gulfstream. He appeared to be alive.

"Of course he's alive. They want information from him. They will torture him to get it, then kill him. Zimo, this is a disaster, and you will pay for this failure. I will, however, take into account your past successes and your proven loyalty. Also, you can help redeem yourself by mitigating this situation."

"Sir, give me the chance and I promise I'll make it right."

"I expect nothing less from you, Zimo."

"Sir, do you want me to detonate the device in our captured comrade's head so he can't talk?" This was the most logical move for him to ask, and his boss to make, so he had to say it.

However, if Kain said yes, he wouldn't be able to do it. What Kain didn't know was that the captured man was Zimo's brother, Byeong. He held his breath for the reply.

"Zimo, ye... no, wait. I have a thought."

Zimo's heart leaped.

"This may turn out to be advantageous to me, and favorable to your future. The Lentini plane will be going back to the executive airport in Vegas. From there they'll take our guy to a secure place for interrogation. I'm convinced it will be their huge complex in the desert northwest of Vegas. You know the place?"

"Yes, sir. That's where Lentini's phony furniture manufacturing plant fronts for his scamming, prostitution, and drug businesses."

"Correct. If I'm right, Tony Lentini will be there personally to interrogate our man and try to get information to impress me. This will be our chance to take out their whole organization once and for all.

Go to the San Diego Airport and take one of our stand-by under-cover Fed-Ex jets, and get to Vegas now. I'm going to send one of my combat cells there in Vegas to wait for Lentini's plane to land. They'll follow them from there and find out where they take our guy. They will forward the location to you, and you'll join up with them."

"Yes, sir."

"If it's the plant like I think, you will personally see to it that there are no survivors. Everyone involved with Lentini must die at the plant or anywhere else in Vegas. This will be a coordinated attack, both there by you and by another elite team at the compound in Malta. We will annihilate all of them. Just give me a two-hour's notice before you launch your attack on his plant in Vegas so we can hit them at the same time in Malta. Understand?

"Yes, sir. It will be done as you command."

***

Jane parked in a space in front of Oscar's casita a few minutes past midnight. Everything so far worked exactly the way Brody said it would. For her, that was a big relief. She knew they'd be in good hands once Brody got there, but even from a distance, he got them to this casita safely. Jane gently called out to Mary who was asleep in the passenger seat.

"Aunt Mary, we're here."

"What? So soon? Oh wow. You know, I think I might have dozed off."

"Yes, and I'm glad you did. It's been a long and

stressful day. Let's go in and check the place out."
Jane punched in the code on the front door and they
went inside. She heard the door automatically
relock when she closed it. The alarm panel on the
wall beeped and flashed red. She tapped in the code
and was relieved to see the red light turn green to
confirm it was disarmed.

"Mary, why don't you take a look around while I
call Brody? I told him I'd call as soon as we got here."

"Okay. Wow, this place is amazing. So spacious,
and the ceilings must be twice as high as the ones in
my house. You sure this is the casita and not the
main house? I feel like Alice in Wonderland."

"Yes, I'm sure. I got a glimpse of the main house
as we passed by. You should have seen it, Auntie. It's
a for-real mansion. Take your time, I'll be right here
on the phone."

Mary set off to explore, and Jane sat down in a
leather chair in what must be the living room. She
pulled out the burner and dialed Brody.

When the phone rang, Brody had to shake life
back into his right hand before he could manipulate
it enough to touch the green bar on the screen to
accept the call.

"Jane, everything all right?"

"We're in the casita. It all went very smoothly,
and we feel safe, thanks to you."

"I feel guilty and responsible for what you and
Mary are having to go through."

"Stop right there, Brody. Yes, we were
frightened, for sure, but we talked about it on the

way here. We know who is responsible for all this, and it's the scammers, not you. No matter what happens, you're our hero."

"Still, I can't help but think I missed something, and you have my word that I'm gonna make it right. Where's Mary?"

"She's checking the place out. From what we've seen so far it's huge and luxurious. How far away are you? "

"About four hours. I want you two to get some rest now. I'll try not to make noise when I get there. I'll quietly let myself in and find a place to lie down. You can wake me whenever you get up. I'll have to get going right away on a couple of leads to track down. I'll get this fixed as fast as I can, and the guys are working to help me do that. Which reminds me. One of the guys you haven't met is on his way there too. He's gonna make sure you girls are safe while I'm out. His name is Dan Knapp. Oscar is his friend that owns that place. Logistically, he pencils in to be at the casita about the time I need to get up."

"Logistically? I love it when you talk soldier to me. Makes me feel like the whole U.S. military has my back."

"Well, you will have two branches. Navy and Army. How's Mary doing?"

"You should hear her. She's walking around, saying 'Oh my' over and over at everything she sees. Your friend's friend must be very rich. I'll go join her and try to calm her down so we can get some rest before you get here. I miss you so much."

"Good, because I miss you too. Okay, go close your eyes, and when you open them again, I'll be there. See you soon."

"See you soon."

Jane kept the phone tightly clutched in her hand as a way to stay close to Brody while she went to find Mary. After passing through the living room, she found a powder room, office, plush library, room with a pool table, and a full bar. Then she came upon a large separate dining room that led to a massive kitchen and family room with a movie theater complete with a commercial popcorn maker. The place had to be four thousand square feet. She might not ever find Mary.

Through the kitchen was a full laundry and a hallway that led to three king-size bedrooms. All three had sliding glass doors that led out to a barbecue area with a resort-style pool and hot tub. She went into one of the rooms and walked to the sliding glass doors. There Mary sat at the edge of a hot tub with her feet dangling in the bubbling water. Jane opened the door and stepped out into the yard.

Mary looked up and said, "Jane, this place is unbelievable. You have to dip your feet into this hot bubbly water. It's making my whole body relax and putting my mind at ease."

"That's just what I need right now. I'll join you for a bit and then I'll be ready for some real deep sleep."

"I'm having a hard time keeping my eyes open. Did you talk with Brody?"

"Yes. He'll be here in a few hours and will let

himself in and crash on one of the couches till we get up."

Jane dipped her feet into the soothing water and instantly felt the same relaxation Mary described. After ten minutes, she announced she was ready for bed.

Mary said, "Me too," and they dried off, said goodnight, and went to their separate bedrooms. It didn't take more than a few minutes before they were both sleeping peacefully.

***

After Brody hung up with Jane, he called the guys and told them he was going to check out Oscar's place when he got there, and then get a few winks. Nick set his alarm for thirty minutes before the time they calculated Lorenzo's plane would land in Vegas. Shawn would get up earlier and drive over to Nick's to be there at that same time. Nick's home was their command center. They would monitor everything from there.

Brody got to Oscar's place a couple of hours before dawn. He parked next to Jane's car at the casita and walked back out to the front yard to sweep the main house. He saw cameras all along the roof line and could tell they covered every square inch of the property. The cameras were high-tech and wireless and looked exactly like the ones Shawn showed him when they first hit the market.

Shawn was so excited and couldn't wait to show them how they worked. They recorded 24/7, 365 days a year, and every digital image was sent to a secure server and stored indefinitely. The exterior cameras would send an alert to Oscar's phone and his computer if anything larger than a bird moved outside his home. When alerted, Oscar could determine if something or someone looked suspicious, then he could hit a panic button on his phone or computer and set off a very loud siren.

That would scare the B-Jesus out of anyone nearby, and at the same time, notify the complex's security team and local law enforcement. Brody was sure Oscar was watching him right now.

He looked through a window next to the front door and saw that the same type cameras had been strategically located in the areas he could see. The whole system would be synced together, inside and outside. Because Oscar decided to help them, regardless of the possible dangerous consequences, Brody was pretty sure if Dan asked Oscar to give him and the guy's temporary access to all his security features, he wouldn't hesitate to do so. Brody couldn't have picked a better safe house for the girls, even if he had the time to find one. He didn't believe it was a coincidence that Dan had a friend who had his home available for them and was fanatically serious about security. No, he truly believed this was a Godsend.

Brody walked around the rest of the property and proved to himself that all was secure before going into the casita. After resetting the alarm, he went into the lavish guest bath and took a quick military shower. Wash rag, soap, wash rag, towel. He found a comfy leather couch that was plenty long for a stretch out. It took him zero time to go to sleep and bring an end to the life he had lived that day. While dead to the world, his mind and body rejuvenated in preparation to live another life the next day, all sixteen hours of it.

Chapter 19

LOVE AND MORE DRAMA

The next morning Brody began his life anew with a soft kiss. He opened his eyes to see Jane's smiling face. She looked bright, fresh, and beautiful without a smidge of makeup. The white terry cloth robe was open to her waist, revealing only skin underneath. The view jump-started Brody's adrenaline better than the strongest coffee could.

She spoke in a soothing and angelic voice, and it made these simple words the best reason to be alive.

"Good morning, honey."

"Good morning, beautiful. I missed you so much. I wish we could spend the day together, but that'll have to wait."

"We're gonna have plenty of days to spend together. Your phone started buzzing about 20 minutes ago. I took it into the kitchen so you could sleep a bit longer."

"What time is it?"

"Nine o'clock. You better be ready for a huge breakfast. Oscar has this place stocked with everything. I've made pancakes, bacon, scrambled eggs, toast, coffee, and fresh-squeezed orange juice for everyone, and plenty of fresh fruit. There's a veggie tray too. The portions for you, Dan, and Oscar, are doubled because I know how you men can eat. Whatever you have to do today, you need to refuel to be at your best, so no argument."

"It'll help me detox from my fast-food splurge last night."

"Exactly. Here's your phone. You can check in with the guys then make your way to chow."

"You're right, I'm starved. Thank you so much."

"We're a team, sugar. I'm gonna tell Mary that breakfast is ready. We'll meet you in the kitchen."

She stood up and sashayed her butt as she walked away, giving him a wink over her shoulder.

"That's not fair!" He yelled after her. He waited till she was out of sight to sit up and look at his phone. Two missed calls, one from Shawn and one from Dan. He called Shawn first.

"Hey, sorry I didn't answer when you called. Jane confiscated my phone so I could get a few more winks."

"Not only pretty, but smart too. Lucky you. You know I'm monitoring Lentini's plane, office building, plant, family compound in Malta, and Oscar's home. Well, his plane left early this morning from Gillespie Airport as scheduled. It just flew over the Spring Mountain Range and is on a descent pattern into

Vegas. Right on time. Wheels will leave skid marks on the tarmac at nine-fifteen. I'll track them from there, and when they get where ever they're going, Nick will take over. He's already pulling up information on the two most likely places. One probable is the Lentini real estate offices, about three miles off the strip west of the Rio Casino. The other is the Lentini furniture manufacturing plant out in the desert northwest of Vegas."

"Thanks. Tell Nick I'll be ready to roll when he calls with the location."

"10-4, Brody."

Brody stood up just as the doorbell rang. He pulled his gun out from under the couch pillow and went to a side window to see who it was. He didn't want a bullet in the eye through the door's peephole. Dan, knowing Brody as well as he did, stood on the porch in clear view and faced the window he figured Brody would be peeking from.

Brody spotted Dan's smiling mug and gave him their secret sign that everything was all clear, The Finger. He opened the door with a welcoming bear hug. Dan had a pile of gear on the porch and both grabbed handfuls to haul it in.

"I'm impressed, Dan. You have enough weapons and equipment to fend off an army. Thank you, my friend. Hopefully, we won't need it all."

"No problemo. We're gonna keep these gals and Oscar safe. I brought Kevlar vests and Glock 17s for them. Don't worry, I'll train them on the guns and anything else I think they'll need for self-defense."

"All I can say is that I'm blessed to have the best friends in the world."

"I can speak for myself and the other guys when I say we're just as blessed to have you as our friend, Brode. Hey, is that bacon I smell? I'm starving."

"You're just in time. Jane cooked up a big breakfast for us, including Oscar, so let him know to get here before it's all gone."

"I'll send him a text right now. He should be on his way."

"Come on, I'll introduce you to Jane and Mary."

Dan started ahead of Brody when suddenly Brody grabbed him from behind and stopped him.

"Hey, just thought of something I wouldn't want to slip out, Dan. Mum's the word on you saving my life in Seattle. I need Jane to focus on the here and now."

"Got it, no worries. I've saved your butt so many times I don't even consider it special anymore." He laughed with his deep Sam Elliot-type voice.

"And don't think I don't appreciate every one of them. It's just that I find myself overthinking everything when it comes to Jane. I hope you understand."

"Absolutely, buddy, I totally get it."

"Good. I'm going to eat fast so I can get ready to go when Nick calls with Lentini's location. I hope you won't mind carrying the conversation."

"Not a problem. You know I can talk anybody's ear off."

"I do know that about you." Brody laughed.

"When I leave, you're headset will be synced up, and you'll be able to hear what's going on. But…"

"Got it. If Jane or Mary ask what's going on, I say it's all good, just routine stuff."

"Right."

Brody made the introductions in the kitchen, and quickly chowed down. When he finished, he kissed Jane and thanked her for everything. He told Mary he had an idea about who the people were that broke into her house, and he was going to put them under arrest. A little white lie there. They'd be under all right, but it would be dirt.

Mary thanked him and told him to be careful and that she'd be praying for him. He waved goodbye and headed to the door. Just before he grabbed the door knob, someone knocked. Again he looked through the side window. He recognized Oscar from the picture Dan sent to his phone. He opened the door and grabbed Oscar's hand.

"I'm Brody. Thank you so much for all your doing for us. You have a fantastic place here."

"I've been very blessed to have this place. There's no need to thank me, Brody; I should be thanking you for spicing up my life. Is Dan here?"

"Yes he is. Just a few minutes ago. He's in the kitchen."

"Is that bacon I smell?"

"Yep, and you better get some before Dan eats it all. I'll introduce you to the ladies you're helping. Then I have to go. Sorry for hurrying out, but I have some things to check out."

"Totally understand. When this is all over, you have to promise that you'll let me host a celebration right here for all of you."

"That sounds fantastic. I don't know how we can ever repay you."

"This is simply what friends do for each other. I would do anything for Dan. He's been a very dear friend for many years, and I know he would do anything for me. My only request it that you have a great time at my party. Just eat, drink, and be merry, that's all I want."

"You got it, and I hope we'll be partying soon. Let's go into the kitchen."

Brody repeated the introductions for Oscar, then went out to his truck and opened the bed cover of his F-150 Raptor. He was running a check on all his gear when his phone sang. It was Nick.

"Hey."

"Hey, Brody. Looks like something big is about to happen at Lentini's manufacturing plant today out in the desert. When you can, hook up your com and body cam. It'll be the best way for the four of us to communicate. You ready to roll?"

"In about ten minutes."

"That'll work. When I'm done filling you in, Shawn will take over. He'll be guiding you to the plant. Here's the rundown on what happened when Lentini's plane landed. Three men exited the Gulfstream. Two vertical, one horizontal, the Asian you saw Lorenzo carry away. We recognized Lorenzo and Aldo from the descriptions you gave us.

Lorenzo loaded the unconscious Asian into the back seat of a Silver Escalade and closed the door. Aldo got in the back seat on the opposite side. Two guys already in the front seat. As soon as Aldo closed his door, the Escalade drove in the direction of the plant. Lorenzo got into another Silver Escalade and took off in the opposite direction. The direction of Jane's condo."

Brody's heart skipped a beat, and he felt nauseous.

"I know what you're thinking, Brody, but you got them outta there and in a safe place. Concentrate on that and the fact that we're watching Oscar's place, and Dan is there to protect the girls."

"I know you'll watch Lorenzo like a hawk and keep me updated."

"You bet. But something else happened at the executive airport that has to be connected. I saw a white Mercedes-Benz V 300 D Van, like the one you said the Asians used at Mary's house, parked outside the fence at the airport. It pulled out and followed Aldo's Escalade. Just when I was going to tell Shawn to take a look, he told me to see what he was watching at Lentini's building downtown."

"What's that?"

"Four men came out, and Shawn zoomed in. One of the men was Tony Lentini. They got in yet another Silver Escalade, and it headed towards the plant too. Then another identical white Mercedes van a block away pulled out and began following Tony."

"It sure looks like there's gonna be a showdown

out at the plant," Brody commented.

"Seems that way. No vehicle followed Lorenzo, so he left without a tail. We watched both vans stay well behind the Escalades for a couple of miles, then drop off the pursuit. Both of them pulled off to the side of the road and stopped. The only reason to do that is because, like us, they are convinced that the Lentini Escalade with their Asian guy, and the one with Tony Lentini in it, were going to the plant."

"That has to be it."

"Yep, the vans waited about 20 minutes, then headed toward the plant. We'll probably know pretty soon if they intend to rescue their captured comrade, or if they have something else in mind."

"What do you have on Lentini's Vegas plant?"

"It's huge. As big as a Costco in square feet, and it has a full basement. Easily three times the size of the warehouse Lentini had in Seattle. Speaking of Seattle, well, let me have Shawn tell you. Give him the bad news, Shawn."

"Yeah, Brody. Unfortunately, we won't have the use of the satellite that can penetrate through steel, concrete, and ground like we used in Seattle. I won't be able to see in the plant's basement like I could in the Seattle warehouse. It won't be available for another 12 hours."

"It is what it is. We'll make do with what we have. Would've been nice, though. Looks like that's where I'll be going, so I guess my eyes will have to do the penetrating inside the plant when I get there. What else do you have, Nick?"

"The plant is literally out in the middle of nowhere," Nick replied. "A two-lane road tees off from the only main road out there. It goes east for eight miles and terminates straight into the plant. The only road in or out. The plant advertises on the dark web as a drug and sex service depot. It's closed one day a week, Mondays. So it's closed today. You won't be able to get inside by pretending to be a John or other kind of paying customer. Shawn is scanning topographical maps of the terrain to find a way to get you close without being seen."

"Good thing your Raptor is AWD. You're gonna need it," Shawn added.

Nick continued the rundown. "The plant has a 10-foot chain link fence topped with razor wire, about 100 feet out from the exterior walls. It goes completely around the building. The only opening is at the entrance. The entrance has a military style concrete guard shack in the middle of the road. The incoming traffic has to split off to the right side of the shack and stop. An armed guard inspects the vehicle before a heavy steel arm is lifted to let them in. All traffic is scrutinized and inspected going in and out. And, like the military, the shack has a total of four armed guards, two for incoming and two for outgoing. They are there 24/7 regardless if the plant is open or not."

"Hold up a sec. Jane and Mary are coming out."

"That's okay, I'm done anyway until you get close to the plant. When you're done with the girls, Shawn will tell you what to do," said Nick.

"Got it. Thanks."

Mary walked up to Brody.

"Jane told me you're leaving to find the men that are looking for me. I'm assuming that's because they're after Jane too, and I feel so guilty about that. I know you have to do this, and I want you to know that I'll pray that you have strength, wisdom, and God's protection. Come back to us safely, Brody."

"I will. Don't worry, I've got this, and I have the best team in the world."

"I believe you. I'll leave you two alone now. Godspeed."

Jane moved closer to Brody as Mary walked back to the casita.

"You weren't going to leave without a kiss, were you?"

"Never, honey. Perfect timing, though. Looks like all the bad guys are converging in one place and I'll be able to get there before the party starts."

"Oh, Brody. I know you're trying to ease my fear by being so casual and nonchalant about where you're going, and I love you for that, but I'll be worrying until you're safely back to me."

"Well, the fastest way for that to happen is for me to get going. Shawn, Nick, Dan, and Oscar will keep you and Mary safe till I get back."

He wrapped his arms around her, and this time they kissed just with love in their hearts, not passion. Both of their eyes welled up.

See you soon, Brody."

"See you soon, Jane."

She walked back to the casita, trying not to shake, and couldn't recall her heart ever aching as hard as it was right now.

Brody closed the bed cover and got in the driver's seat. He put on his body cam and headset and set his phone on the passenger seat to check the hook-up with the guys.

"Nick, Shawn, Dan, you copy?"

All of them replied with, "We hear you loud and clear, Brody."

Good, I'm ready. Let's do this."

"I programmed SIRI to get you close to the plant road. When you do, I'll take over. For now, just listen to the directions from the English Lady," Shawn said.

A second later, Brody heard a royal, pompous tone that is common with the British, ordering him to, "Proceed to the route."

***

About two hours later, Shawn cut in. "You can turn SIRI off. In about a mile, take the narrow dirt road on your right. The paved road to the plant is still two miles further up the road."

Brody saw the dirt road ahead and turned right.

"Good. Between the tracker in your jaw and your body cam, it's almost like I'm right there with you. The dirt road runs in the same Easterly direction as the plant, and is almost perfectly parallel to the plant's road. Here comes the tricky part."

"What's that?"

"You'll stay on this road for six miles where it dead-ends. You'll have to get out and maneuver through the brush to find a gradual slope that goes into a wash about 50 yards wide. You'll need to test it and see if it's solid enough to drive on. I'm hoping you can because the walls are high enough to hide the car. Otherwise, you're hiking the rest of the way in."

"Got it. I should be at the wash in a few. What's the status on Lentini's Escalades and the Asians' vans?"

"Both Escalades arrived at the plant at 12:45. The two white Mercedes vans rendezvoused at a small private airport 20 miles north of Lentini's plant. I'm getting a clear view from one of the satellites. Thank God for clear weather. For a small airport, I'm surprised to see that it has two very large hangars. There appears to be a lot of activity. I can see at least 20 quads getting serviced and loaded up with combat gear and weapons. As far as total manpower, there are eight men in each van, and it looks like another 27 that were already at the airport. So about 43 men, all Asian. Nick's working on finding their connection to all this. There's no doubt they're using the airport as a staging area for an assault, and I'm guessing their target is the plant."

"Odds are you're right. I'll check back when I get to the wash. You still got eyes on Lorenzo, right."

"Yes, he's still heading right for Jane's condo. I'll let you know when he gets there.

Ten minutes later, Brody stopped at the end of the dirt road and got out. He found the slope and walked down to the wash. It was just as Shawn had described. The wash was hard and firm, forged from when the raging river that carved it out dried up hundreds of years ago. He was just getting back into the Raptor when Shawn's voice came through his earpiece.

"New development, and this can't be a coincidence. It's the middle of the night at the Lentini family compound in Malta. I've been tracking a large cargo jet from the Korean and Chinese border that was heading straight for the Lentini compound.

"Where is it right now?" Brody asked.

"It's over the top of the compound and dropping paratroopers out the back. At the same time, four large boats are speeding toward the heavily guarded Lentini docks. This has the earmarks of a well-coordinated air and sea assault. Nick and I are watching from a thermal imaging satellite.

"Where are the paratroopers?"

"On the ground, swarming like ants all over the outside of the Lentini's residences. They're taking out all the exterior security guards and are already breaching each house simultaneously. The occupants won't have a chance. Some of the paratroopers have broken off that assault and are heading toward the docks.

"So they're hitting it from both sides, land and sea?"

"Bingo. Numerous explosions and gunfire all around the compound. Between what's going on there and the military buildup at the airport near Lentini's plant, I'd say Tony L and family are about to be history. Looks like whoever is behind these Asians is intent on wiping out the entire Lentini Empire.

"Sounds like this might be our lucky day."

"And then some. We won't have to do anything except sit back and watch Lentini get wiped out," Shawn replied.

"We don't know for sure if they'll be successful at the plant, but at least the Malta Lentinis are being checkmated. But that still leaves the person behind the Asians, and Damon mentioned the Senator is connected with him. Right, Nick?"

"Right, Brody. I've been working on trying to find out who that is, but all I've come up with so far is ghosts."

"So, we'll still have to figure that out. Could be once this fight is over and the Asians are successful, they'll have no motive to go after Mary anymore. But we'll have to know that for sure. Since I'm here, I'll set up an observation post and move in after the fireworks are over. Maybe I can find someone alive in the plant and extract information. Okay, Shawn, the wash has solid ground. Where do I go from here?"

"Drive down and go to your right. I'll tell you when to stop."

"On my way. Keep me updated on the attack in Malta."

"Roger," Shawn said.

The wash was amazingly flat and smooth, and he easily accelerated up to 40mph. He wanted to get to the plant before the action started and meandered about six minutes, dodging trees and huge boulders. After a few more minutes, Shawn told him to pull up and stop.

Brody unloaded all of his gear and then maneuvered the Ford to a large Palo Verde tree in the middle of the wash. He parked underneath its thick foliage for cover, fairly certain the Asians didn't have access to the sophisticated military satellites that Shawn and Nick did. But they could send drones out to scope the area just before their attack on the plant.

He gathered tall weeds and branches off nearby trees, and packed them in around the Ford. He stood back about twenty feet and was confident that no drone would see it. Unseen and untargeted was his theme for the day.

He climbed up the wash wall with all his gear to level ground, and saw the plant a few hundred yards away. Shawn was watching him.

"Brody, see those thick scrub oaks on your left? What do you think?"

"Perfect cover." Brody hauled his gear over to the oaks and settled in.

"From there you're about 350 yards from the plant on the south side with a view of the entrance, the south side, and a partial view of the rear on the west because the building angles towards you.

"What won't I see?"

"The north side of the plant. I expect the assault will come from that direction because of the straight line of open desert from the airport. They'll probably head in a tight formation. When they get close, they'll split up, encircle the plant and cut off the road and only exit," Shawn strategized.

"Sound military tactics there," Brody said.

"They'll establish a perimeter closer in and that will put them between you and the plant. They'll have their backs to you and logically feel safe that nothing's on their six."

"That makes sense. I'll have their rear flank covered and room to get to the Raptor and escape if the need arises. I'm strapping on my weapons, including night goggles. No telling how long this will last. I have my scoped M82 and binoculars so I can zoom in on the action."

The sand at the base of the oaks was dry, light, grainy and easy to maneuver. He pushed handfuls in front of him, creating a berm to rest the rifle on. That done, he laid down and got in position, completely entombed by the biggest oak. Well, maybe a bad analogy, but he couldn't think of a better one, considering how he was hidden.

"Hey, Brody," Nick said. "Update on Malta, but I gotta say, I was confused that they took the risk and didn't coordinate both attacks. Seems like a mistake to me. An attack in two or more locations is best done simultaneously for the element of surprise.

"Maybe logistically, they didn't have a choice," Brody replied.

"Yeah. If they had to attack Malta first, they covered that flaw two ways.

"How?"

"One, they jammed all cellular signals, radio transmissions, and land lines in and around the compound so nobody could get a call out and tip off Tony. Secondly, they were obviously prepared to attack Lentini in Vegas very soon after they launched in Malta. They are saddling up at the airport. It's definitely scorched Earth over in Malta Brody."

"Still gunfire and explosions?"

"No, that stopped. All the Lentini homes are burning. We can see they overwhelmed Lentini's men at the docks too. No gunfire or explosions there either, just a bunch of dead bodies lying in and out of the water. The boats have docked, and the paratroopers are loading onto them," Nick said.

"That was a smart ingress and egress plan, fly in and boat out," Brody replied.

"I hope we don't ever have to fight those guys," Dan added.

"Now that you have eyes on the plant, let me fill you in on what I know," Nick continued. "I pulled up the city-approved construction and interior design plans. It's a freaking fortress. The exterior walls are 40 feet high, two feet thick, with steel reinforced concrete, and that's all built on top of a 20-foot deep basement."

"Where's the parking lot?" Brody asked.

"The main entrance on the west side. Very large

parking lot. Makes sense because that's where the road dead-ends. It has a solid steel man-door that opens to a 20 by 20 square-foot room with one large window. Directly across from the door is a counter like you'd find in a hotel."

"Similar layout to the one in Seattle?"

"Affirmative. No doubt money is collected there and people get processed and directed to areas of the plant. There's a door on the right that leads out to the main floor and to a stairway that goes to the basement.

"All the illicit activities take place there, I'm assuming."

"Agreed. The north and east sides of the building are solid walls, no doors or windows. The south side that you're facing, Brody, is unique. One large hangar-size opening in the middle with two electronically operated one-foot thick steel barn doors that interlock when closed."

"I'm looking at them through my binoculars. They're huge."

"Yes, you could roll a 747 out of it. It's gonna be a challenge to get inside the place if those doors are closed. Behind them is the main floor. It's a cover for furniture making, completely stocked with carpentry tools and various types of wood stored just along the north wall."

"Appearances only."

"Precisely. My research didn't come up with even one store or online site selling furniture from there. Along the east wall is a laundry. The large floor space is bare in the middle. Don't know what they use that for. The basement is laid out like the one at the Seattle warehouse, only much bigger, and it looks like it has one of those rooms with the drains in the floor."

When Brody heard that, he didn't expect he'd get a full body chill and butterflies in his chest, but he did.

"There are 40 one-bed, one-bath apartments, huge bathroom/ shower rooms, two large rooms with tons of electrical hook ups, and two large storage rooms. The whole basement is set up to run their scamming, drugs, elderly hit squads, and prostitution business, and who knows what else. That's all I have."

"Thanks for the update," Brody replied. "I have a clear view of the areas you laid out for me. Good work. Through my binoculars I can see the two silver Escalades parked just inside the open hangar door. I also see a couple of passenger vans and a large delivery type truck along the far wall. The largest area inside is blocked from my view. I see a few people wandering about inside."

"Armed?" Nick asked.

"Affirmative. Outside are a couple of cars and about 10 pick-up trucks parked up against the fence at the east side of the plant. Like you said, Nick, this place is three times the size of the warehouse in Seattle. Plenty of room for whatever illegal activity the Lentinis do there," commented Brody.

"Yep. And I imagine Tony's downstairs with Aldo

interrogating the Asian. I wonder how that's going."

"You're right Nick, Nobody is rushing around inside or outside in panic, preparing for an attack. The six armed men scattered around the outside of the building couldn't be more casual. Two are leaning against the building smoking cigs. Two others are sitting in chairs, drinking beer. Only the last two are actually patrolling the area, but they're horsing around more than anything else. They don't have a clue what's coming their way," said Brody. "They're gonna get caught with their pants down on this one."

"Whoa. And sooner than they know. The quads have left the small airport and are heading your way fast. Must be trying to close the time gap between the attack at Malta and here," Shawn told them.

"They still don't want to take a chance that someone from Malta will tip off Tony," Brody interjected.

"Exactly. They're traveling single file, just like we thought. Top speed is around 50 mph, so they should be there in about 20 minutes," Nick replied.

"Hey, Nick, look at this," Shawn interrupted, motioning to his surveillance camera at the Lentini office building that Tony left about an hour and a half ago.

"Hey, Brody."

"Yeah, Shawn?"

"I guess we shouldn't be surprised. Nick and I are watching flames and smoke billowing out of Lentini's real estate office building. Very intense.

Fire trucks are rolling up, but are staying back at a distance. It's almost like every square inch inside the building went ablaze at the same time."

"Fire chief on the scene?"

"Yep. He just issued a statement to the press that the fire is so intense they're doing containment only. The place will be ashes by the end of the day."

"Not surprised. With the Malta attack and the attack that's coming to this Lentini plant, it only makes sense they'd take out his office building too," Brody responded.

"I'm switching from binoculars to the scope on my Barrett M82. I'll have enough fire power to protect myself on this side of the plant if I have to.

"Dan, you copy?"

"Yeah, Brody."

"How are things at the casita?"

Chapter 20
CASITA UPDATE

"No worries, my friend. All's peaceful and quiet here. The girls are holding a vigil of sorts, but at least it's at the pool. Oscar is schooling me on his security systems and the panic rooms. Remember the pathetic home-style bomb shelters they were putting in people's backyards in the late fifties that wouldn't even withstand a single stick of dynamite? Well, these rooms are impenetrable. The way they're built, reinforced, and supplied, we could survive a direct nuclear blast and live in them safe and secure for decades. Oscar told me there's room here for all of us should that happen."

"Really? What a guy. You picked a good friend there, Dan," Nick commented.

"Sure did."

"Brody," Shawn said. "Let me add to Dan's good news. I've been watching the general area and especially a two and a half mile radius of Oscar's property. I haven't seen any suspicious vehicles or abnormal activity of any kind inside or outside that circle. Should there be, I'll give everyone there at Oscar's plenty of warning to get in the shelters."

"Thanks, guys. To be honest, it's hard to put the worry about the girls' safety outta my mind. But trust me, I know how important this is and I'm focused and ready to meet any challenge out here."

"We know you are," Nick replied.

"I'm gonna hydrate and do some more camouflaging. I'll check back in a few."

"Roger, we'll keep you posted," said Shawn.

Brody gobbled up two power bars and chugged down some more water. The Vegas desert was as harsh as anywhere in the Middle East, so staying hydrated meant staying alive. Some of our soldiers in the war in Iraq got so dehydrated they peed out blood shortly before passing out from heat stroke.

After replenishing his body, he threw more sand over himself, then looked through his rifle scope for any change in activity around the plant. After a few minutes, he got anxious, but before he could say anything, Shawn broke the silence.

"Lorenzo drove up to Jane's condo garage door. It opened after a couple of minutes, and he drove in. Must have one of those transmitters that send all the possible codes to the opener till it hits the right one. He's been in there about five minutes. Hold on. The garage door is opening. He's backing out to the street. He turned in the direction that would take him to the plant. No surprise there. I'll let you know if he changes direction."

"Thanks."

This is actually a good development, Brody thought. He knew he was going to have to have a life and death showdown with Lorenzo. He couldn't leave that animal out there alive knowing who Jane was and where she lived. No way. *Come to Papa, Lorenzo, and your final resting place.*

"Where's the convoy?" Brody asked.

"Less than ten minutes out. Looks like they plan to get real close before they split up and circle the place. Wait a sec. They just launched two drones. They're climbing and heading your way. We saw you get in under that oak and dig into the sand. If we didn't know you were there, we couldn't see you. But we do see your hot head using the thermal imaging. You might want to throw some water on it just in case. I don't think the drones will have thermal capabilities, but why take the chance?" Shawn added.

"Pouring water on my head now. Make a difference?" Brody asked.

"Amazing, where did you go?" Shawn joked.

Brody looked up over the roof of the building to the North. "Yep, here they come. I see a narrow cloud of dust rising up from the north like a large dust devil," Brody informed them.

Minutes later, that same tight swirling dust devil was spreading like a wall all across the northern horizon. The single file quad line was splitting up and sending branches left and right to encircle the plant. The lackadaisical and clueless guards at the plant must have heard the roar of the quad's motors coming their way, because they were hysterically running around grabbing their AK-47s they left leaning against the building.

Brody saw the fear in their body language. He'd seen it many times before. They tried to disguise it by screaming, "Over here, over here." Even as far away as he was, he could hear the shouts. Men did that in the hope that they could get someone to come and reinforce their position for their own selfish safety. Doesn't work, just makes everyone more confused and vulnerable.

This proved to be the case once again when one of the guards looked the wrong way and was torn to pieces by machine gun fire that came from the first quad leading a branch around the front of the building at the main gate just outside of the fence. At the same time, the other branch of quads came circling around the rear of the building. Brody could see the first quads on the west and east sides come around the ends of the building and head straight for him. Luckily, once they reached about 100 yards away from the south side of the building, they turned towards each other and formed a line facing the fence and the building.

The firepower that was unleashed on the plant gave new meaning to shock and awe. Small hand-held rockets, 50 caliber machine guns, and grenades were fired continuously. The only way any human could escape this murderous onslaught was when their soul left their dead body. Advantage Asians.

Tony Lentini's men did the only thing they could. They fired back until their cold dead fingers froze onto the triggers of their guns. Before they died, some of their errant rounds went past the quads that were lined up in front of Brody and whizzed by him.

The bullets struck a musical chord when they ricocheted off the rocks or hard sand next to him. They made that signature zing sound as they echoed away into oblivion. Brody took advantage of all the loud sounds of gunfire and shot down the two drones still hovering over the battle zone. It was good practice and strategy. He was eventually going to have to move from his position, and those peeping drones would have spotted him.

Just when it appeared the slaughter was going to be quickly over, things changed.

High caliber bullets poured out from inside of the hangar at the quads as the heavy steel hangar doors were closing. They closed together extremely fast, but not until a rocket was fired inside by one of the quads and exploded. Gas, fire, and smoke belched back out before the doors completely closed. Certainly that would have caused considerable damage inside.

Now that the hangar doors were closed, the fire power from the quads had no effect on them or the thick concrete walls of the building. The same type steel that was on the hangar doors was activated by a panic button somewhere and closed down over the large window at the front office. Stale mate. But the Asians weren't going to sit around.

Two Ford Super Duty F-450 XL four wheel drive pickups drove around from the North and stopped at the main gate and at the rear of the building. Guys jumped out of both trucks and hooked up thick steel chains from the trailer hitches to the exterior fence. Once secured, the trucks took off and pulled down the entire fence as easily as tipping over a standing row of dominos. As the fence was no longer an obstruction for the attackers to deal with, the guys stood their ground and waited for a favorable change to the Mexican standoff.

Suddenly that change happened, but it wasn't favorable.

Brody felt the ground shake around him. He could tell it was coming from the rooftop of the building.

"What's happening, Shawn?"

"I see it. There's a massive steel plate sliding on the roof and opening up a huge hole. Men are pouring onto the roof from the corners of the hole. They're spreading out along the four-foot-high parapet wall to all four sides of the roof."

"Any update on Lorenzo?"

"He's on the main road heading to the plant road. Should be there in about forty minutes," Shawn answered.

Nick cut in. "Brody, that sky-hatch wasn't on any of the plans I saw. It must have been added secretly after the building was finalized."

"And the plate blends in perfectly with the roof.

No distinction between them from what we could see from the satellite," Shawn added.

"No worries, guys. Just means this isn't going to be over as fast as it looked like a few minutes ago. I see the heads of the men on the roof peaking over the parapet. They're raining down some serious firepower on the quads stuck out in the open. A couple of them got hit by rocket grenades and are completely destroyed. The remaining are trying to find cover."

The scene reminded Brody of old TV westerns where the Indians circled the wagon train and there was a back and forth till one side was overwhelmed or gave up.

"The ground is still shaking, but not as much. The steel hatch opening must have been part of it, but there seems to be something else happening. There's a deafening roar now coming from the roof." Brody said.

Just then the source of the roar became visible. An AH Apache Helicopter. *How the hell did Lentini get one of those?* It shot straight up from the roof like a jack-in-the-box. It reached a height of about a hundred yards above the roof and hovered there. Brody zeroed his scope in on the cockpit. He recognized the pilot. It was Tony Lentini.

The Apache fired a Gatling gun mounted on the bottom of the chopper as well as rockets at the quads while spinning around in a circle. Advantage Lentini.

However, what seemed like a brave act only

proved one thing. Tony was a macho fool. Brody could see the crazed and angry expression every time he spun back around into the view of his scope. Lentini was clearly possessed with revenge towards his attackers. Stupid. He could have easily kept going and flew away out of range before the Asians trained their guns at him. Then he'd be safe and long gone.

Lucky for Brody he didn't. Brody had no priority as to who he would take out between these two groups. He hated both of them for going after the girls. But it was Tony's scamming operation that caused all this to happen in the first place, so Brody figured it was only right to kill him first if given the opportunity. And that opportunity had just presented itself in spades.

Brody waited for the chopper to spin back around so he could get a clear shot at Tony. *Come on, come on, come on...ah, there it is.* Brody lined up his crosshairs and fired a 50 caliber round at the maniac's head before he could spin the chopper out of his view again. The rifle butt kicked into his shoulder hard, confirming action, which also confirmed an opposite reaction. That was the spiraling bullet out of the muzzle, through the chopper's windshield and into Tony's head.

Brody watched through his scope's magnified lens as Tony's headless body fell forward onto the control stick. The move drove the Helicopter straight down back through the roof and into the building. It exploded into a huge fireball, killing all

Tony's men on the roof and whoever was on the main floor. Probably everyone in the basement too.

No one could have survived that fiery volcano, the heat of which burned Brody's face from 350 yards away. If that weren't enough, multiple huge explosions followed from inside the building. Likely from the gas tanks of the Escalades or other vehicles parked inside, as well as any ruptured natural gas lines.

One of the latter blasts dislodged the hangar doors, creating a sizable gap. Tony's insane ego not only took himself and the plant out, but it opened the doors for the Asians to finish the job. The Asians would breach the gap and get inside once the fuel-driven inferno burned out.

Brody spotted something that would substantially decrease their wait time to get inside. Water gushed out of the building. There must have been a fire sprinkler system installed and it was now spraying thousands of gallons on the boiling fire.

A few of the quads maintained position on all the flanks, but the bulk of the force that was still intact converged on the hangar doors and waited for the flames to die out. No one could be left alive in there, but whoever was in charge of the Asian attackers was going to make sure.

Brody's plan to get information from one of the Asians was looking slim to none. It even looked less promising when the Asian guys began loading up their dead and wounded on the backs of the undamaged quads. They weren't leaving anyone behind. All he could do now was wait and see what happened next.

***

"I'd say the Lentini's threat to Mary and Jane has been eliminated, except for Lorenzo," Brody told Nick. "I'll deal with him when he gets here. Have you found anything about the Asians and why they were at Mary's?"

"Sorry, Brody. I've searched all my data bases and asked everyone I know if they might know something about a powerful foreign group operating here in the U.S. Hard to believe, but no one has heard anything about them," said Nick. "I'll keep at it, but I think our best bet is to try and get one of those guys out there on the quads to talk. I know there couldn't be lower odds anywhere in the universe, but you'll have to try."

"Agreed. It's not looking good, but my best opportunity may be happening soon," Brody replied. "The fire in the building is almost out. The sprinklers are still spewing tons of water all over the place, and it's dissipating the residual smoke too. They'll be going in soon, and one of the men on perimeter watch might be distracted enough for me to capture him."

Brody switched back to his binoculars. He could see a guy standing up on a quad with a big red Z painted on the hood and back panel. He was giving orders and directing a couple of eight-man teams to go into the building now that the fire was out.

Looks like I found the boss.

Brody's instincts were right on, because he was, in fact, looking at Zimo. The two teams covered each other and went in.

***

Five minutes went by and nothing happened.

"Brody, Lorenzo's getting close. I'll give you a heads up when he's on the plant's road," Shawn warned.

"Roger," Brody confirmed.

Ten minutes later the armed teams came out of the plant soaking wet. Several of them gestured to the man still standing in the Z labeled quad with their thumbs up. Indicating what? They had no prisoners with them, so thumbs up must have meant they made sure no one was left alive. That was Brody's conclusion.

The Asian Brody believed was their leader held a radio to his mouth and spoke. Just then all the quads around the building started their engines. The ones in front of him went left and right the way they had come, and headed back north around the burned-out building. Everyone left except Mr. Z. He watched as the last of his quad brigade drove out of sight. Then he stepped to the ground, lifted the strap of an AK 47 over his head, and held the gun across his body. Finger on the trigger, he cautiously entered the building.

Yep, he's the captain. Last one to leave the ship. He's proving to himself that his orders were adhered to. Trust, but verify. Even though Brody hated the Asian personally, he had to respect his style of leadership. It was much like his own.

As the Asian disappeared through the opening between the hangar doors, Brody couldn't believe his luck.

"Nick, Shawn, you see that?"

"Yeah we saw the one guy that's left go into the building," shared Shawn.

"What was I just saying about the odds of pinning down one of those guys for information?" Nick asked.

"Lowest in the universe," Brody replied.

Dan chimed in. "With this slight break, let me quickly tell you that Jane is jumping out of her skin, as well as Mary, but they're being strong. They asked me several times about how you are and how it's going. I told them you're fine, and it was going better than expected."

"Thank you, Dan, you don't know what a relief that is for me. I know they're worrying, but thanks to you, now not so much."

"Stay focused, bro. We all want you back here as soon as possible." Dan added.

"I'm laser focused. Guys, I'm going to move in close to the hanger doors. I'll take cover behind one of the blown-up and disabled quads. I'll have to wait for Lorenzo to get here before I can confront the Asian. I don't want to be caught in a crossfire."

"You'll get your chance soon. Lorenzo turned onto the plant's main road, and he's heading straight to you at a 100 plus miles an hour," Shawn said.

"Got it," Brody confirmed.

**

Brody nestled into the undercarriage of a quad on its side. Unfortunately, parts of the former occupant were scattered around him. That and the pungent smell of death coming from inside the building was reminiscent of his times in the Middle East. He had to blink several times to be sure he wasn't actually there. *Darn it, this is America. This shouldn't be happening here.* He couldn't help but think that since 9-11, or really, as far back as the Kennedy assassination, the whole world was up for grabs. And especially the USA.

The quad he was hiding behind had holes in the floor that allowed him to cover the plant road. He spotted a jagged opening the Asian would be coming out. Who would come into his view first, Lorenzo or the Asian?

"Lorenzo!"

"Brody?"

"I see him, Shawn."

Obviously, Lorenzo noticed the smoldering plant and battlefield as he approached and slowed down to veer off the road into the desert behind a Palo Verde tree. He exited the Escalade, and Brody saw a Smith & Wesson XVR 460 Magnum handgun in his catcher's mitt of a hand. This was a serious weapon, basically a mini version of Brody's own M82. A vest wouldn't protect him against that. He couldn't risk Lorenzo getting off the first shot. This was kill or be killed.

Lorenzo zigzagged as he ran up and took cover in the concrete guard shack about 30 yards from Brody. The bastard was not only huge and quick, but also smart. The way he maneuvered himself to the shack Brody couldn't line up a clear shot. He knew he'd only have one chance for the kill shot or risk retaliation from his Smith. Brody knew for a fact that just wounding the huge Lorenzo wasn't going to stop him.

Then Lorenzo looked away from Brody's position at the one remaining operational quad parked by the hangar doors with the red Z on it. No doubt in Brody's mind that Lorenzo was going to kill whoever came out of the building and got in that quad. This was going to be a three-way fight, and the only advantage Brody had was the other two didn't know he was there.

Brody played the logical scenario out in his head. Lorenzo had the element of surprise and would have the first shot at the Asian captain when he came out of the building. When Lorenzo came out in the open to inspect his kill, that would be the opportunity to kill him. Nick, Dan, and Shawn knew not to interrupt Brody's concentration. They were confident he'd make all the right calculations and be the last man standing. But if there was ever a situation where Brody needed live back up, it was now.

Meanwhile, Zimo had been busy.

Chapter 21

THE LOOSE ENDS

As soon as Zimo entered the building and looked around at the devastation, he knew that people died two different ways here. He'd seen it before. All the people on the main floor died quickly with the fire ball and explosion and wouldn't have felt any pain. The basement was a different story. There the people would have suffered horribly, not because they burned, but because they had suffocated.

When the helicopter crashed through the roof, the full fuel tank ripped open, spreading the fuel throughout the entire main floor. This was helped along by the downdraft of the rotors until they stopped turning. Then, one of many possible ignition sources ignited the fuel, creating what is known in the military as a fuel-air bomb. Those bombs suck all the oxygen out of the air and they essentially smother someone. No different than putting a pillow over one's face.

As Zimo walked through the basement he saw

evidence of just that. Everyone was dead, and he would confirm that to his boss, Kain, but that wasn't why he kept searching the basement. He knew from the building plans that the interrogation room where his brother would be had been built as a self-contained panic room. He'd learned everything about it by hacking the computers of the architectural firm that built it. The room would protect anyone inside from the fuel-air bomb, all the explosions, and more.

He told his troops to leave that room for him. Finally, he found it in the far-east corner.

I'm coming to save you, my brother. Hold on just a bit more.

Outside the room was an electronic failsafe switch that would open the bomb-proof door, hidden in the concrete floor. You had to know exactly where to get to it. The floor was poured just one inch thick right over the vault with the switch. No one could tell; it looked 20 inches thick like the rest of the floor, and perfectly uniform.

Zimo went to the spot where he knew the vault was and used the small sledgehammer he'd brought with him to break up the floor. In a few seconds, he got to the vault and hit the switch. The door opened.

When Aldo saw the door open, he figured it had to be one of his people letting him out after all the explosions, so he relaxed his hold on his Glock. That was all Zimo needed to put a six-round burst of his AK into Aldo's lungs. Aldo hit the floor convulsing, trying desperately to get his bullet riddled lungs to work. Zimo took the gun from Aldo's hand and saw the painful and panicked look on his face as he tried to suck in air into his lungs faster than it was escaping. That losing struggle went on for a few more agonizing seconds before he suffocated.

A just exit for a terrible excuse for a human being who certainly didn't have an ounce of humanity in him, Zimo thought as he rushed over to the table where his brother was tied. He had suffered the beginnings of sadistic torture, but it stopped a while ago as evidenced by the dried blood at the back of his head. Zimo saw why.

The device in his brother's head had been triggered. He had been dead for some time. "No! No! No!" He screamed.

Weak from despair, Zimo went unsteadily back upstairs and into the front office that was surprisingly stable after the explosions and fire, except that the main door was breached. It had been reinforced as a secondary panic room on Tony's orders. He pulled out his secured phone and called Kain.

"Brody, there's a cellular phone transmission and reception from inside the plant. I've seen this type of encryption before and I'm hacked in. I'm getting and recording the conversation. Right now the phone is stationary. I'll let you know if it starts moving," Shawn said.

"You're the man," Brody quipped.

Kain immediately answered Zimo's call with, "Zimo, report!"

"Yes sir. All three phases of the mission to eliminate the Lentinis and their operations have been successful with minimal losses.

"I'm not concerned about losses. Get on with it," Kain barked.

"Yes sir. The Lentini family compound in Malta is completely destroyed and the entire family and employees there have been killed. Lentini's Vegas office building is destroyed and all employees that were working in the building at the time or at home, are dead. And as you ordered, sir, I personally spearheaded the attack here at their manufacturing plant. It is also destroyed, and everyone is dead including our man who was captured."

"Excellent, Zimo, and yes I know about our man. I couldn't risk that he would talk and ruin my plans, so I activated his device. No big deal. Again, great job."

Kain's words turned Zimo's blood cold, giving him a chill. Then just as fast, his blood began to boil. He would avenge his brother's death and kill Kain.

"Thank you, sir. Will you allow me to correct my failure in San Diego and get that Mary Charbenau woman? I'll personally bring her to you."

"No, Zimo, that won't be necessary. She is no longer a threat. It was Tony Lentini that concerned me. The information he was acquiring could have disrupted or even jeopardized the plans I've already put in motion. You have vindicated yourself by wiping out the Lentinis and securing my plans. Not only that, but I'm promoting you as my second in command. Your job there is done, but another one begins that will bring a glorious legacy to you, me, and our people."

"I am honored, sir," said Zimo through clenched teeth.

"Zimo, our people will see me as a king, and you as my royal prince," continued Kain. "We will claim the world for ourselves and our people forever. You should be proud."

"I am, sir, and I'm honored. What is it you want me to do, and should we meet in person to discuss it?" Zimo asked.

I'll keep pushing to get close to him, and then I'll finish him.

"That won't be necessary right now, maybe later. This is what you need to do. You and your men will go to the port of Long Beach, California. The *Water Crest* will dock there in five days," said Kain. "The ship has ten containers loaded with a chemical protein that will poison the world's drinking water. You're in charge of putting it into all of the world's water supply and killing off our enemies. You will continuously taint the water for eight weeks to be sure we've infected everyone with the protein except, of course, our people."

"A great honor," said Zimo.

"Indeed. I've just received permission from all the world leaders to let you do that, the idiots. The greedy bastards will welcome you with opened arms. Zimo, this is very important. There are two containers on the ship labeled BPA free and they contain the antidote. You are to secure those containers for our people just in case they are accidentally contaminated. You will take your men and go to Long Beach and wait for the ship. Any questions?"

"No sir."

"Good. Zimo, I'm reconsidering meeting with you. I think there will be time before the ship arrives, and I would like to personally give you a reward for your good work and loyalty."

"That is very generous sir. I would like that very much."

"Great. I'll try to get you here to New York. I'll let you know."

"Thank you sir. I'll be waiting," Zimo said.

For as long as it takes.

***

"Brody, the phone inside the building is moving toward you," Shawn warned.

"Copy."

Seconds later, Brody and Lorenzo saw the Asian step out of the building and walk towards his quad. Brody looked back at Lorenzo and was happy to let him make that first move. Being in between, Brody had to swivel his head to see who was going to get the set point. He was sure Lorenzo was going to serve it up as an ace, because the Asian wouldn't see it coming.

Zimo pulled off the AK-47 and set it in the back of the quad, then jumped in behind the wheel. Lorenzo waited a beat to see if anyone else was coming out, then burst out of the shack on a dead run straight towards the Asian, who was temporarily unarmed. Lorenzo charged forward to close the distance and get as close to Zimo as possible before he fired. The Asian's peripheral vision must have caught Lorenzo coming and he quickly reached back for the AK.

However, before he could maneuver and shoot, Lorenzo was on top of him, firing his handheld cannon. The Asian took several hits, twisting and jerking to the melody the bullets played on his body. Lorenzo was just five yards away when he fired the last shot that found its way below Zimo's body armor. A gut shot. The Asian fell over on the ground and made his final imprint on this earth as this life was slowly leaving him.

Brody wasn't sure his M82's 10-round magazine would be enough to stop Lorenzo, but it was time to try. He stood and aimed the rifle at Lorenzo's body mass, not risking a headshot even though Lorenzo's head was as big as a pumpkin.

Lorenzo heard or sensed Brody's movement and instinctively launched himself straight up. Brody had seen that same move made by a deer when it heard the metallic click of the safety being unlocked on his gun before he could fire at him. Lorenzo flew up and over the top of the Asians' quad. While still in the air, he contorted his body like a gymnast and grabbed Zimo's AK. It was an amazing feat by the giant. Any Olympic judge would have been impressed. A ten, for sure.

But while the giant showed off, Brody quickly

adjusted to Lorenzo's flight and fired. A misty cloud of red exploded from Lorenzo's back into the air before he went out of sight on the passenger's side of the quad.

"You hit him, Brody. He's crouched down by the right front tire, moving slowly and having a hard time getting his arms and hands to work. That round may have broken his back, ribs, or even cut his spinal cord," Nick said. "Now's your chance. You should be able to see some of that big body from underneath the quad."

Brody got down to look. "I see him behind the front passenger tire from the waist down." Brody fired two more rounds, one through the passenger tire where Lorenzo's hip should be, and the other one into his fully-exposed left knee. Lorenzo toppled over onto the ground and lay there on his side in obvious pain.

"Two more hits Brody. Blood is pouring out of his back, hip, and knee. He let go of the AK. He's rolling back and forth in a fetal position. Come around the back of the quad for a clear shot. No fire or police en route. They must have disconnected those alarms to keep from being scrutinized. But get outta there as fast as you can after you finish him," Nick said pleadingly.

"Will do." Brody cautiously moved around to the Asian's quad. He kept the back passenger corner between himself and Lorenzo, just in case. He saw Lorenzo lying on his side, bleeding profusely with a bone sticking out of his back. Brody aimed the rifle down to finish off the man who had gone after Mary and his Jane.

Lorenzo looked up at him and, in an agonizing voice, pleaded. "You can't just shoot me like this in cold blood. Please, call an ambulance and just leave. I'll go back to my home in Italy, and you'll never see me again. I promise you, please."

Brody said nothing, then fired four shots, two to his head and two through his heart. Then he checked for a pulse and wasn't surprised to find one. The man was truly a bear. Brody took out his K-Bar and cut through Lorenzo's carotid to let his pulse pump the remaining life out of him and onto the desert sand. Now Brody would never again have to worry about him going after Jane or Mary.

Suddenly, Brody heard an almost imperceptible sound. He turned his weapon towards it. Searching. There, he heard it again. Unbelievable!

The Asian was still alive!

Brody, gun ready, cautiously went over to check. The Asian's eyes were shut tight from pain. Yes, he was alive, but barely. Brody saw the gut shot and knew he didn't have much time left.

"Hey, who do you work for?" Brody asked loudly.

"Water," the Asian said through choking speech.

"Guys, you hear that? He's asking for water. I know with the gut shot, the thirst he's having is unimaginable, but if I give him water, he'll die right now."

"You're right. Use it. Tell him you'll give him water if he talks," Dan said.

"Okay, I'll give you water if you tell me who you work for."

"Water. Don't drink water. You die. Stop Kain… Washingtondccc… you all… die. You kill Kain for…for…me…pleeeasse…" the Asian said with his last breath. His face relaxed with his eyes still closed in a forever slumber. Brody checked his neck.

"Strange, there's still a weak pulse."

Just then, the Asian's eyes popped wide open and made Nick jump in his chair. Brody checked his neck again, and this time, there was no pulse. The Asian was staring into another realm.

"What the heck was that?" asked Nick.

"The same thing that's going to happen to all of us," Brody said.

"What do you mean?" Nick asked again.

"Someday, we'll all wake up… dead," Brody announced.

"Brody, I'll never understand you, brother," Shawn said.

"I don't think any of us will," Nick agreed.

"Okay, guys, I'm getting outta here and going back to Oscar's. See if you can make sense of what the Asian said," Brody said.

"We're on it," Shawn said.

***

Brody was driving back to the casita when Shawn called. "Brody, Dan. Nick and I have good and bad news. We have the transcript of that cell conversation I told you about from inside the plant. It gives us the name of the Asian Lorenzo killed—

Zimo. No name for the other guy, but I know he was in Washington DC at the Four Seasons Hotel. Even got the room number, 6156. Brody, do you think Zimo was trying to tell us that guy he was talking with is Kain?"

"I'd bet on it. He did say Washington DC," Brody responded.

"There's a lot more, and I think it explains what Zimo was trying to tell us."

Shawn told them about the plan to contaminate the world's drinking water from a cargo on a ship called the *Water Crest* in Long Beach.

"Nick's all over this, and he's making things happen at light speed. He forwarded a copy of the phone transcript to the people he trusts at Homeland Security, FBI, CIA, NSA, etc. He's also telling them everything Damon told us. Especially that one of our own Senators may be colluding with this guy Kain," said Shawn.

"What a psychopath," Dan commented.

"No joke. The agencies are investigating and sharing information right now," Shawn continued, "but they're doing more than that. The FBI and Homeland Security are joining forces to do an undercover operation at Long Beach when the Water Crest docks. They want to catch the people when they show up to claim those containers. They are also all over room 1656 at the Washington DC Four Seasons with wiretaps and surveillance. We've done our part to expose this thing and now it's in the hands of the proper authorities. Even though this story is huge, United Nations-type huge, they promised to keep us in the loop."

"That would be the right thing to do," Brody agreed.

"Brody, there's a part of the transcript you're really going to like, without a doubt, the best part," Shawn said. "They think this Kain character told Zimo that he was no longer concerned about Mary and not to go after her."

Brody had to swallow hard before he could speak. "I can't wait to tell them. Hey, Dan…"

"Don't worry, Brody, mum's the word. It'll be a special gift from you to them they'll never forget."

"Thanks. I should be there in a few minutes."

"Hey guys, don't forget, Oscar promised us a big party at his place when this is over. Nick, Shawn, he'll want you guys and Sofia here too," Dan added.

"Sofia and I wouldn't miss it," assured Nick.

"Neither would I," Shawn said.

"After Brody breaks the good news to the gals, I'll get with Oscar on the specifics and let you know."

The guys thanked Dan, and told Brody they were going to shut down the command center in Nick's office for the night, but would keep an open line to the first guy Nick called at the FBI for updates.

***

Brody called Jane and told her he was on his way. She was waiting outside when he pulled up. They didn't speak; just stood there holding each other tight, not wanting to let go.

Finally, Brody whispered in her ear, "I have some

great news to share with you and Mary. Let's go make her smile."

"Love to."

They passed Dan on their way out to Mary's favorite spot by the pool. When Jane wasn't looking, Brody gave him a knowing wink.

When Mary saw Brody, she jumped up from her lounge chair, spilling her margarita all over herself. "Oh my, I'm going to smell like a lush," she said with a laugh, and wiped herself down with a towel. Then she gave Brody a big hug.

"Well, I have it on good authority that the people who were looking for you, Mary, are no longer looking. You are now free to live your life as before and without fear. How's that sound?

"Oh Brody, really?"

"Yes, really. I won't go into details, but you can trust me and the guys on this one."

"Oh, I'm so happy. I wasn't worried about myself. It was you guys and Jane that I was so worried about. I thank God that He answered my prayers."

"I agree, I really think he was looking out for all of us," Brody said.

"Does this mean we can go back to my condo?" Jane asked.

"Yes, life back to normal." Dan stood off to the side, listening.

"Hold your horses, everyone. I just got off the phone with Oscar. He insists you all stay here for the big celebration he promised to throw. He's already ordered the caterer, etc., and will have it all put together by tomorrow afternoon. He did have a special request. He's met someone recently and would like to invite him to the party if it's okay with everyone. How about a show of hands in favor?"

All hands went up.

"Thanks, that'll make him very happy. I'll call Nick and Shawn and tell them to get on the road early tomorrow morning if they can. They've already committed to be here so I don't think that will be a problem."

"I hope no one minds if I do a little celebrating right now. Margaritas, everyone?" Jane asked. A chorus of "Here, here" rang out. Brody went into the kitchen to help with the drinks and maybe get a different kind of stimulation as well.

The evening continued with easy conversation, laughs, and many smiles. Then it ended with Jane and Brody retiring to her room, Dan to his, and Mary to hers. The next morning began with bright sunshine, clear cloudless skies, and a slight breeze to cool the skin. It was so perfect that they all decided to have breakfast outside by the pool. Oscar joined them since he was taking time off from work.

***

After breakfast, Oscar had fun decorating and arranging furniture and plants to complement the festive setting. He asked Dan and Brody if they'd string lights over the main seating area by the pool where the food, music, and dancing would take place. He was going all out and enjoying every second of the happy mood. The party was scheduled to start at 6 p.m. That gave Shawn, Nick, and Sophia plenty of time to get there. In fact, they were on the way and should arrive by 4 p.m.

Oscar made up rooms in the main house for their stay and for his guest, who would be there around 3 p.m. He was excited to introduce everyone to him. They had met at the Bellagio poker room, where Oscar dealt Texas Holdem. He was a personal assistant to a high roller, and when Oscar became the high roller's favorite dealer, he'd been invited to join him and his assistant for dinner and drinks. That's how their friendship started and grew. His friend had been out of town in Mexico recruiting workers for his boss, and was going to come straight there from the airport.

Oscar designed the party to be casual with a Hawaiian flavor. Flowery dresses and shirts with colorful leis for everyone. Everyone had a blast preparing for the party and anticipating Oscar's spread. The variety of foods alone would put the most expensive Las Vegas Buffet to shame. Jane and Mary arranged beautiful centerpieces from the flowers Oscar had delivered. The string lights were installed with Dan as the expert lead, and Brody feeding him the strings and a 10-inch slotted screwdriver. Piece of cake. Dan descended the ladder and set the screwdriver down on the table where Jane and Mary had put their first completed centerpiece.

They all stood together admiring their work when Oscar stepped out of the sliding door of the casita and announced that his friend had arrived. They all turned to look.

"Everyone, this is my friend..."

Brody and Dan froze. They immediately recognized the man who was sporting a new L tattoo on his neck. And he recognized them too.

Carlos! Carlos! The man they freed from the Seattle warehouse. Carlos, the rat who must have made the call that launched the attack on the warehouse to kill them.

Carlos knew his boss, Mr. Tony, wanted them dead. He'd be a hero and move up even more in the organization if he took them out. This was his chance. He reached inside his suit jacket for the very same gun Tony told him to get out of the SUV back in Seattle.

Brody now knew who the high roller was that Carlos worked for. Tony Lentini. Hundredths of a second ticked by like minutes. All movement was like a slide show slowly advancing frame by frame in a black and white past. Brody saw in horror the way Carlos's hand quickly snaked inside his expensive suit jacket, obviously reaching for a gun. He'd seen the move many times before.

Brody and Dan were too far away to launch an effective attack. They wouldn't be able to get to Carlos before he started shooting. One of them would have to die to save the others. Brody knew it was going to be him.

Just before he charged, one of those hundredths of a second ticked off and he looked down. There was the screwdriver. Without another hundredth ticking off, he grabbed it and threw it at Carlos as hard as he could, just like he was trained to with his K-Bar knife. Hopefully, the substitute screwdriver would give him the same results.

As the screwdriver left his hand, he charged right behind it straight for Carlos as fast as he could. The screwdriver was in the air when Carlos fired his gun. The bullet and screwdriver passed each other.

The screwdriver's blade found its target and buried itself all the way up to the handle into Carlos's chest before he could get another shot off. Brody got to him just as Carlos looked down at the handle in disbelief and began convulsing and coughing. Blood poured from his mouth. The blade must have punctured a lung and pierced part of Carlos's heart.

The criminal crumbled down to the floor, dead before he got there. Everyone stood silently in shock.

Then Jane screamed. "Oh my God, Brody! Mary's been shot."

Brody ran back and knelt down next to Mary, who was lying on her back. Blood bubbled from her chest, soaking her blouse. She was choking on her own blood.

"Oscar, call an ambulance, then the police. Dan, get my medical kit out of my truck."

"On it."

"Mary, you stay with us; you stay strong. You're gonna be okay," Brody told her, but couldn't make himself believe it. He'd seen these wounds before.

Jane knelt next to Brody, holding Mary's hand.

"Yes, Mary, you're going to be fine," Jane said. But she couldn't stop the tears from flowing down her cheeks.

Mary struggled to say something.

"Don't try to talk," Brody told her.

"It's okay. I have to. I can see in your faces that you two are scared and worried about me. Please listen carefully. This life here on Earth wasn't the goal I was born to, it was only the means to reach the real goal. And that is everlasting life promised to us by Jesus. I want you to understand that, and don't be sad. I've lived a long and blessed life, and I'm ready to go."

"Maybe so, but not today. We'll get you patched up and then you'll be around for a long time to come. Let's talk about how you feel. Can you breathe?" Brody asked.

"Yes, but it's painful. I feel very cold," she replied.

Brody knew that meant she was losing too much blood.

Dan came back and set the med kit down next to Brody.

"Mary, I have to roll you on your side to see if you have an exit wound, okay?"

"Yes, whatever you have to do. Why am I so cold?"

She's going into shock.

"Jane, get me a couple of blankets."

Brody gently lifted Mary and saw it was a through

and through. He'd have to stop the bleeding at both holes.

"Okay, Mary, I'm going to apply a pressure dressing on your chest and back until the ambulance gets here. Dan, go to the kitchen and put some ice in two Ziplock bags."

Dan passed Jane who was coming back with blankets, and told her that Oscar said the ambulance and police were on their way.

Oscar came back outside, visibly shaking, and said, "I'm so, so sorry, everyone. I don't know why Carlos did that." He stood there staring down at Carlos saying over and over, "I'm so sorry, I just don't know why."

Dan came back with the ice packs.

"That's okay, Oscar. Not your fault." Dan knew that Carlos was trying to shoot both him and Brody, but wouldn't open that can of worms at the moment. "Right now," he continued, "all we have to do is tell the authorities the truth. Which is this. He came through the door, pulled a gun, and fired at us. He was killed in self-defense. It's up to the police to figure out why. Could have been that you're rich, and maybe he gained your trust to rob you. Let's go outside and wait for them. We'll have to put them at ease when they get here. They'll be responding to a shooting, so they'll be nervous and on edge. Brody, I'll direct the paramedics to you."

***

In the following hours, Mary was taken by ambulance to the hospital. Jane and Brody followed in his car. The police took charge of the crime scene at Oscar's. Oscar and Dan remained to answer questions and assist. They'd take Mary, Jane, and Brody's statements later.

Mary was rushed into surgery with internal damage to one lung but no other organs. Significant internal bleeding concerned the doctors. Brody and Jane held each other and waited for news, praying that it would be good.

Shawn, Nick, and Sophia arrived to the chaotic situation at Oscar's. Dan filled them in amid Oscar's constant apologies. The guilt was eating him up, and he begged everyone to stay at his home and promised he would try to make the best of the horrible situation. The situation started to ease considerably when four hours later, they got a call from Brody saying that Mary was out of surgery and in intensive care. The prognosis was good. They stopped all the bleeding and repaired her lung. They expected her to make a full recovery.

With the good news and the fact that Mary would remain sedated until late tomorrow, Brody and Jane decided to go back to Oscar's. On the way, Jane wanted to, no, needed to, talk.

"You saved all of our lives. You're my hero, and I love you for that."

"But?" Brody asked.

"But, I think about how close we all came to being killed, and it's a miracle that Mary wasn't. I heard Dan say the guy might've been trying to rob Oscar, but he was aiming the gun at you. Is this related to

Mary getting scammed, and was he trying to kill you because of what happened in Seattle?"

"Yes. Jane, I'm going to tell you everything, and I won't leave anything out. Not only that, I promise to always answer any question you have for me with the truth, no matter what."

Brody spent the rest of the ride plus a substantial amount of time sitting outside the casita in the car, telling Jane every detail of what happened from the time Mary told him about being scammed through to today.

"Oh, my God. You could have been killed in Seattle. I'm shaking right now."

"That's why I held back. I didn't want you to be worried about me."

"I understand. But no more secrets between us, no matter the pain. Promise?"

"Promise."

"So this Carlos was an unbelievable fluke, and there isn't anyone else looking for you, or us, right?"

"Yes, Carlos was a crazy fluke. No, there isn't anyone else. All of Lentini's people were killed at his plant in the desert. Unfortunately, the innocent as well as the evil ones. There's still the scammer problem, and people that want the world to themselves. I don't know what my role is going to be in that, but I have to do something. The United Nations was formed after the Second World War to prevent people like Hitler from doing what he did. It's a shame that the organization isn't doing the job. The world would be a safer place if they did. On another subject, let's stay here until Mary gets out of the hospital, then go back to San Diego to live our lives together."

"Is that a proposal?"

"Yes, it is. I know this is probably not very romantic and questionable timing, but I don't know how to do things except right to the point. I love you more than I know how to put into words. But I'll try. The moment we met, you changed me. Everything about you filled my heart and mind with a need that only you can satisfy. I hope that tells you how much I love you. Jane Peltier. Will you be my wife?"

"Yes! And I believe this is another thing we have in common. I like being right to the point, too," she said, grinning.

EPILOGUE

Eight months later, on a sunny day at the base of the giant cross on Mount Helix, San Diego, with its 360-degree view of God's earthly creation, Brody and Jane were married. Mary and Sofia stood strong and proud next to Jane as her beautiful bridesmaids. Nick, Shawn, and Dan wore full-dress uniforms next to Brody. It was the perfect place to commit the rest of their lives to each other, and Him.

Jane got a transfer from her Las Vegas bank to a branch in San Diego months after Mary got out of the hospital. She sold her condo and made Brody's bungalow their home. She planned to work a few more years before retiring. Then the two of them would enjoy each and every day as if it were a Saturday!

***

A news story broke that a U.S. Senator was convicted on numerous charges, including fraud, theft of government funds, murder, and crimes against humanity. At least 40 other leaders in countries around the world were also convicted on the same charges. The United Nations held a special session to assure the people of the world that this would never happen again.

***

Brody, Nick, Shawn, and Dan also vowed to uncover scams and scammers and turn them over to the proper authorities.

***

Unfortunately, Kain escaped before being captured. He is now the world's most wanted man. Brody and the guys are helping to search for him.

***

Brody figured it was his destiny to stop Kain and people like him. After all, his last name was Alexander, which in Greek means...Defender of Mankind.

ABOUT THE AUTHOR

L E Kennedy is a Navy veteran who was proud to serve his country during the Vietnam War. Now, he's a father, husband, grandfather, and great-grandfather who is proud to serve his family.

He played his first Seven Card Stud poker game working in a Detroit car wash at age 12 and was hooked for life. He couldn't wait to turn 21 and play poker at the Stardust in Las Vegas. It took nine years, but he was there playing poker on his birthday. It has been a dream of his to win a poker bracelet at the World Series of Poker in Las Vegas. In 2018 he did cash in the super senior event, placing 126 out of 2,400 entered. He will continue trying for as long as he can.

He's always been a daydreamer, and he thinks that's why he views the world through a lens of imagination. He remembers situations in his life in great detail, and he think that's why people say he tells a good story. He likes storytelling, and has always wanted to write one down for people to enjoy. This is it, and he hopes whoever reads this will enjoy it and hopefully benefit from some of his life's philosophies.

God Bless,

L E KENNEDY

Made in the USA
Las Vegas, NV
09 September 2023

77299958R00193